DARK HALLS

DARK HALLS

JEFF MENAPACE

MIND  MESS
PRESS

2019

"The flesh is weak, Johnny. Only the soul is immortal."
—Alan Parker, *Angel Heart*

1

The woman hid in the barn. She'd managed to lift and slide the iron beam onto the brackets of both barn doors, sealing herself in, but the villagers would not be deterred, their incessant, murderous shouts carrying a force equal to—perhaps greater than—their efforts to smash through.

The barn doors bowed inward with each charge, the iron beam holding, refusing to bend. The woman looked on with little comfort in this fact, for the iron beam's refusal to bend grew irrelevant—it was the brackets holding the beam on those barn doors that appeared ready to give. Each explosive charge from outside would yield a crack on the surrounding wood that held the brackets, each explosive charge pulling the brackets further and further free, the barn doors bowing that much more inward, revealing a slice of the growing mob outside, their faces rabid with blood lust.

A final charge and the brackets came free, the iron bar hitting the dirt floor with a dull clang, the barn doors bursting open, both from impact and the storming mob rushing in after.

The woman screamed. She screamed as they pounced, and she screamed as they butchered her. Pitchforks plunged. Machetes hacked. Knives slashed. They tore off her arms. They tore off her legs. They tore off her head.

A hatchet split open her limbless, headless torso. They removed her heart …

2

Oven, Ryan thought during the walk from his car towards the human resources building in his new black suit. Although it was still morning, the August sun was already out in force and doing a commendable job of baking him in the dark material. Once he got back in the car, the strait-jacket and noose (tie) were coming right off and getting tossed in the back seat, air conditioner blasting the whole way home. If he got the job? You can bet your ass some old-school Metallica would be blasting too.

Portfolio under one arm, Ryan pulled at the heavy glass door of the HR building with the other and entered. A blast of cool air immediately hit his face, and he all but purred.

The elderly receptionist noticed his gratitude. "Could fry an egg out there, huh?"

Ryan returned a polite smile. "Sure could." He tugged at his tie to let the blissfully cool air find its way down his torso. Thin circles of sweat had already gathered in the center of his chest and beneath his arms, but the conditioned air soon prickled his damp skin—gave him "goose bumps" as his mother would say.

"Can I help you?" the receptionist asked.

"I'm Ryan Herb," he said, readjusting his tie. "I have a ten o'clock interview."

The receptionist pulled her glasses to the tip of her nose and scanned the appointment book. Her perfume was wincingly awful and generously applied at that. Ryan took a step back and pretended to tie his shoe to get away from it.

"Okay, Ryan," she said, "if you just take a seat over there, Mr. Hansen will be with you in a moment."

Ryan exhaled, popped up, and thanked her. He made his way over to three large sofas lining each of the walls facing him. Two coffee tables holding an assortment of magazines sat in the middle. He scanned them quickly, looking for any that may be education related. He spotted a couple. Would he reek of it if he picked one of them up—among several issues of *Sports Illustrated* no less—and pretended to be reading it with great interest when the head of HR came out? Fortunately, the decision became irrelevant seconds later—Mr. Hansen, head of HR, appeared with his hand extended, and Ryan couldn't have been more grateful; he was a blink away from grabbing one of those *Sports Illustrated*s.

"Hi, Ryan. Jerry Hansen."

Ryan took hold of Hansen's right hand and stood. He shook it firmly during his ascent and then more so once he was upright. Ryan was a good five inches taller than Hansen at an even six feet, and his lean physique was the polar opposite of Hansen's. Still, despite the man's exceptional rotundness, Hansen clearly took great care in the remainder of the package. His dark suit sported a pink silk tie and pocket square. Thick gray hair freshly trimmed and parted neatly to one side. Chubby red face shaved smoother than a child's. He carried a strong smell (*lots of smells today*) of bathroom soap. Ryan wondered whether he had just shaken the hand of a guy who'd recently wiped his ass. He hoped Hansen was a lefty.

"Nice to meet you, Mr. Hansen," Ryan said.

Hansen held up a hand and frowned playfully. "Please, call me Jerry…"

Mr. Hansen was my father's name.

"…Mr. Hansen was my father's name."

Ryan smiled. "Nice to meet you, Jerry."

3

Ryan followed Hansen down the corridors of the HR building. Their destination was a room that had missed the memo on décor. There was one window, one large oval table with chairs, and what seemed like nothing but the color brown.

"Fancy, huh?" Hansen said.

Ryan feigned a laugh.

Hansen took a deep breath and continued. "Yeah, well, this building is kind of an impromptu human resources department for the time being. Anonymity is the name of the game right now until we can get the school year started; I'm sure I don't have to tell you why. This place actually used to be an advertising firm."

"Is that right?" Ryan asked, hoping his feigned interest didn't sound as bad in Hansen's ears as it did his.

"Yup. Advertised breakfast cereals, if I'm not mistaken."

Ryan smiled; easier to feign interest without words.

Hansen did not return the smile. He instead asked: "You *are* aware of the details surrounding our…" He paused, then settled on: "*Situation?*"

Ryan kept his reply intentionally short. "Yes, I am."

Hansen nodded once and took a seat at the head of the table. The table's length was long enough for Ryan to have his pick of chairs, but he chose the one to Hansen's immediate right. He placed his portfolio on the tabletop and folded his hands over it.

"Still, I'm sure there are *some* things we can't avoid discussing, yes?" Hansen said.

"Of course," Ryan said. Though he wasn't entirely sure, Ryan had the sick feeling Hansen was alluding to the school's tragic past, and in a mute effort to steer things in a brighter direction, Ryan began to open his portfolio…and Hansen immediately reached out with his thick little hand and closed it again.

"I don't need to see that, Ryan," he said. "As far as I'm concerned, you've got the job."

The words registered with Ryan, but any joy he should have felt was marred by confusion. He felt like a man who'd won something by default.

Hansen seemed to have little trouble in reading Ryan's puzzlement; it almost looked as though he'd counted on it.

"I feel we need to discuss other matters first," Hansen said. "Matters about the school's history."

Oh hell, he does *want to talk about it.*

"I know all about what happened here," Ryan said.

"Do you?" Hansen asked, leaning back in his chair, folding his fingers across his ample belly.

"Yeah, well, I think I do…I mean, who doesn't, right?"

"And yet you still want to work here," Hansen said. *Said*—not asked.

Ryan frowned inside. These were questions he had not prepared for. He was prepared to talk about classroom management, his philosophy on education, No Child Left Behind, and all the other routine topics they ask about on such interviews. The school's tragic past was not the elephant in the room he'd hoped it would be.

"Yes," Ryan said. "Absolutely."

Hansen leaned forward and placed both elbows on the desk. He looked hard at Ryan, but with a smile.

"Do you mind if we keep the next few minutes somewhat…blunt?" he asked.

Ryan shrugged. "Fine by me. I'm good with blunt."

Hansen pushed off the desk and rocked back in his seat. He sat in that position for a moment, rocking gently, metal squeaking, fingers steepled together beneath his double chin.

Was this act of sincere rumination for effect, Ryan wondered, or was Hansen really at a temporary loss for words? Ryan's gut reluctantly settled on effect; Hansen appeared the storyteller type.

"You want this job because you can't get anything else, am I right?" Hansen asked.

Ryan searched for an answer. None was forthcoming.

Hansen seemed to sense this and swiveled his chair to the right, taking his eyes off Ryan and placing them on the bare wall as he spoke. "Remember, we're being blunt here, Ryan, so I hope you're not taking offense to this."

"No offense taken," Ryan said. "My skin is thick."

"Good. Because I'm sure you're a damn fine teacher. Problem is, you just graduated. Yes, it helps that you're a little older than the average graduate, but the truth is that no cushy district is willing to give you a contract unless you sub for two zillion years, give or take. And even then, who knows? Heck, most people who *do* try to go down that road fail to gain enough Act 48 and continuing-ed credits to gain their level two certification, and by then they have no choice *but* to remain a sub; their level one certification is no good anymore. Heck, at that point you'd be better off working a steady gig at McDonald's, where you'd get better wages and benefits than you would as a sub—by a long shot."

Call me choir, brother, Ryan thought, *cuz you're preaching to me.*

Hansen took a breath and continued talking to the wall.

"Of course you *could* find a stable gig in the city to gain those credits, but then finding shirts and sweaters to fit over a bulletproof vest can prove somewhat cumbersome, wouldn't you agree?"

Ryan reluctantly grunted his agreement. Working in certain parts of Philadelphia's inner city was indeed like working in a war zone, where personal safety unfortunately took precedence over a student's education. And he should know; much of his field experience had taken place there. Loved the kids—*loved* the kids—but the structure of their environment and influence…it was as though nature was nurture's bitch.

Hansen continued: "So, you find us. The secret behind our desperate need for teachers is hardly a secret anymore, and you figure, why not? It's in a lovely suburb. The pay and benefits are nice. The school's just been rebuilt, brand spanking new. Sounds like a great gig, yeah?"

"Sounds like if this 'head of HR' thing doesn't work out for you, then you have a decent future as a fortune teller, Jerry," Ryan said.

Hansen accommodated Ryan's wit with a chuckle, spun back in his chair, and faced Ryan. "Well, I'm afraid my comments are simply based on the majority of hopefuls like yourself who have walked in and out of these doors this past week."

Ryan frowned. "So, you're not as desperate for teachers as you've made out?"

"I wouldn't say that. Many come in from neighboring states. New Jersey, Delaware…folks who haven't been bombarded with all the gossip and cuckoo talk that goes on around this area. Still, the majority tends to deflate before the interview is even done."

"Why?"

"Well, once they find out about all the…*things* that have occurred here…" He shrugged. "I guess it just spooks them."

Ryan frowned again. "Surely these applicants knew about these 'things' before they applied, yes? They couldn't have been going in blind?"

"Yes and no," Hansen said. "They knew some stuff—*some* stuff."

"We're still being blunt, right, Jerry?"

"Of course," Hansen replied quickly. He seemed eager to hear what Ryan was about to say.

"Why would you tell them more than they needed to know?" Ryan said. "You need teachers, and yet it seems like you're scaring them away."

Hansen stuck out his lower lip in a judicial spout, pausing a few seconds before saying: "They've got a right to know everything that's happened in that building before signing a contract."

"Sure, I understand that," Ryan said, "but it sounds to me like you're telling them about the deadliness of lung cancer right before offering them a cigarette."

Hansen seemed amused by the analogy. He asked: "What do you know about the school?"

Ryan could feel a line of sweat running down his back. It was hotter in this room than the lobby. He straightened his posture and cleared his throat. And then Hansen's earlier words suddenly came back to him, and his focus shifted.

"Wait a minute," he said. "Did I hear you right earlier? Did you say I *had* the job? It's mine?"

Hansen nodded.

"Great," Ryan said. *Meeting over, I hope.* "So where do we go from here? I imagine I have some papers to sign…?"

Hansen ignored Ryan's question and repeated his own. "What do you know about the school?"

The room *was* hotter than the lobby; Ryan was sure of it. Maybe it was Hansen's breath.

"Mr. Hansen—"

"Jerry."

"*Jerry.* I don't understand why you're harping on this. I'm okay with the school's history; it doesn't bother me in the slightest. I don't believe in curses, and I assure you that those wacky locals who picket the school and the old HR building will have no effect on me whatsoever. I just want to teach."

Hansen turned away from Ryan and spoke to the wall again. "Your response is admirable, Ryan. And I believe you'll work out fine here. But the reason I am"—he held up both hands and made quotation gestures to the wall— "'harping on this' is because of liability issues. It's my job to ensure that every employee I hire for employment in this district—in this *school*—is capable of fulfilling each and every job requirement that is expected of them. We can't afford to have people freak out halfway through the year, if you know what I mean. *You* may think I am trying to spook you and the others, when, in actuality, I'm merely trying to test your resolve."

Ryan went to counter, but Hansen instantly carried on. "Before the school's fire, we had several teachers—veterans—lose it for no apparent reason. These were folks I was quite familiar with; they carried the inner strength of an oak."

"Were these the suicides?" Ryan asked.

"Yes. And each and every one of them took place within the walls of the school itself. A gym teacher hanged himself from a basketball hoop. An art teacher cut both wrists and crawled into one of her closets where she bled to death—a student, bless him, found her—and a science teacher leapt out of his second-floor window headfirst."

Not exactly within the walls of the school, that last one, Ryan thought, and then immediately chastised his dark sense of humor.

"Yeah," Ryan said. "I remember reading about it."

Hansen whirled back around in his chair. He was oddly excited. "The medical professionals in the community believe that curses are ludicrous, of course; they felt that the suicide victims had to have been unstable in one way or another, despite their years of diligent service."

"What about you?" Ryan asked. "Surely you don't believe in curses and whatnot…"

Hansen shrugged. "To tell you the truth, I don't really know anymore. I'm one of a few original employees left around here; I knew the victims well. They certainly seemed fine to me."

Ryan loosened his tie. "I'm still here, Jerry. And I still want the job."

Hansen sat back in his chair and began tapping his fingers in rhythm across his belly. Ryan watched Hansen studying his fingers as they twiddled on his stomach. You could argue that the man was deep in thought. But Ryan felt confident Hansen already knew what he was going to say next, he was just waiting for the perfect moment to deliver it. Storyteller indeed.

"The murders?" Hansen finally said. "You know about the murders?"

This is hands down the most bizarre job interview I have ever been on in my entire life. I can see why the others left halfway through the interview. They weren't freaked out about the school's history. They were freaked out from Jerry "Manson" Hansen here.

"Yes, I read all about the murders."

Hansen continued as though Ryan had said no.

"Six murders in the past sixteen years. At an *elementary school*, for Christ's sake. Kids killing kids."

Ryan repeated himself. "Yeah, I read about those. One boy stabbed and killed two of his classmates in '87. Another beat a fellow student to death with a baseball bat during recess in—"

"'99," Hansen broke in. "The last one was 2003. Another stabbing. *Three* children killed this time. Four wounded. The student, the perpetrator—good grades, good boy, never a lick of trouble from him—apparently had asked to go to the boys' room. Instead, he went to the cafeteria, somehow managed to secure two large kitchen knives, returned to his classroom—a knife in each hand—and did his thing. I guess that was when the locals felt enough was enough and…" Hansen finished his sentence by pretending to light a match and set something on fire, sound effects and all.

Ryan nearly cast Hansen a disgusted look after his stunning portrayal of an arsonist, yet reeled it in—despite Hansen's previous assurance that the job was already his, he knew a considerable amount of ass-kissing was still required.

"Unbelievable, isn't it?" Hansen asked. "These were children, for God's sake. Murderers before puberty."

"Victims before puberty too," Ryan added.

Hansen acknowledged Ryan's comment and looked as though he may have regretted his words.

Ryan, desperate to change subjects, asked: "Have you decided what grade you're going to be putting me in?"

"You'll be teaching fifth grade in our west wing. You'll have three team members, but, unfortunately, no mentor. In fact, *all* of your team members will be first-year teachers. I'm sure you understand."

No mentor??? Fuuuck…

"Sounds fine to me," Ryan lied. "I'm sure everything will be fine."

Hansen stood and walked to the solitary window in the room. He looked out of it as though something had caught his eye.

Only Ryan knew better. He knew Hansen's act by the window was merely an attempt at biding additional time so he could choose a new line of questioning, to reintroduce the subject Ryan was so desperately eager to avoid.

"I really like your optimism, Ryan," Hansen said. "I think you're going to do fine. It must have been quite a shock to find out you got the job minutes into your very first interview, yes?"

No mention of voodoo this time. Perhaps I was wrong.

"Shock is right," he said. "A pleasant shock, however."

Hansen smiled but kept staring out the window. "You have something I admire," he said.

"What's that?"

"Ignorance."

Ryan wondered whether he'd heard him correctly. Had he just been insulted?

"*Ignorance?*"

Hansen broke his gaze from the window and returned to his seat. "You're not afraid," he said. "You're not afraid because you're ignorant."

Ryan shifted uncomfortably in his chair. Hansen sensed this and quickly elaborated.

"I'm not using the word 'ignorant' in a negative connotation, Ryan. Please don't think for one moment that I was questioning your intelligence and whatnot. The simple truth is that you aren't afraid because you don't know what it is you're up against, and for that I envy you. It's your *ignorance* that makes you fearless."

Ryan felt better and worse after Hansen's explanation. Better because he now understood that he was not being insulted; worse because he could not understand, for the life of him, why the director of human resources was trying to convince him the boogeyman was real.

"So, you *do* believe in curses," Ryan said.

"No," Hansen quickly responded, "I am a man of science. I trust my eyes; I trust logic."

"Doesn't sound that way to me," Ryan said. "You just said you envy me because my ignorance protects me from whatever naughty stuff wanders up and down the halls of Pinewood Elementary."

"You asked me whether I believed in curses, and I do not," Hansen said. "There *is* something wrong with Pinewood, though. Something…" He paused, frowning as he dug for the right words. Then: "*Bad.* Something inside that school is *bad.*"

It took you that long to think of "bad"?

"But it's a fresh start now, right?" Ryan said. "Highland Elementary is gone. Pinewood is the future. Full of promise and free of the stigma that plagued it, yes?"

"Just new bricks and paint; that's all Pinewood is," Hansen said. "Whatever it was is still there."

Man of science, Ryan's ass. He could all but smell Hansen's fear of the unknown. He needed to bring him back and end this insane interview before Hansen ended up underneath the table sucking his thumb.

"I'm still here, Jerry. It's been five more minutes, and I'm still here." Ryan took a breath, let it out slow. "I certainly agree that what happened over the years was tragic. But I do not, for one minute, believe that something '*bad*' inhabits that school."

Hansen smiled and whispered: "*Ignorance.*"

Ryan's temper flared, slackening the leash on his required ass-kissing. "You can call it ignorance if you want, Jerry, but I don't recall many people blaming Freddy Krueger or the Blair Witch when the incident at Columbine occurred. Same with Virginia Tech—no talk of '*bad*' things there." Ryan had now thrown Hansen's woeful adjective back at him twice. He needed to check himself.

But Hansen hardly noticed. In fact, he perked up. "They were high schools and colleges, Ryan. We're an *elementary* school. What compels children to slaughter children on *three separate occasions* over the span of twenty years?"

Ryan just shook his head, figuring it best to stay mute.

"Not to mention the other stuff," Hansen added.

"Suicides are tragic," Ryan said, "but hardly an excuse for the occult or whatever the locals wish to call it."

Hansen stood and walked to the window again. He peered out of it pensively.

Fucking drama, Ryan thought, rolling his eyes behind Hansen's back.

"That's not what I was referring to," Hansen said. "People watch the news, they read the paper. They learn about the big stuff, the stuff that's impossible to ignore. The murders, the fires, the suicides. But they never learn about the little things, the small stuff. The stuff the school kept a secret from the media as best it could."

Ryan gave a little shrug. "If it's small, then what's the big deal? I mean, I would imagine its significance pales in comparison to what you refer to as 'the big stuff,' yes?"

Hansen turned his head from the window slightly and looked at Ryan with one eye. "That depends: do you go for the horror films with the big budgets and elaborate special effects, or do you prefer the subtle, psychological horror?"

Ryan splayed a hand. "I don't know; I suppose I prefer subtle horror, the psychological stuff."

Hansen controlled his smile to something small and appropriate. "Me too." He turned and faced Ryan completely. "The murders were tragic. *Horrific.* All those children dying, and at the hands of other children, no less. It was beyond comprehension. But you see, that was the big stuff, the special effects; the subtle, psychological horrors were the motives of the children who committed those murders."

"And they were?"

Hansen splayed his short stubby arms. "There were none. Not even any recollection of the atrocities they committed. Nothing from all three. No recollection. Zip."

"They were probably lying," Ryan said.

Hansen went on undeterred. "These were children who underwent *extreme* psychological testing after what happened during their respective incidents. Not one of them recollected the horrors they committed. And believe me, there are dozens of psychologists, therapists—they even tried hypnotists—ready to swear on their lives that they believe every word those children said. Lying? I think not."

"Psychopaths are excellent liars, Jerry, children and adults alike."

"Not one single doctor signed off on that possibility. You don't think they would have caught it? These were good kids. Strong students. Popular. No history of deviant behavior at home or in the classroom."

Ryan kept quiet for a moment. He wanted the interview over, and he wanted Hansen to be a memory he could share with his buddies tonight over a beer. Still, one thing seemed odd to Ryan. Where was the principal? This director of human resources seemed to have more insider gossip than the token busybody on the corner, yet the principal—the one who likely had even more meaty bits to share than old Hansen here— was curiously absent.

"Where is Mr. James?" Ryan asked. "I would have thought he'd be here."

"Gone," Hansen said. "Off to greener pastures. Deborah Gates will be taking his place. Miss Gates is a first-year employee with the district as well." Hansen paused a moment. Then: "I expect you're wondering how a director of human resources like myself has so much insider knowledge about an elementary school."

Ryan smiled. "Like I said, Jerry; you could be a fortune teller."

Hansen's mood became too somber too fast to acknowledge Ryan's repeat quip. The subject of the school's former principal had obviously affected him.

"Edward James was—*is*—one of my closest friends," Hansen went on. "He went through it all—acting principal for every single catastrophe that occurred at the school. You'd think after all that happened, he would have been replaced or quit, but no one else wanted the job, and Ed absolutely insisted on staying on. He confided in me about everything. Ed walks with a limp now. I suppose the reason for that limp was his last straw."

"A limp?"

Hansen only nodded.

Christ, he's going to make me ask. "So, what happened?"

"One of the small things," Hansen replied, and stopped there.

Oh, for the love of— "Such as…?"

4

"Ed was leaving the school well after six on a Friday evening," Hansen said. "He was a clean freak, Ed was. Couldn't stand litter or clutter, and it wasn't uncommon to have the stray paper or pencil or candy wrapper or whatever escape the janitor's attention." Hansen leaned back in his chair, ample belly jutting, his shirt buttons struggling to hold hands. He was too deep in thought to even notice or care. "So, Ed spots a couple of errant crayons on the floor outside a classroom and wanders on over to pick 'em up. Once again, it's after six, smack dab in the middle of January, so it's dark out already. The school's lit some, but it's anything but bright. All the classroom lights are out. It's a wonder how he even spotted the damn crayons. So, as he bends over to pick them up, he hears whispers coming from the dark classroom in front of him. He thinks it's kids hiding, playing a joke, who knows, right?"

Ryan nodded without thought.

"Either way, there's no damn reason *any* kid should be in the school that late, especially since everyone but Ed was gone. So Ed enters the classroom and flicks on the light. He sees just one boy. One boy, all by himself, his back to Ed, sitting and facing the corner of the room with his legs folded like he's being read to or something."

Ryan leaned in.

"The kid is real close to the corner of the wall—almost crammed into it—and he doesn't even flinch or take notice of Ed when those bright classroom lights come on. He just keeps on whispering to himself and staring into that corner."

"What was he whispering?" Ryan asked.

"Ed didn't know," Hansen replied. "The school was pin-drop quiet, but Ed claimed he couldn't make out a single word the boy was saying. So, of course Ed calls to the boy, but the kid doesn't answer. He just stays put and keeps on whispering into that corner. So, Ed inches towards the boy and calls to him again. Nothing. He can't call the boy's name because the kid's back is turned and he can't get a look at his face."

"Who was the kid?" Ryan asked.

Hansen ignored the question. Did, in fact, look mildly annoyed that Ryan had suggested flipping to the last page.

"So," Hansen went on, "Ed is now a good five feet from the boy, standing behind him. The boy still hasn't moved an inch and still hasn't acknowledged Ed. He's still whispering something, only Ed claims they weren't words, at least none that he'd ever heard before, and Ed was as learned as they came, spoke three different languages.

"Finally, Ed gets a bit frustrated, steps forward, and taps the boy's shoulder. The boy turns around and locks eyes with Ed…and that's when Ed froze stiff."

Ryan hated to admit it, but Hansen had him now. "Why did he freeze?"

"Ed was tough," Hansen said. "Ed *is* tough. Did two tours of Vietnam that had him seeing things that most people could never stomach. But when that boy turned and looked up at Ed, well, Ed claims that was the first time he'd ever been truly afraid. Like down to his core. Ed claims that boy's eyes were pure white, like they'd rolled back into his head, and his mouth was…was too big."

"*Too big?*"

"Ed claims the boy was smiling, no, *grinning* up at him, and that the boy's mouth was too big, like it had too many teeth."

Ryan became aware of the tie around his neck. He loosened it with a finger.

"What did the boy say?" he asked.

Hansen shrugged. "Nothing. He just stared up at Ed with those white eyes and that impossibly big grin and stayed as mute as a broken radio. Ed said nothing himself; he was too damn scared."

"The limp," Ryan said. "What does this have to do with the limp that finally made him call it quits?"

"Ed eventually summoned the courage to speak to the boy," Hansen replied. "'Are you okay?' 'What are you doing here?' Et cetera. And the boy just kept staring up at Ed—still the white eyes; still the big grin—but his right hand pulls out a pair of scissors. Before Ed can even blink, that little bastard jams those scissors right into the top of Ed's foot. The boy turned out to be only nine years old, but he jammed those scissors in so hard they went right through the leather instep of Ed's shoe and straight into the bone, splitting it like a crab shell."

"Jesus," Ryan breathed. "Who was the boy?"

"A student," Hansen replied. "A fourth-grader who had somehow managed to make his way into the building after hours."

"So then what happened?"

"Well, there's Ed screaming and cursing and hopping on one foot, and there's this boy, on his feet now, grinning up at Ed with those eyes, head tilted slightly to one side as though he's amused by Ed's dance, his pain. The boy then starts to whisper again, only this time it's a bit louder, a normal speaking tone. And Ed—despite his pain—ignores his foot and shifts all his attention back onto the boy, to what the boy was saying."

"What was he saying?"

"It wasn't gibberish; Ed was adamant about that. He insisted it was a language of sorts. It had inflections and lilts and pauses…how did Ed put it? Sideways English?"

"*Sideways English?*"

"Yeah. Ed said it was like English, but it wasn't. Like someone took a proper sentence and threw it in a blender before trying to read it." Hansen smiled a little at recalling this.

"You've got a heck of a memory, Jerry."

Hansen nodded. "Well, I still talk to Ed. Every now and then we discuss what happened. He doesn't really mention the murders or the suicides much, but he sure as hell dwells on that one boy."

Ryan casually glanced at the clock on the wall. He had been here an hour. Far longer than he'd expected. Still, that didn't stop him from asking: "How did Ed end up dealing with the situation? By that I mean, what did Ed do after the boy stabbed his foot and started babbling in 'sideways English'?"

Hansen appeared pleased with Ryan's deeper inquiry. Didn't even try to hide it. And why not? The only thing the storyteller loves more than an audience is a captivated one.

"Like I said, Ed was tough. And nine-year-old boy or not, he grabbed that kid by his *throat* and slammed him up against the wall. Ed started screaming at the boy, chastising him, but the boy's expression never changed. He just kept grinning and speaking that speak with eyes as big and as white as golf balls. And Ed admitted to me that despite his rage, he was still scared shitless by this child he was holding by the throat. Ed said it was like holding some talking doll that was broken and wouldn't shut up. So, his fear caused him to strike out."

"He hit him?"

Hansen nodded. "Yup. Not a slap either. Closed fist, right on the bridge of the boy's nose."

Ryan sat back and gave Hansen a funny look.

"It's true. The boy's nose popped like a big pimple, and blood went everywhere. Ed immediately dropped the boy and took a step back, horribly ashamed at what he'd done."

Can't fucking blame the guy. Some kid stabs my foot then goes all Linda Blair on me, I'm swinging too. As a first-year teacher seated with the head of HR, Ryan thought it best to keep that last thought to himself.

Hansen continued. "The boy's eyes welled up from that punch, rolled from white back to their natural blue, and before you know it, there was just a plain old fourth-grader in the room, sobbing from a punch on the nose his principal had just given him."

"Jesus," Ryan said. "So that's why Mr. James left? Because he assaulted a child?"

"No, no, no—the boy doesn't even remember Ed hitting him. Doesn't even remember how he *got* to the damn school in the first place. Much like the children who committed those murders over the years, the boy remembered *nothing*."

"And I imagine there's a fleet of specialists willing to testify under oath to that," Ryan said.

Hansen's eyebrows knitted, looking as though he couldn't be sure whether Ryan was patronizing him or not. Still, he replied: "Yes—that's right."

"How did something like this escape the media?" Ryan asked. "I admit it is small compared to the other stuff, but it's pretty darn shocking, if you ask me."

"Ed buried it. The parents of the child were initially upset, of course, but agreed once they heard the details of what happened and got a good look at Ed's foot. Pretty soon it was as good as fiction. Ed buried lots of stuff when he was there. The small stuff. But after this…after this, Ed was done."

Ryan was now at a crossroads. He wanted to leave. He had been here way too long, and knowing now that he had the job, he saw little point in continuing his chat with Hansen if all they were going to do was exchange ghost stories. The problem, however, was that Hansen had hooked him with the last story, the bastard.

Still, Ryan could not be blatant about his desire for more; asking a storyteller like Hansen for more yarns was like asking a gun fanatic whether he wanted more ammo. Ryan needed to be subtle in his approach, squeeze out one or maybe two more quick gems if he was ever going to have that beer with his buddies tonight.

"This small stuff you keep mentioning, Jerry—this small stuff that most are unaware of…is there something *I* should be aware of before attempting to do my job? Something that may prevent me from doing my job to the best of my capabilities?"

Not bad.

With both elbows on the table, Hansen interlocked his short, stubby fingers and rested his chin on them, hammock-like. He then frowned as though trying to figure out a riddle. After a substantial pause, chin still resting on his finger-hammock, jaw closed, answering through his lips only, he replied: "I don't know."

Ryan wanted to laugh out loud. After all the man had shared, *now* he was at a loss for words?

"*No?*" Ryan could not help but blurt.

19

Hansen unlocked his fingers and lifted his chin. He sat back and breathed deep. "*Nobody* knows, Ryan. Nobody knows *what* to expect. Hell, if we had expected any of the prior tragedies to occur, we could have avoided them altogether, right?"

Good point.

"I will say this," Hansen began. "Trust your instincts and grow eyes in the back of your head. A bit clichéd, I know, but it's the truth. I would also suggest trusting *no one* in addition to your instincts."

"That's…kind of unusual advice for a first-year teacher. I mean, I would imagine a rapport with my peers, and especially my grade-level team, is highly encouraged. That would be tough to come by without a little trust," Ryan said.

Hansen offered a little smile. "So give them a little, but not a lot. You seem like a good guy, Ryan. I'll probably be fired for telling you this stuff." He laughed at his own wit. "But the truth, at least as far as I see it—"

(*Grain of salt, anyone?*)

"—is that weird stuff happens in that school when your guard is down; keep it high and tight."

Hansen stood and held out his hand. The interview was finally done.

"Welcome aboard, Ryan," he said.

Ryan took Hansen's hand and gave it a firm shake. "I've really got the job? Just like that?"

Hansen smiled and said: "Just like that. Pam—one of my HR reps—will have some paperwork for you to sign. She's at the school now, waiting for you. She'll be able to give you a brief look around, show you your classroom. The building officially opens this Monday. You can start setting up your room then. You'll have until the 28th to get everything ready. After that you'll have a week of orientation. Classes officially start on the 5th."

"Thank you, Jerry."

Hansen extended his hand again. Ryan thought it odd, but took it anyway. Hansen held the shake longer than before, smiling at Ryan like a parent might when their child boarded the school bus for the first time. It was a smile that held both well-wishes and worry.

5

Exiting the human resources building, Ryan cared little that he was back in the oven after being pampered by the building's conditioned air—he had a *job* and was temporarily impervious to discomfort. And it was this imperviousness that kept him from doing the upper-body striptease en route back to his car that he'd promised himself earlier. After all, he still needed to meet Pam the HR rep at Pinewood. Job now secured or not, he figured it best to keep the straitjacket and noose on for professional appearance's sake. The striptease could wait until he was on his way home.

Ryan was seconds from putting his key into the driver's side door of his car when he felt eyes on his back. He turned and found a woman staring at him. Her expression was an easy yet curious read. She looked disgusted with him.

"Hi," Ryan said.

The woman said nothing, just fixed him with that look of disgust. Ryan shrugged, unlocked his car, and went to open the door.

"Why would you work there?" she finally asked. Her voice was unsteady. The voice of a woman who'd recently been crying or was on the verge of crying.

Ryan pulled his hand away from the car door and faced her. He guessed her at perhaps forty, her unkempt appearance making Ryan's guess generous. Her posture was fidgety. Her face, her eyes in particular, dark and bagged—that of a woman who hadn't known sleep for some time.

"Work where?" Ryan asked.

"Why?" she asked again. Her fidgeting grew. Ryan thought it looked as though she was trying to ignore a bug crawling up her leg.

"I just left a human resources building," Ryan said. "How do you know where I'll be working?"

The lady took a few steps towards him. Ryan felt uneasy as she approached. Surely he wasn't afraid of this woman?

Local loonies, dude. Can't be too sure.

"I know where you'll be working," she said. Her tone was harsh, the clear yet curious disgust for Ryan climbing with his tiptoeing around her query.

Ryan placed his portfolio on the top of his car. "How do you know I got the job?"

Two bugs crawling up her leg now. Blatant disgust now partnered with anger.

"You got the damn job," she said. "There's a reason no one wants to work there, you know. A reason that no one wants to send their children there, too."

Ryan sighed. *Hansen's sister, perhaps?* he mused. *More story time ahead?*

"Well, apparently I'll be teaching a full classroom in less than a month," he said. "Go figure."

"You'll never get that far," the woman replied. "The district demands we build a new elementary school, but why in the name of God would they *re*build?"

"Convenience, I suppose. Don't have to search for a new location. Foundation is already built. It's just a matter of putting the pieces back together."

"Some pieces don't fit. Some pieces *won't* fit."

Ryan sighed again. "So I've heard. Listen, I hate to be rude, but it's got to be about a hundred and fifty degrees out here—if I stay any longer, I'm going to start seeing purple spots before my eyes."

Ryan flashed on an old Bugs Bunny cartoon. Elmer Fudd was freaking out after Bugs had convinced him he had "rabbititis" by painting the room with an array of spots, a sure symptom of the horrible disease. *Spots! I see spots before my eyes! Dr. Killpatient! Dr. Killpatient!*

Ryan politely waited for a response. He also bit the inside of his cheek to keep from smiling, Mr. Fudd and Mr. Bunny tickling him as they always had. Figuring no response was forthcoming—only the constant, hateful glare—Ryan opened the car door, tossed his portfolio inside, and was halfway inside his vehicle when the woman finally responded. And Ryan was certain he'd heard her wrong.

"My son's a retard," the woman had said, or so it seemed.

Ryan froze, one leg inside the car. "I beg your pardon?"

"My son is a *retard*," she said again.

He *had* heard her correctly.

Ryan pulled his leg from the car and faced the woman again. He measured his response. What type of mother called her son a "retard," for Christ's sake?

"I'm…not sure that's a very politically correct way of stating something like that, ma'am," he opted to say.

The woman shifted continuously from her left foot to her right. Three bugs on her leg now. "Doesn't matter what you say. I know how it is. My son is a retard. He's a retard because of that fucking place you insist on working in."

"Retard" and now "fuck?" Classy lady, this one. Does this nut job really have the audacity to blame the school *for her poor son's misfortune?*

The woman read the skepticism on Ryan's face as plain as if he'd spoken it.

"I had a perfectly normal son until the day he entered third grade at that…that shithole you call a school."

"Shithole" now, huh? Very classy indeed. Also a little unnerving if he was being honest with himself.

"Only *one* week after school had started, I get a call from the counselor," the woman went on. "She claimed he couldn't even write his own name anymore. Couldn't even solve the simplest of arithmetic problems. He couldn't even color a goddamn coloring book without making a mess of it!"

He was drugged.

"Did you have any pharmacology tests done?" Ryan asked. "Perhaps he ingested something toxic?"

"Of course I did! They found nothing! The only thing those tests *did* find was that…was that his IQ had dropped fifty points."

The shock on Ryan's face arrived before he could leash it.

"*Yes!*" the woman exclaimed. "*Fifty* points! One minute he's about to start learning multiplication, and the next minute he's struggling to tell me what two-plus-fucking-two is!" The woman was crying now. A twinge of sympathy poked at Ryan's heart. Still, he remained ever wary of the woman.

"I'm so very sorry, ma'am," Ryan said. "That's very tragic. I don't know what could have happened to your boy, I really don't. However, I still believe referring to your son as a 'retard' is not—"

"I *know* what happened! Everyone in this *town* knows what happened! And he *is* a retard! He's a retard because he's not the child God gave me! God gave me a perfectly healthy boy. The boy I own now is damaged. Something *unholy* in that school damaged my boy."

Ryan dropped his head and shook it. *Time to squash this.*

"Again, I'm truly sorry, ma'am. I wish you and your son the very best." He turned his back to the woman, entered his car, and shut the door as she started to speak again. He backed out of his spot, watching her talk—*yell*—at his driver's side window as he did so.

Ryan caught one last sight of her in his rearview as he pulled away. She was now roaring at the world in all directions. Roaring at the sky, to God, perhaps.

Ryan still did not believe in ghosts or curses or witchcraft or whatever the hell the local loonies were currently settled on, but he did have to admit that the woman had one over on old Hansen. Hansen had him for an hour and had done little but strain Ryan's eyes from rolling them so much after every melodramatic spin Hansen put on each of his—admittedly amusing at times—tales.

This woman had had him for less than five minutes, and Ryan would be lying if he said he wasn't pulling away feeling—admittedly, but with no trace of amusement this time—a little spooked.

6

Rebecca Lawrence poured herself a cup of coffee and sat across from her mother at their kitchen table. "Do you think I got the job because I'm your daughter?"

Carol Lawrence lifted her own cup of coffee to her mouth and spoke a second before the rim touched her lips. "Does it matter?"

Rebecca shrugged. "Maybe a little. I mean, it's nice to have a job, but I was just wondering whether they would have offered me the job had I not been your daughter."

"Life lesson, my dear: sometimes it's not what you know but *who* you know. Besides, you know how desperate we are for teachers."

"Gee, thanks, Mom. So, now I got the job because I'm your daughter *and* they're desperate?"

Carol laughed. "Whoops—guess that came out the wrong way."

Rebecca smiled. "Forgiven."

"What *I'm* wondering," Carol said, "is if you're going to be weirded out by having your mommy teaching in the same building as you."

"Doesn't bother me in the slightest," Rebecca said. "In fact, I'm sure I'll be quite the popular newcomer when it comes to gossip time—being the daughter of one of the only remaining employees from Highland Elementary and all."

"You're making me feel old."

"Revenge for the 'desperate' comment."

They shared a pleasant smile, sipped from their cups, and sat silently for a moment. Then: "Are you nervous?"

"A little," Rebecca replied. "First grade is a big jump from fifth when I student-taught."

"You'll be fine. Just be sure to establish good structure and routine right from the beginning. Those first few weeks are crucial."

Rebecca nodded back, then dropped her gaze to her coffee and kept it there when she asked: "Do you believe any of the stuff that's said about the school?"

"What stuff is that?"

"That it's cursed or haunted or whatever."

Carol raised an eyebrow. "I would hope that I raised you well enough that you didn't believe in those sorts of things."

"You did, and I don't, but…"

"But…?"

"Come on, Mom, think about all the horrible stuff that happened there. You were there for it all. Are you telling me it didn't make you wonder from time to time?"

Carol laughed. "Wonder whether the place was *haunted*?"

"Never mind."

Carol finished her coffee, stood, and went to the counter for a refill.

"Do you believe in God?" Rebecca asked.

Carol turned, coffeepot in one hand, empty mug in the other. Her eyebrow was up again. "How did this go from a 'first day of work' chat to an 'is there a God' chat?"

Rebecca shrugged again. "I don't know. Just kinda came out after all the voodoo talk about the school, I guess."

"Fair enough. I *do* believe in a higher power, but I've got no time for organized religion. And I *always* encouraged you to follow your own path; you know that." She returned to her seat next to her daughter with a fresh cup.

"Are you happy that I don't follow an organized religion like you?" Rebecca asked. "That I don't go to church?"

"Not at all. But I *am* proud that you made up your own mind on the matter without others influencing you."

Rebecca dropped her gaze to her coffee again. "It does make you wonder, though, doesn't it? All the crazy stuff that happened in that building? It's like something out of a movie."

"It is definitely movie material, that's for sure. I suppose I'm just happy they decided to rebuild and that I've got my old job back. Subbing during the interim was no fun at all."

Rebecca sat back in her chair and ran a hand through her long blonde hair. "I still don't know why they decided to rebuild," she said. "After a vigilante act like that fire, you would think they would have left the school alone. Bulldozed it or something."

"There's only one other elementary school in the district, honey. Couldn't exactly pack all those kids in neighboring towns into one school. Would *you* want to teach a class with fifty kids?"

To Rebecca, such a thought was more terrifying than the more immediate prospect of ghosts and curses. "*Hell* no."

Carol laughed. "Well, there you go then."

"But to *rebuild*," Rebecca said. "That's what the locals are still so upset about, isn't it? Rebuilding instead of relocating?"

"There *was* no place to relocate. Everyone seems to gloss over that fact, even though the *multiple* town meetings emphasized this truth over a dozen times."

Rebecca grunted. She'd attended a few of those town meetings with her mother and was guilty of forgetting this fact herself. She switched gears in her questioning. "I don't think I ever asked you why you stayed on so long at the school. So many teachers left during the tragedies, but you never even considered it, did you?"

"Of course I *considered* it. But then what type of example would I be setting for the children? 'Kids, ghosts and monsters aren't real, but I'm getting the hell out of here while the gettin' is good' doesn't exactly reflect well on me, does it?"

Rebecca laughed.

"More importantly," Carol went on, "teachers are informal parents to their students. We help raise them. They look to us for guidance, and support, and even love. To abandon them after such a traumatizing moment in their lives is just that: abandonment. I never want a child to feel such a thing during their formative years, no way. Not on my watch."

Rebecca all but beamed at her mother. She didn't think it was possible to respect her more. "That's awesome, Mom. It really is."

Carol gave a theatric bow of the head. Rebecca laughed again.

"Enough crazy talk," Carol said. "What activities do you have planned for your first day?"

7

Ryan stuck his key into the front door of his mother's house, unlocked it, and entered.

"Ma?" he called out. "You home?"

Cynthia Herb emerged from around the corner of her kitchen and greeted her son with eyes that defined anticipation. "*Well...?*"

Ryan sauntered towards his mother with the swagger of a celebrity, swinging his suit jacket over his shoulder and pumping his eyebrows to complete the effect.

"You, my darling mother, are looking at the new fifth-grade teacher at Pinewood Elementary School."

Cynthia rushed forward and hugged her son. "Oh, sweetheart, I'm so proud of you!" She then held him back at arm's length. "They let you know already? So soon?"

Ryan nodded. "I know, I know—it was a shock to me too. I thought they'd at least have me back for a second interview before saying anything. I guess they really are desperate for teachers."

Ryan's mother punched him on his arm. "Oh, stop it—that's not why they hired you."

Ryan tossed his new suit jacket towards the back of one of the living room chairs, but missed, and the jacket fell to the floor. Ryan was indifferent, but his mother snatched the jacket right up and punched him again.

"I love how you treat your clothes," she said, dusting the jacket off with one hand.

"Hopefully, I won't be wearing that damn thing anytime soon."

"Yes, well, your mother *paid* for it and would appreciate it if her son showed a bit more respect."

Ryan kissed his mother on the top of her head. "I'm sorry, Ma. You're right."

This seemed to temporarily mollify her, but did not stop Cynthia Herb from making sure every last dust particle and strand of cat hair—she had three—had been wiped from her son's black jacket. Satisfied, she handed it back to him and said: "Hang it up. And hang your slacks up too. Do it nice."

Ryan was already in the kitchen with his head buried inside the refrigerator. "I will in a second, Ma," he called over his shoulder. "Anyway, like I was saying, the guy didn't even look at my portfolio. We barely talked about the curriculum or anything. In fact, I thought I heard him wrong when he told me I had the job right off the bat."

Cynthia gave in, carefully hung the jacket over the back of a kitchen chair, then said: "Right off the bat? That's odd—you were there for over an hour. What did you talk about?"

Ryan's head emerged from the fridge. In his right hand was a can of soda; in his left, a porcelain bowl covered in plastic wrap. He waved them around as he spoke.

"To be honest, the guy was kind of weird. He seemed like he was more into scaring me than offering me a job."

"Scare you?"

"Yeah, you know—all the crazy stuff that happened there over the years…It seemed like that's all he wanted to talk about. Said he wanted to make sure I didn't scare easy and *'freak out'* halfway through the school year. I have to admit, some of the things he told me *were* pretty messed up."

Ryan's mother walked toward her son and took the porcelain bowl out of his hand. She placed it in the microwave and pushed a few buttons.

"I could have eaten it cold," he said.

"What kind of 'messed-up' things?" she asked. "Did he talk about the murders and the suicides?"

Ryan tapped the top of the soda can a few times before he cracked the tab and took a sip.

"Yeah, he mentioned them a little. But he talked about some other stuff too. Stuff most people don't know about. Did you know a nine-year-old boy stabbed the principal in the foot with a pair of scissors? Apparently, this happened after hours. School was empty save for the principal and the kid. Creepiest part wasn't so much the kid stabbing the principal, but what the kid was doing right before he stabbed him. Apparently, according to the principal anyway, the kid was under some kind of crazy trance, like he was possessed or something. Eyes all rolled back white, speaking in tongues, grinning like a psycho."

"You're kidding me."

"I kid you not, Ma. The principal cracked him a good one after he did it, too. Banged him right on the nose. Creepiest thing was that the kid had no recollection of the stabbing whatsoever."

Cynthia folded her arms tight to her chest, a pacifying movement she often did when uneasy. Softly, she said: "Just like all the other children over the years."

"Yep. I'm telling you this guy Jerry Hansen—that was his name, the HR guy—he was like a fat little Vincent Price. One ghoulish tale after the other."

The microwave beeped, and Ryan retrieved the bowl. It was rice, veggies, and diced chicken, and half of it was in his mouth before it had a moment to cool. He garbled a curse with his full mouth and immediately took a big swig from his soda to put out the flames.

"Serves you right," Cynthia said. "You eat too fast."

Still chipmunk-cheeked, still chewing, he blew his mother a kiss.

"Did you get to *see* the school? Or were you just in HR?" Cynthia asked.

Ryan swallowed. "No, I got to see it. I met someone else from HR there for paperwork and stuff. Got a decent look around. Saw my classroom."

"And?"

Ryan shrugged. "It's a classroom."

"How does the school look?"

Ryan shrugged again. "Looks like a school."

Cynthia made a face. "Smartass. I'm talking about the damage that was done after the fire."

"No traces as far as I could tell. Like it never happened."

"I imagine the district is hoping everyone else will soon adopt that line of thinking."

Ryan shoveled in more food, thought of the crazy lady who'd approached him by his car outside the human resources building. *Wouldn't count on it,* he thought.

"So, now you've got a job," Cynthia went on. "No subbing, no long-term subbing, but a *real* contract. A permanent gig."

Ryan chased his mouthful down with more soda and burped lightly into his fist. "A permanent gig, Ma. I can finally get out of your hair and start looking for my own place."

"Oh, sweetheart, you know I don't mind having you here."

Ryan knew that she didn't. His mother was quite possibly his closest friend. They had been by each other's side through much hardship over the years, and their loyalty to one another was unequivocal.

"I know that, Ma, and I don't mind living here; I really don't." And there was truth to this. Home-cooked meals? Laundry? A mother whose company you actually enjoyed instead of avoided? The only downside was, of course, the whole dating situation. Awkward thing to meet a nice girl out on the town, only to tell her you'd moved back in with your mother. True, he'd done so because every penny he earned from the plethora of shit jobs he held down went to tuition, and there was a kind of nobility in that, he supposed, but still, young men who lived with their mother would always carry a certain stigma, likely pioneered by that infamous proprietor of the good old Bates Motel.

"However," Ryan went on, "I think that at thirty, the time has come for me to move out of my mother's basement before I start attending *Star Trek* conventions and the like."

"You just got a late start, sweetheart. You floundered for a little while, but you eventually found your feet. Your life is just starting."

She smiled a mother's smile at him, and Ryan's heart turned to goo.

He hugged her tight, pulled away, and pretended to punch her lightly on the chin. "Thanks, Ma. I think I'll keep you around a little while longer."

"Wait until I'm worth more money before you get rid of me."

"I'd get the house."
"You'd have to split it with your sister."
"Balls."

8

Ryan stood at the head of the classroom, facing all twenty-eight students, all of them boys. No girls.

Whenever he spoke, they laughed at him. When he tried to speak louder, they only laughed louder.

And then silence. But *only* silence; the children's behavior did not change. They still taunted and pointed at Ryan, unaware that their once resounding laughter no longer had a voice. A silent film of students taunting their teacher.

Ryan tested his own voice and found it useless, too. He was sure he'd spoken, felt the subtle vibrations of his vocal cords working; it was the volume that was broken. *His* volume, maybe? Had he gone suddenly deaf? Was the reason the children no longer registered the truth that their laughter had lost its voice was because it hadn't? Good lord, did the fault lie with his hearing?

Ryan went to speak again, louder now, to ask—*beg*—the children to stop laughing for just one damn minute and tell him whether they could hear what he was about to say.

Ryan opened his mouth, but got no further. Anything he had to say, mute or otherwise, held no chance of coming out once he saw their eyes. They had gone white, all of them. Their laughter, still silent—everything still inexplicably silent—continued more so, their mouths—*bigger now?*

Are they…bigger???—seemingly stretched beyond anatomical capacity in the throes of their uproarious fits.

Ryan slammed the bottom of his fist on his desk and cried out. And his voice was heard, by him *and* the children; their laughter stopped, but the grins—*too big, too fucking big*—remained.

Silence again. And Ryan went to speak again. And, like moments before, he got no further. The children had begun to chant in whispers, all of them in unison, not one out of sync.

The volume of their chant grew, loud whispering now, like hisses from a den of snakes, their eyes still impossibly white, grins still impossibly wide, the zeal in their expressions growing with Ryan's blatant fear.

Working in the same unison of their chant, each child simultaneously withdrew a pair of scissors from their desks, each pair twice the size of their prepubescent hands, each pair as sharp as a surgeon's blade; the irrational but rational order of the mind in dream state making this last fact a certainty without the need to touch the scissors' steel.

His feet now of course leaden, denying him movement, Ryan turned helplessly towards the classroom door. He saw the old principal, Mr. James, staring back at him through the small rectangular window of the door—the inexplicable logicalities of the dream world assuring Ryan that it was indeed Mr. James staring back despite his never laying eyes on the man before.

And oh, how Mr. James was enjoying himself. Pointing and laughing at Ryan through that little rectangular window above the classroom door, his laughter as hard and as maniacal as the children's had been.

Ryan turned back to his class, noticed that all twenty-eight boys had now drawn back their arms, scissors cocked. Ryan held up his hands, pleading.

All twenty-eight fired, Ryan waking with a cry before the blades found their target, recalling the cruel and illogical truths of the dream world he'd just experienced, now more than a little grateful for one more: you always woke a second before impact.

──────── ◆ ────────

Ryan had never pissed the bed before. Even during his most booze-infested nights of debauchery when younger, he had never pissed his bed.

He now wondered, with no amusement, whether he'd popped his cherry tonight. He was soaked.

Ryan quickly rolled out of bed, stood, and patted himself down. His boxer shorts might have been the *only* thing that was dry. The rest of him—tee-shirt, hair—was soaked through with sweat. His bedsheet and pillow too.

Any relief Ryan might have felt for not pissing the bed was short lived. The remnants of the dream still hammered his pulse and stuck him with a twinge of shame. To be so physically affected by a nightmare.

"Fucking Hansen," he muttered.

Ryan headed up the basement stairs and tiptoed into the kitchen. There was one bottle of water left in the fridge, and he chugged it down in one go.

"Ryan?" His mother calling down from upstairs.

"Yeah, it's me, Ma."

She came downstairs in her night-robe. All three cats followed her down, took turns weaving in and out of her legs, meowing, hinting that getting a jump on breakfast might be a great freaking idea, please.

Cynthia frowned at her son or, more accurately, his appearance. "Are you okay?"

"I'm fine."

"You're as white as a sheet. Are you sweating?" She placed her palm on his forehead. "You don't *feel* warm."

Ryan pulled his head away and placed the empty water bottle on the counter. "I'm not sick, Ma; I just had a bad dream, that's all."

Cynthia frowned again. "A nightmare?"

"And then some."

"You never get nightmares."

"I know."

"What was it about?"

Ryan turned on the kitchen faucet, bent, and splashed water on his face. "All the crazy stuff the guy from HR told me about today," he said to the sink.

"Here—" Cynthia pushed a dish towel at her son.

Ryan groped for it blindly, grabbed it, thanked her, and toweled off.

"I guess the fat little Vincent Price got to you after all," she said.

Ryan returned what amounted to a courtesy smile and tossed the towel on the counter. "I guess he did." He then frowned. "Did I wake you? I was trying to be quiet."

"I heard you shout."

"I shouted in my sleep?"

"Well, I *hope* it was you. Otherwise there's someone else in here with us."

"Jesus." One of the cats, Sebastian, an orange tabby, jumped on the countertop. Ryan absently stroked him while reflecting on his dream, on the sobering fact that its intensity made him cry out in his sleep. "Must have been a hell of a shout if you heard me from upstairs. Did you not take your Benadryl tonight?"

A problem sleeper who'd tried every drug on the market to find shut-eye, nothing, at least according to Cynthia Herb, worked as well as good old over-the-counter Benadryl. Zonked her good. "No, I got my fix. It still woke me, though. It was a hell of a yell, honey. You sure you're all right?"

Ryan flashed on the dream again. He then flashed on the odd time he brought home a girl after a night out, a girl who didn't mind getting playful in his mother's basement, Ryan confident those quarters were soundproofed with Benadryl and two flights of stairs. His face reddened as he now wondered how many times he or his lady friend for that evening might have woken his mother during such an occasion.

Pleasant thought. What, the nightmare didn't fuck with your head enough?

"Yeah—I'm good, Ma."

Cynthia went to the cabinet, retrieved a glass, filled it with water from the automatic dispenser on the fridge door, and then handed it to her son. "Here—have a little more water and then try going back to sleep. It's still early."

"Any more water and I *will* piss my bed."

"Huh?"

"Never mind." He took the glass of water but didn't drink it.

She patted his cheek and smiled. "See you in the morning. *Come on, babies,*" she then called to the cats. Two of them followed her back upstairs. Sebastian stayed put on the kitchen counter, staring hard at Ryan. *About that early jump on breakfast thing,* that feline stare said.

Ryan fed him, the act an attempt at taking his mind off his dream. He bent and stroked the cat who was eating greedily from his bowl.

"You ever have bad dreams, Sebby?"

Sebastian continued to devour his food.

"No, I suppose not, ya spoiled little bugger."

He gave the cat a final stroke, smiling at the simple pleasure he was taking in his early meal. "Don't tell your mother," he joked. "You owe me one, buddy."

9

Rebecca Lawrence arrived at Pinewood Elementary early Monday morning, before the building had officially unlocked its doors. The back seat of her car was stuffed to capacity and looked as though she was planning a trip cross-country. She was excited, she was anxious, she needed to pee, and she wanted a cigarette.

Rebecca had attempted to quit smoking on her twenty-second birthday. It was a bumpy attempt at first, with the occasional one slipped here and there, usually out drinking with friends (those times were the worst; it was not unusual for her to go through half a pack in a night) or in times of stress. Now, however, as a teacher who would no doubt be preaching health and well-being to a bunch of six-year-olds, she figured it best to drop the habit completely before stepping foot one into her classroom.

And so now, at twenty-three, she had officially kicked the habit, but the urges still taunted her, especially during those social outings and moments of stress, the latter currently taunting without mercy. Should she sneak one now? She was quite sure she still had half a pack buried somewhere in her glove compartment. How old and stale they likely were crossed her mind, and the risk of carrying the odor of smoke into the building on her first day for a quick drag or two of something that probably tasted like shit buried the idea. She opted for her go-to during such times: gum.

She dug in her pants pocket for the pack she always kept, unwrapped a piece, and began chewing with a purpose. Better.

She checked her watch. Five to eight. Five minutes until the building opened, or so she was told. Anxiety continued to tickle her belly. The kids weren't even arriving for another week and a half, yet the fingers of anxiety continued doing their thing.

She chewed faster. Sometimes her mind was her greatest foe. Her ability (habit) to entertain every little worst-case scenario—*what if the staff hates me? What if I finish setting up my room and it looks like crap? What if what if what if*—was likely the reason she still lived at home with her mother. Was assuredly the reason she had not entertained a serious boyfriend in over two years. Home was safe. Being single was safe.

Oh, she'd had her flings in high school and college, even a year or two after graduation, that stretch of time when most refuse to accept that college life had ended and the real world had begun, but she never secured anything serious. Her friendships too were similar. Sometimes frequent, sometimes fun, but never reaching "bestie" status.

She hoped that would change with her new vocation. A vocation that, despite her mother's standing as a well-respected educator in the area, Rebecca had never considered in her youth. However, like so many others of her generation, she had sampled just about every damn class that her college offered in her quest for a calling, that calling finally presenting itself during a summer elective on elementary education. She loved it from the start, and the rest, as they say, was history.

She was now officially a teacher, about to step into *her* school and set up *her* classroom, hoping to get it properly prepared for the day when *her* students arrived. It was all too much. Screw the gum. She was having that cigarette.

Rebecca rolled the window down and spat her gum at the feet of Ryan Herb, who just happened to be walking by.

10

Ryan Herb stopped and looked down at the piece of gum that had landed at his feet. He turned to his right and looked into the open driver's side window.

"Lost its flavor?" he asked.

Rebecca's face grew sunburn hot. "I am *so* sorry. I didn't see you there."

Ryan looked in her back seat. "I'm not surprised with all that stuff you've got in there. You've probably got a few blind spots."

Rebecca returned a small laugh. "I could barely see out of my rear window on the way here."

Ryan smiled. "You should see *my* car. So, I take it you work here? All that stuff is for your classroom?"

"You take it correct." Rebecca suddenly felt silly carrying on a conversation while still seated in her car. She got out. Ryan took a few steps back to accommodate her.

Rebecca extended her hand. "I'm Rebecca. I'm going to be teaching first grade."

Ryan shook her hand. "Ryan. This your first year?"

"Yep. You?"

"Yep. Probably a little older than the average first-year teacher though."

"How old are you?"

"Thirty. Bit of a midlife career change, I guess you could say. What about you?"

Older guy. She liked that. "Twenty-three. Fresh from the classroom. What grade will you be teaching?"

"Fifth."

"I student-taught in fifth."

"You did? Seems odd they'd put you in first. Two different worlds if you ask me."

"At least it's not kindergarten. I might have had to draw the line there."

Ryan smiled. "No argument there. Kindergarten would kill me."

Rebecca gave an innocent smirk. "I imagine that was an inadvertent pun on your part."

Ryan looked stumped for a moment. Then: "Oh right!" He laughed. "So, I take it Mr. Hansen gave you his spooky little speech as well?"

"Who?"

"Jerry Hansen. Head of HR? Little fat guy?"

"Oh, him. Yeah, I remember him."

"He try to scare you with the school's history during your interview?"

Rebecca nodded. "He certainly didn't tiptoe around the issue. Not like he told me anything I didn't already know, though—my mom taught at Highland for over twenty years. "

"No shit?" Ryan blurted. "She still teaching?"

Rebecca nodded.

"One of the sole survivors," he quipped. "I may just pop into your classroom later for a bit more gossip."

Rebecca blushed again at his mention of dropping by her classroom later. The guy was cute. She already imagined telling people how they'd met. *Spat gum at his feet, I swear to God.* An amusing little courting tale if there ever was one.

(*Getting a bit ahead of yourself, aren't you, girl?*)

She reeled herself in. "Sure, whatever," she replied with a little shrug, hoping it read *stop by or don't—no biggie.*

(*Reel it in, don't cut the line, dummy.*)

Ryan smiled politely, said, "It was nice meeting you," turned, and headed towards the school.

Rebecca bonked her head with her palm. "Sorry about the gum," she called to him.

He turned, gave the polite smile again, then turned back and kept going.

Dummy, she thought again.

11

What in the hell do I do with all this shit? Ryan thought to himself after finally unloading everything from his car into his classroom. It was a chaotic mess. More a hoarder's paradise than a classroom. When he'd student-taught, Ryan had joined his co-op teacher in the middle of the school year, with the room already set up and running. Now it was *his* job to make the classroom look like a classroom. A daunting job indeed for a guy who could count on one hand the number of times he'd made his bed in the morning. He needed an ally.

Ryan left his classroom and stepped out into the hallway. It was closing in on noon, and the school saw fit to keep the air-conditioning on hiatus until the official start of the school year. Even if he did find someone to help him with his room, he doubted they'd be so willing after they got a whiff of him. He smelled like a wet dog.

Ryan started down the hallway. The walls were bare and lifeless. No doubt in a few weeks they'd be alive with all things learning, but for now, they held little warmth, unlike the damn school itself. He must have sweated off five pounds in his classroom alone. He made a note to bring a few fans with him tomorrow. And water. Lots of water. His mission of finding help for his classroom now took a back seat to hydration.

He decided to take a little stroll. If he found someone willing to help him,

(maybe the girl you met outside? Rebecca? She was easy on the eyes, wasn't she?)

great, if he didn't, he could certainly find his way to the teachers' lounge. During his brief tour with Pam from HR this past Friday, Ryan had noticed a soda machine in the lounge. Right now the prospect of a cold soda was the whole world. Onward.

Ryan's journey throughout the building had him opening and closing classroom doors that weren't locked, poking his head into corners and spaces that seemed undiscovered. Although he knew that at least one other person—Rebecca—was in the school, there was a creepy quiet about the building that felt as though it was sleeping. It transported Ryan back to August days in his youth, when the still and baking heat gave an isolated feel to the world, as though it too was sleeping.

The teachers' lounge was in the school cafeteria. Ryan entered and found two things, one a joy to behold, and one a surprise. The joy to behold was the soda machine, glowing and humming to his left (it had occurred to Ryan during his journey to the lounge that if the school felt air-conditioning was unnecessary, so too might it feel that getting the measly soda machine in the teachers' lounge up and running held little priority as well. But it was. He only prayed the thing was stocked).

The surprise was the large rectangular table for faculty dead ahead. There were people seated around it. Three of them. Two men and a woman. None of them acknowledged Ryan's entrance. Perhaps they hadn't heard him enter.

Ryan cleared his throat. All three at the table turned their heads towards him simultaneously and stared. Their expressions projected nothing.

Ryan smiled. "Hi."

All three said nothing. Just continued staring back. Ryan was well aware of the cliques that formed among teachers, much like the students themselves. Passive-aggressive behavior and even mild back-stabbing was unfortunately common in his new vocation. Had he stumbled upon one of those cliques now? Subtly hazing the new guy with their closed mouths and judgmental stares?

Unlikely, he quickly thought. Unless the three at the table were among the few veterans of the infamous school. But chances were good they too were new. And if so, it would make sense they'd be keen for allies, wouldn't it? He knew he sure as hell was.

"I'm Ryan Herb," he tried again. "I'll be teaching fifth grade."

Still nothing. Just stares.

Ryan frowned inside. *Is there a problem?* was on his lips, but he bit it back, trying for one last olive branch. He noticed none of the three had a soda, or anything for that matter, in front of them. "Hot in here, isn't it? Can I offer anyone a soda?" He placed his hand on the soda machine to his left.

Ryan felt as though he'd placed his hand on a stove. A searing pain burned his palm. He jerked his hand free and cried out. Then instantaneous darkness, the room, its shades pulled, becoming black as night.

Ryan stumbled backward in the darkness, felt the door at his back, turned, shouldered the door open, and stumbled out into the cafeteria, actually falling onto his knees.

The brightness of the cafeteria was a relief. An even greater relief was the queer fact that the searing pain in his palm was gone, as though it had never been. But of course it had, and with no biting back anything now, he found himself blurting out: "What the fuck was *that*?!"

A form of hazing the new guy, maybe? Rigging the soda machine to be white hot?

Killing the lights? He imagined the three in the lounge to be in hysterics now. *It was the ghosts of Highland that did it, kid!* He spun and immediately re-entered the lounge.

The lights were back on. And Ryan might have grudgingly told the three that they'd gotten him good, only he had no one to tell.

The table was empty. Like the pain in his palm, so too had all three, inexplicably, disappeared.

Wait. Wait, wait, wait, wait…

He stepped further into the lounge. The layout of the room was wide open. No places to hide, the huge rectangular table for faculty filling the bulk of it. Ryan bent and checked *under* the table. A silly step for adults to take to milk the extent of the joke, but he checked all the same. There was nobody under the table. He was alone.

Aloud now: "Wait, wait, wait...just wait a damn minute. I did not just imagine this."

The lounge now shared the quiet of the rest of the school. The still quiet that made him think of lazy August days in his youth.

Quiet. Quiet...

The quiet. There was no hum from the soda machine to his left. He turned and looked at the machine. It no longer glowed. He risked touching it again. It was not white hot. Not cold either. It was the same temperature of the room. He leaned forward and traced the thick black cord snaking its way out and down the back of the machine where it lay on the carpet, unplugged.

"This...this is..." He didn't know what this was.

12

"That's it, I'm done," Rebecca said to no one as she finished unpacking her final box.

Her classroom resembled a supply room, and a messy one at that, but at least everything was unpacked and out of the boxes. She would make sense of things tomorrow. Today's goal had been just to unpack. Cross it off the list.

She wondered why Ryan had not stopped by to say hello yet. Get some gossip, as he'd put it. It was nearing noon and hot as could be in the school. Surely he'd be wanting a break sometime soon? Should *she* drop in on *him*? Make it no big thing. Breezy. How's it coming? Need any help? That sort of stuff. But nice about it. More sincere. Certainly not the stupid play at indifference she'd given earlier when he'd suggested dropping by for that gossip.

"*Hey!*"

Rebecca jumped and spun towards her classroom door. Speak of the devil …

"Hey yourself," she replied. She went to smile, offer some of that charm she'd lacked this morning, only the guy's appearance changed things. He looked more than a little rattled. "Are you all right?"

He ignored her question and fired off his own in rapid succession, not waiting for her replies. "Are we the only ones here? Have you met anyone else yet today? Have you *heard* anyone else?"

"I don't know," she said. "I've been in here working all morning. Why?"

He remained in her doorway. He looked down the hallway, first left, and then right, as though worried someone was following him.

"Are you all right?" she asked again. "You look a little flushed."

Ryan felt his face with both hands, then ran them through his sweaty hair, gripping tight and holding for a second at the end. A classic stress tell.

"I'm fine. Just the heat, I guess." He gave an uneasy smile, said, "Thanks," and left.

Rebecca waited until he was out of earshot—although a part of her hoped he might hear—before saying: "Well, *that* was weird."

13

"It's gonna happen from time to time, you know."

Ryan, back in his classroom, was lost in thought, replaying recent events in the teachers' lounge when the male voice in his doorway broke his trance.

He spun and saw a short old man dressed in faded green attire. Pants and a tee. His exceptionally bald head was slick with sweat. His face reminded Ryan of one of those dogs with so many wrinkles you can never get a good look at their eyes. In the old man's hands was a broom, nearly as tall as he was.

"Huh?" was all Ryan said.

"You wanna work here, you better get used to it," the old man said again. He had a way of talking that looked as though he fancied eating his lower lip, as if each word that exited his mouth left something tasty behind that begged licking. Dentures he apparently did not care to hide.

"Used to what?" Ryan said. "What are you talking about?"

The old man cocked his head as though disappointed with Ryan. He leaned on his broom, said: "Oh, you gonna play dumb, are you? You know what I'm talking about, son. I see it in your eyes just like I seen it in the eyes of all the others who been here before you. Not to mention you bolted out of that lounge like your ass was on fire." He laughed at his own wit.

"This building is brand new," Ryan challenged.

The old man snorted. "You're trying to bullshit a bullshitter. You know what I'm talking about, son," he said again.

Ryan did, and he told him so. "You worked at Highland?"

"Sure did. Long time."

"You were there just now when I was in the teachers' lounge?"

"Yep."

"I didn't see you."

The old man stopped leaning on his broom and took a few steps into Ryan's classroom.

"Tell you the truth, I didn't see you at first neither. Just heard you hollerin' about somethin'. I come out and you're on your knees looking like you was praying." The old man's southern twang was now clearly evident. After so many years in Pennsylvania, Ryan guessed he held on to that twang for hometown pride's sake. Where exactly that hometown was, Ryan couldn't give a flying fart. Not now, at least.

"I wasn't praying," Ryan said.

"Good. Cuz it won't do you no good anyway."

"Who *are* you?"

The old man took a few more steps towards Ryan and held out a bony hand mapped with thick blue veins that wormed their way up his forearm. Ryan took it. The old man's grip was unusually strong for his age and size, hardened from years of labor.

"You can call me Karl," he said. "I'm the head janitor here. Been here forever and will probably be here long after."

Ryan would have ordinarily dismissed such a comment as an old man's quip. Now, he wondered whether it meant something far different.

"I don't…I don't understand what happened back there," Ryan said. His defensive tone was gone. He now spoke in what amounted to a frightened whisper, a child begging his folks for proof there were no monsters in the closet.

Karl could offer no such consolation. "Of course you don't. Can't say I really do either. I just know that you got spooked, and I'm here to tell you that if you're the type that spooks easy, you should pack your stuff and leave now."

Ryan flashed on Hansen, the man's attempt to spook him. Anger brought back his courage. "I don't usually spook easy, but Jesus, man, *something* happened to me back there."

"Something like what?"

"I wanted a soda from the teachers' lounge. I saw some people sitting in there—"

Karl interrupted him. "Nobody here but you, me, and that pretty blonde girl at the other end of the building."

The heat in the classroom became a chill. "*Can't* be, man. I swear on my mother's life I saw *three* people sitting in that lounge."

"You say hello?"

"Yeah, I did. They blanked me though. Just stared at me."

Karl sucked his dentures. Leaned on his broom again. Ryan went on.

"So, then I go to get a soda from the machine—"

"Hasn't been filled yet. Haven't even plugged it in."

"Yes, I realize that now, Karl, thank you. May I continue?"

Karl smiled.

"So, I went to get a soda from the machine because when I first stepped in there—I am *positive*—that damn thing was on, Pepsi logo shining larger than life in my face. So, I touch it, and my hand burns like acid. Then the room goes pitch black. After that I panicked and ran out."

"That all?" Karl asked.

"No, that's not all. If you were watching like you said, then you'd remember that I went back in."

Karl closed his eyes and nodded slowly, signaling that he did indeed remember.

"Yeah, well, when I went back inside, the lights were back on, and..." Ryan paused a moment, feeling a hint of silliness saying it aloud for the first time. "And there was no one there. I even looked under the damn table like an idiot. Oh, and the soda machine *was* unplugged, of course. No Pepsi logo shining in my face."

Ryan splayed his hands. There it was—take it or leave it, old man. And to Ryan's surprise (or maybe not so much surprise; the old man *had* been somewhat Hansen-esque in his cryptic mutterings thus far), the old man took it. Took it and actually looked as though he sympathized with Ryan.

"I believe you, son," he said. "I believe every word you just said."

Ryan felt something like relief. It was fleeting, though. The old janitor believed him. Hurray. Who the hell would believe *them*?

"What did you say your name was, son?" Karl asked.

"Ryan."

"Ryan, there are only four people left from Highland that are still working here: me, Carol Lawrence, Barbara Forsythe, and Stew Taylor.

"Now, me and Barbara, we been here the longest. Barbara's the head secretary. I'm sure they'll bring another in to assist, but Barbara will be the one to tell you what time it is in Russia. There's nuthin' that woman don't know about nuthin', and I can guarantee she knows more about Highland than I ever will. You might find her a bit standoffish—hell, some might even call her a proper bitch—but that's only cuz she's an old fart like me and been doing the job too damn long. Tough old bird, though. Could easily retire at her age, and with all the crazy shit that's happened around here the past twenty-some years, you'd think she would. But she stays on. My guess is that the job has become all she knows; wouldn't have the first clue on how to pass the time if she did hang 'em up for good.

"Carol Lawrence, now, she's been here a spell herself. Been through all the craziness over the years just like Barbara and me. Lovely woman, Carol. Has a classroom floor you could eat off of. Never had to break even the tiniest sweat when I got to cleaning her room at the end of the day. She's another one that didn't have to come back. Veteran like her could probably get a job anywhere. Came back though, bless her."

"She's the mother of the pretty blonde at the other end of the building," Ryan said.

Karl's face lit up. Not that it changed much; it still looked like one of those wrinkly dogs Ryan still couldn't name,

(*Sharpie? No, that's a magic marker, stupid*)

but for the first time, Ryan got a look at the old man's eyes. Like little slivers of green almonds under those canopies of flesh.

"Is that right?" Karl said. "Well, how 'bout that? I imagine we got us another fine teacher on our hands."

"What about the last one?" Ryan asked. "What did you say his name was? Stew?" Eternally bad with names, something he would have to remedy when the school year started, Ryan had only remembered the name because of Stewie from *Family Guy*.

"Stew Taylor. He's the health and phys-ed teacher. Big son-of-a-gun. Handsome fella too. Looks like Denzel Washington, some of the ladies at Highland used to say. He was good friends with John Gray. John was the other gym teacher at Highland who…" Karl paused a moment, searching for the right words, "…took his own life."

Ryan replayed the interview with Hansen. He remembered his mentioning of the gym teacher's suicide. "Was he the one who hanged himself from a basketball hoop?"

Karl looked at the floor and traced a cross on his chest. "Yeah, that's him."

"So, why did this guy Stew stay on, you think?"

Karl looked up. "Don't know. My guess is that he's like the other two: tough as nails and willing to stay for the sake of the kids. I think there's a part of him that stays for John, too."

Ryan nodded and dropped his own head out of respect.

"Now, I just painted a pretty good picture of those three, wouldn't you say?"

"Yeah."

"Well, here's the thing: They been here long, and I been here long. We've all been through some serious shit. Seen stuff most people wouldn't see in a million lifetimes. And I'm here to tell you that I don't trust a single one of 'em."

Ryan's chin retracted. "Why?"

"I'm not pointin' any fingers, son, but there's somethin' wrong with this school, and somebody *brought* it here."

Ryan snorted. "Wait a minute. Are you implying that one of the veterans you just mentioned is bad luck? Come on, man."

"No, that's not what I'm saying. But I *am* saying that whatever it is that lives in this place didn't get here by itself. The folks I just mentioned been here the longest, since the very first tragedy. No record of any such stuff happening before they came on board. Take from that what you want, but I *do* know that I haven't survived as long as I have in this place without looking out for number one and trustin' *nobody*."

"So, if you don't trust anyone, then why are you telling me all this?"

Karl smiled. "Cuz you're new, son. And I seen the look on your face when you ran out of that lounge."

"What *did* I see, Karl? I don't believe in ghosts."

Karl shrugged. "Neither do I. But that don't mean they don't believe in us."

Ryan fought the urge to roll his eyes. If Karl had turned out to be Hansen's father, he wouldn't have been a bit surprised. "So, did *ghosts* kill all those kids? Did *ghosts* make all those teachers commit suicide?"

"You're puttin' words in my mouth, son. I never said such a thing. But there's something here that can make folks do things they wouldn't normally do, make folks see things they wouldn't normally see. If you want to call that ghosts, then go ahead, but I think that's making it too simple. I think whatever's here is just too damn mean to be labeled anything in particular."

"So, by your logic, *you* could have brought the 'mean' thing here," Ryan said.

Karly smiled again. "Now you're gettin' it, son. Trust no one."

"So, are you like the other three then?" Ryan asked. "Are you still here because you're tough as nails and care about the children's future?"

"Nah," Karl said. "I'm still around cuz I wanna see whatever the hell it is that lives here die before I do."

14

Rebecca left the school at half past two. She was happy with the progress she'd made in her classroom, but was still preoccupied with thoughts of Ryan and his strange behavior earlier.

She had known him for all of five minutes, but her curse of overanalyzing everything, coupled with her frequent waves of self-doubt, had her digging around in her head for something *she* might have done to deter him from spending more time with her this afternoon like he'd suggested. Her regrettable play at indifference when they first met? No. She wasn't *that* bad. Even her self-doubt could see that. Some might have even called it playing hard to get. And even if it was that, wouldn't the guy have simply refused to stop by at all? One might assume that his very brief visit might have been his own turn at a play of indifference, only it seemed anything but. It was weird. Very weird. But the guy was cute, and cute superseded weird in Rebecca's school of philosophy.

She was on the road for no more than thirty seconds before justifying lighting up that cigarette. It took little convincing to come to the conclusion that she *needed* it. She needed it because she had worked hard in the classroom, and she needed it because she was stressed by the thought of a cute guy she had just met being turned off by her. She nodded her head once emphatically, opened her glove compartment, and grabbed the old pack of Marlboro Lights.

Her earlier prediction that one of the stale cigarettes might taste like crap was pleasantly untrue. It wasn't good, but it wasn't bad either. She cracked her window, took a deep drag, and exhaled into the wind.

Dammit, why was he being so weird? What did I do?

15

Ryan was playing basketball in an empty gymnasium by himself. The lights in the gym were off, but he could see.

On the sidelines was Karl. He was wearing a referee's uniform and had a whistle around his neck. The basketball hoop before him appeared larger than a standard hoop. The backboard was not glass, but a black chalkboard. On that blackboard the crude white lines of the classic Hangman game were there, larger than life. So far only a base and a pole had been drawn onto the board.

The net to the hoop was absent. In its place was a man hanging from a noose. He was dressed in a track suit—a gym teacher.

Despite the hanging gym teacher's presence, Ryan inexplicably continued to shoot at the basket. Each time he did, the man hanging from the noose—who was still alive—would wince as the ball flew towards him. Each shot Ryan made would cause another Hangman line to appear. Karl blew his whistle every time Ryan scored.

Soon, the Hangman drawing was one shot away from completion. The remaining piece—the head—was all that was needed. Without delay—again, inexplicably, the irrational but rational order of the mind in his dream state once again in full effect—Ryan shot the ball and scored.

Karl's whistle blew.

Ryan turned his back to the hoop and began bouncing the ball with powerful, triumphant thuds. Each time the ball hit the floor, it did not produce the sound of rubber on hardwood, but instead produced something dull and heavy and wet. The sound of someone slapping a roast onto a cutting board.

Ryan looked down at the ball in his hands. He saw the tongue first, hanging from the side of the gym teacher's open mouth, purple and swollen. The eyes on the severed head were rolled back white, the neck hitting Ryan's chest with powerful jets of red.

Ryan dropped the severed head and spun back towards the hoop. The gym teacher's body was gone. The black backboard was now glass, as it should have been. Karl was gone too. The lighting in the gym grew darker. Ryan tried to leave but could not; fear leadened his feet. He felt a tap on his shoulder.

Ryan turned and found himself facing the headless gym teacher. In the gym teacher's right hand was his own head, held by a clump of his own hair. The head still pulsed blood from the neck, the purple tongue still dangled. The eyes were no longer white but blue and wide, straining as they looked up at Ryan, accusatory.

Ryan opened his mouth to apologize but could produce nothing. The gym teacher turned his back on Ryan and whipped his own severed head against the concrete wall behind him where it exploded into a mass of a red and blue and black.

Ryan found his voice and cried out, sitting bolt upright in bed. He was soaked again.

16

Rebecca and her mother sat in their usual spots at the kitchen table with their coffee.

"That *is* weird," Carol Lawrence said to her daughter. "You haven't spoken to him since?"

"Nope. He was really sweet when I saw him in the morning, but then when he showed up in my room later, he looked totally freaked out."

Carol sipped from her coffee. "Well, maybe you'll see him today and get an explanation."

Rebecca grunted and sipped her own coffee. "We'll see."

"So he was cute, huh?" Carol asked with a little grin.

Rebecca found her mother's grin contagious. She grinned back. "Yeah, he was."

"I can't wait to meet him." Her grin was now devilish.

"Mom, if you even *think* of trying to embarrass me…"

Carol laughed.

"Oh, Becks, I wouldn't do that. Or would I?"

"You're evil. Anyway, he's probably married or has a girlfriend or something."

"Married?"

"He's thirty."

"Did you see a ring?"

"I didn't think to look."

"Well, get a good look today."

"I'll try. I promised him some juicy gossip. We'll see if he ever takes me up on the offer."

Carol frowned, confused. She set her coffee cup down. "Gossip?"

"The stuff that happened at Highland. When I told him who you were and that you were my mother, he seemed keen on hearing a story or two."

Carol raised her cup and drank slowly. Then: "You know I don't like to discuss what happened there, Rebecca."

Uh oh. It was Rebecca now; no Becks. Mom was serious.

Rebecca reached across the table and took her mother's hand. "I know that, Mom. I told him you didn't talk about it. I guess I was just trying to be friendly. I mean, I did just spit gum on the guy's shoe. I didn't mean to—"

Carol placed her hand on top of her daughter's. "I understand, sweetheart. I'm not angry. It's just a very difficult subject for me to talk about. Watching children murder children is something that will never leave me."

Her mother's frank choice of words punched a hole in Rebecca's gut. "I'm sorry, Mom. I won't bring it up again."

Carol patted her daughter's hand and smiled. "It's fine, Becks. I completely understand why you did what you did."

Back to Becks. Good.

Carol stood. "Okay, I'm off. I've got some errands to run. What time will you be heading in today?"

"Pretty soon. What about you? When do you plan on getting your classroom ready?"

Carol brought her cup to the sink, then flashed her devilish smile again. "When you're stuck in orientation next week."

Rebecca gave a playful frown. "No fair."

17

Cynthia Herb looked at her son with concern. He was pale. His eyes were dark from lack of sleep. She'd heard him hit his snooze button at least half a dozen times this morning.

"Ryan, are you all right? You look like hell."

Ryan poured himself a cup of coffee at the kitchen counter. "Thanks, Ma."

"I'm serious, honey; you don't look so hot."

"I don't *feel* so hot."

"So then what are you doing up?"

"Work."

Cynthia plucked a stray cat hair from her nurse's uniform, then stood next to her son at the counter. "I thought you didn't have to be there officially until the 28th."

Ryan brought his coffee into the den and slumped onto the sofa with an old man's groan. "My *room*, Ma. I have to get my room ready."

Cynthia followed him. "You told me practically nobody showed up yesterday. Can't you take a day off?"

"Maybe some teachers can, but I need every single day in that room to make it look like I know what the hell I'm doing."

"Can't you get some ideas from other teachers?"

"Not if I don't show up for work I can't."

"Fair enough. Still, you don't look well. Let me take your temp." Cynthia started for the junk drawer in the kitchen. Ryan promptly stopped her.

"I'm fine, Ma. I just didn't sleep well. I keep having these weird dreams."

Cynthia stopped and faced her son again. "Another dream about the school?"

Ryan nodded and sipped his coffee. "I don't get it. None of the stuff that happened there bothers me in the slightest. But ever since I got this job, I've had two nightmares that would make Stephen King hard."

Cynthia frowned at her son's crassness. Then: "Well, maybe it does bother you and you're not allowing yourself to admit it."

Ryan made a face.

"It's possible, Ryan. Some horrible things happened at that school. Maybe it bothers you on a subconscious level."

"But that school doesn't exist anymore."

"But it's still the same building, so to speak. Still the same land."

"Jesus, Ma, you sound as bad as Karl and Hansen."

"Karl and Hansen?"

"Never mind. I'll be fine."

Cynthia kissed her son on the top of his head. "Don't stay there too late today. Get a little bit done, then come home and get a good night's sleep."

Ryan grunted.

Cynthia Herb left, only to poke her head back in a moment later. "There's something on your car," she called to Ryan.

"Huh?" Ryan called back, but his mother was gone again. He stood and walked towards the front door. He peered through one of the adjacent windows, fixing on his car in the driveway. There was indeed something on his car. An envelope tucked underneath one of his windshield wipers.

"Fucking solicitors," he grumbled. He went outside, caring little that he was wearing nothing but boxer shorts and a faded Philadelphia 76ers tee. *The Herb House*, his mother used to tease him, *where pants are optional.*

A beige 8x10 envelope was under the wiper. He lifted the wiper and took the envelope. There was nothing on the front or the back. No address;

no writing of any kind. Ryan held it up to the sky and tried to use the sun to see its contents. He got nothing.

Ryan opened the envelope and pulled out its contents. It contained a large photograph of several people standing in rows, smiling cheerfully. At the bottom of the photo were the words *Highland Elementary Staff 2002.*

Ryan's first thought was: *Who left this for me?* His next thought was: Why *was this left for me?* And his final thought—*realization*—chilled him to his core. *Those three teachers in the front row are the same three I saw in the teachers' lounge yesterday.*

18

Rebecca's justification for smoking this time was that she'd felt bad making her mother upset during breakfast. And no stale ones this time. A *fresh* pack needed buying if she was going to justify her stupid habit. It was just common sense, if you asked her.

Fresh cigarette lit, car window cracked, Rebecca began her second trip to Pinewood. She had two goals today: one necessary, the other self-indulgent.

First she would make order of the bedlam that was her classroom. All materials would find an orderly home and become labeled accordingly. Books would be shelved and within reach of little hands. And finally, what amounted to her own little custodial station would stand in the corner behind her desk—a helpful tip passed on to her from her mother. She was teaching first grade, after all. Kids that age were content to let runny noses drip to the floor. Feared asking to go to the nurse, preferring instead to barf smack in the middle of class. Or, God forbid, feared asking to use the bathroom, and, well…

The second, self-indulgent goal was to find Ryan the cute weirdo and give her mind the valium it craved by getting to the root of his odd behavior the other day. That and to do as her mother suggested and check for a wedding ring. Fish for anything that might suggest a girlfriend. Her ongoing battle with self-doubt notwithstanding, Rebecca felt certain there had been the tiniest of sparks between them yesterday. She was going to make every effort to see whether those sparks were mutual.

She was about to get her chance sooner than later.

Pulling into the school's lot, Rebecca spotted Ryan exiting a black Toyota Corolla. Her belly swirled.

———— ✦ ————

The photograph of Highland Elementary's staff from 2002 was on Ryan's passenger seat, tucked safely away in the beige envelope from which it had come. Not once on the drive over did Ryan think about what he would do with his room today. His sole mission was to confront Karl with the photograph. After all, he had been the one who'd planted the photo on his windshield, hadn't he? It had to be him. There was simply no other explanation.

But Karl would be doing some explaining all right, not the least of those explanations being just how the hell the old man had found out where he lived. Were such records available to employees? Check that—to janitors? Sure, HR and the like had his address. But the custodial staff?

Ryan had driven to the school on autopilot, his mind miles away. He saw the traffic signs and the oncoming cars, and yet he didn't. What he did see upon arriving—how could he not?—was the school sign, huge and proudly displayed on the lawn adjacent to the main entrance. Although now, not so proud. It had been vandalized. What used to read "Pinewood Elementary" now read "Pinewood *HEl*Lementary," a clever *H* and an extra *L* crudely painted in red ink.

Ryan stopped his car smack in the road before the entrance, engine idling. He gaped at the sign. "You gotta be kidding me," he said aloud, shook his head with a snort, and then continued into the lot.

Photograph firmly in hand, Ryan was locking up his Corolla when he spotted another car pulling into the lot. He recognized the driver right away. The girl he had acted the fool in front of yesterday. His business with Karl this morning was top priority, but the memory of acting like an ass in front of a pretty blonde provoked his defenseless male ego, and he found that remedying such a situation became a priority as well.

———— ✦ ————

Rebecca pulled into the lot. Ryan appeared to be smiling genuinely her way. Her belly swirled faster. She noticed a large beige envelope in his right hand.

She parked close but not next to him. She hoped she didn't smell of smoke when she exited her car. Cursed herself for not thinking to pop a mint or chew a piece of gum. Wait—no gum. Gum was bad.

"Hi," she said. "Think we'll be the only ones here again today?" Her delivery sounded fine in her own ears. Warm and friendly. No silly indifference this time.

Ryan continued smiling. "I don't know. You'd think there'd be more here when you consider that the majority of the staff is new."

"Good point. Maybe they all changed their minds about working here after all."

His smile dipped some, his eyes dropping for a moment. Almost as though her comment had bothered him. Come on, no way this time. If it had, then maybe the guy simply *was* weird. Thin-skinned to boot. Looks were nice, but confidence was king in Rebecca's world.

She felt better when his genuine smile returned and he said: "Speaking of which, I think I owe you an apology."

She played dumb. "Apology?"

"I said I'd drop by your classroom yesterday for some spooky school gossip and I didn't. Well, technically I suppose I *did* drop by, but I wasn't exactly myself."

"You did seem a little bothered by something." No point in playing dumb this time.

Ryan nodded. "I was. Something very…*odd* happened to me yesterday in the teachers' lounge. It spooked me."

"What happened?"

"To be honest with you, I'm not really sure. I'm still trying to get my head around it." He changed gears. "Did you notice the sign out front?"

She hadn't. "No, why?"

"Someone painted an *H* and an *L* on it. It now reads Pinewood *Hel*lementary. Clever, huh?"

She knew she wouldn't be able to see the sign from where she stood, but she turned and looked anyway. "Are you serious? Who did *that*?"

"Who knows? I know when I left my interview last week, I had a lady give me grief about working here. It was probably just another local pissed off about the school being resurrected."

Resurrected. Odd choice of word.

"What does your mom think about all this?" Ryan asked. "Not the sign, I mean—I doubt she knows about that already. I meant the backlash from the locals about the school."

Rebecca hesitated. She wanted to keep talking, but she didn't want to involve her mother. Not with how upset she seemed about their discussion this morning.

"She doesn't really like to talk about it," she replied. "I mean, she *has,* but usually she gets upset after."

"Understandable. Well, anyway, I apologize for my behavior yesterday. How about I come down to your classroom later and make amends by helping you with the least desirable task you've got ahead of you today? No psycho act this time." He smiled.

Rebecca smiled back, her belly now on the purée setting.

"Promises, promises…" she said.

"Scout's honor." Clearly never a Scout (Rebecca had been one in her youth), Ryan held up his left hand, thumb covering his pinky finger, three fingers together in a lefty take of the traditionally right-handed gesture.

And this blunder was just fine with Rebecca. It allowed her to spot no ring on his finger. Her belly topped out at liquefy.

19

Ryan didn't have any trouble locating Karl, mainly because Karl located him. Ryan had been in his room for no more than a minute when Karl popped his shiny bald head in. He was wearing the same faded green pants and the same faded green tee.

"Morning, son. You're here early."

Ryan did not return the pleasantries. He brandished the beige envelope containing the photo like it was damning evidence in a trial. "Explain this."

Karl took a step back, frowning at Ryan's fervor. "What is it?"

Ryan opened the envelope and pulled out the photo. He handed it to Karl. Karl took the photo, studied it, then shook his head.

"Shame," was all he said before handing it back to Ryan.

"What is?"

"Shame that those nice folks had to die."

"They *all* died?" Ryan asked.

"No—just three." He held out the photo. "These folks here." His bony finger touched three teachers in the front row one at a time.

And hadn't Ryan suspected this? On some level that he struggled to comprehend, hadn't Ryan known that Karl might confirm such an impossibility?

"My God, Karl. Those three. Those were the three I saw yesterday in the teachers' lounge. I'm sure of it."

Karl put a hand on Ryan's shoulder. "Calm down, son."

Ryan shrugged the hand off. Disbelief (how? Just fucking *how* did he manage to see three dead teachers in the teachers' lounge yesterday??? It was beyond insane) fueled his anger. "Why would you leave this for me?"

"Me? I didn't give you that photo, son. In fact, I was just about to ask you how you went about getting it yourself."

Ryan threw his head back and barked out a solitary laugh. "Oh, give me a fucking break, man. Who else would have left it? You were the only one I told about what happened yesterday."

Karl shrugged, strangely calm in the eye of Ryan's storm. "I don't know. Someone trying to help, I imagine."

"*Help?* Help with *what?*"

"I told you there's some diggin' that needs doing around this school. Answers that need finding. Maybe this photo here is kinda like your map to get you started."

Ryan closed his eyes and shook his head. "You're fucking with me. I can't figure out why—or, more importantly, *how*—just yet, but you are. Just admit that you left the damn photo on my car. Admit you left it and I won't be angry."

"Can't do that, son; it wouldn't be the truth. Think about it a minute: you never described the teachers you saw in that lounge—just two men and a woman. *Hundreds* of teachers have come and gone over the years. How on Earth would I know which ones you saw specifically? Which photo to give you?"

Ryan opened his mouth to argue but had nothing. He closed it.

"I will say this," Karl continued, "whoever did leave that photo, I don't think they meant it as a threat."

"Really? Because I sure as hell feel threatened, for many reasons. Chief of them being that whoever left that photo for me knows where I live."

Karl handed the photo back to Ryan. "I didn't leave it, son. You have my word." "I don't believe in ghosts, Karl—" He held up the photo. "I don't believe ghosts

left this for me."

"So then what did you see yesterday?"

"I don't know. But I *do* know that whatever the hell it was does *not* have the ability to drive to my fucking house and place an 8x10 envelope under my windshield wiper."

"You're scared, son. And I don't blame you. I told you this place can make some folks see things they normally wouldn't see. Thing is, most folks *don't* see it. Hell, most of the people that left Highland left because of the killings, the suicides, not because of things they seen. But you...you *seen* 'em. Or at least you're starting to. And somebody—or some*thing*—knows that...maybe they're trying to get your help."

Ryan closed his eyes and shook his head again.

Karl went on. "I told you I was still here cuz I wanna see the evil bastard that's living here—whatever the hell it is—die before I do. I meant that. Problem is, I seen what the bastard's done, but I never seen the bastard himself. Maybe that's what's kept me safe so long. Maybe I just can't see it. But my guess is that you *can*. And like I said, somebody here knows that. And while I can't tell a grown man like you what to do with his life, I can say that if *I* could see? If I could see, I would certainly do something about it."

Ryan opened his eyes. The room swayed.

"It was just the one time, Karl," Ryan said. "I just saw it the one time."

"You'll see more," Karl said. "If you plan on staying here, I promise you; you'll see more."

"I don't want that responsibility."

"Too late. Looks like it wants *you*."

20

First date. Ryan and Rebecca took their seats in a padded booth across from one another. They were in a local tavern no more than a few miles from the school. It was happy hour, and they were settling in for a well-deserved drink, Ryan unquestionably the more deserving of the two given recent events.

Ryan had kept his conversations with Karl a secret from Rebecca as he was almost certain that if he shared their little chats, he'd wind up sitting alone. Emergency call from a friend or her mother perhaps. Sorry, got to go. Don't call me; I'll call you.

Ryan *had* chatted with Karl again after that Tuesday morning when he'd confronted the old man with the photograph. Had, in fact, chatted quite a bit this week. A lot was more of the same, but some new nuggets were divulged. Karl gave the background of the three in the picture, and they were indeed the three who'd committed suicide in the building.

Jane Ballentine, art teacher, was the woman. Mike Johnson, science teacher, was man number one. Man number two? None other than John Gray, gym teacher, the one who'd hanged himself from the basketball hoop in the gymnasium. The one he'd dreamt about. Sort of. After all, the gym teacher in his dream did not resemble the man in the photograph; Ryan had yet to confirm the former's identity. But he'd still known who it was, hadn't he? Even in the bizarre realm of his dream, he knew the man was John Gray.

One particular nugget Karl divulged looked as though it was something the old man had regretted sharing not long after it was out. Apparently, all three suicide victims had claimed to see things in the school that others could not.

Jane Ballentine, the art teacher, claimed to see wounded children roaming the halls, caked in blood, sobbing for help. Not long after, Jane Ballentine slashed both wrists, crawled into her classroom closet, and bled to death.

Mike Johnson, the science teacher, claimed to see a woman veiled in black, cutting the throats of children in his classroom, as he stayed late one night to grade papers. Again, not long after, Mike Johnson leapt headfirst out of his second-story classroom window.

John Gray had claimed a boy had approached him in the gym, asked John to follow him to the boiler room in the basement of the building. John did, but got no further. The boy had vanished, leaving John alone in that boiler room, questioning his sanity. John had told Karl and a few others about what had happened and then told them that he intended on going back to that boiler room the following night to do some digging.

The next day John Gray was found hanging from the basketball hoop.

Ryan's question after Karl had relayed this, and he'd all but blurted it, was: *What did John find in that boiler room?* to which Karl regretfully had no answer. No one had the answer.

As for the reason Karl looked as though he'd regretted telling Ryan about the three teachers claiming to have seen things before they took their own lives? Ryan had figured that out quickly, and with no satisfaction whatsoever. If all of these teachers had died for something they claimed to have seen, then why would Ryan be any different? Who was to say he wouldn't be the next to go?

"Can I have a glass of pinot?" Rebecca asked the waitress when she came to their booth for drink orders.

The waitress smiled, nodded, then looked at Ryan. Again, given recent events, Ryan wanted a scotch. And a double at that. But on a first date? He'd held his tongue on Karl's campfire tales. And so too did he think it wise to not give Rebecca another reason to get that emergency call from a friend or her mother. Double scotch? Guy clearly likes his booze. No thanks. Ryan opted for a light beer.

"So, how's your room coming along?" Rebecca asked.

"All right, I guess. I was always terrible at that sort of thing. In school we had to design our own classroom on paper and explain why each little drawing went where, and how it benefited the learning experience of the kids, et cetera, et cetera. I think it was one of the few projects I got a *B* on."

"Oh, I remember doing something like that. Yeah, that wasn't too fun."

"Did you like Penn State?" Ryan asked.

"I loved it. I still miss it from time to time. How about you? You miss West Chester?"

"Not really. I started back when I was twenty-seven, so my partying days were dwindling. Couple that with the fact that I was living at home with my mom the whole time…" He shrugged. "I guess you could say I actually went to college to learn."

Rebecca laughed. "How do you like living at home?"

"The obvious pros and cons. My mom is a great lady, so it's bearable. I think she likes it too. She likes the company now that my dad's gone."

"Did he pass away?"

"No—just divorce. Amicable too, if you can believe that. He's a good guy. I still talk to him often. What about you? You like living at home?"

"I don't mind it. It helps financially, of course, but my dad died a while ago, and like you, I think my mom likes the company."

Ryan showed sympathy. "I'm sorry to hear that. How did he die?"

"Massive stroke. I was in middle school."

Ryan winced. "I'm sorry," he said again. "Must have been hard on you guys" felt like the thing to say.

"It was. To be honest, I think my mom is still in denial about it, even after all these years. She doesn't like to keep photos of him around or anything. Just his ashes in a big urn in her bedroom. I have a picture, though. Wanna see?"

"Sure."

Rebecca went into her purse and pulled out her wallet. She showed Ryan a picture of a handsome man with dirty blond hair.

"Good-looking guy," Ryan said.

"Yeah, he was great."

⸻ ✦ ⸻

Their drinks arrived.

"Cheers," Ryan said, raising his beer bottle.

Rebecca clinked her wine glass against the neck of his bottle. "Cheers."

They swigged healthily then sat silent for a moment.

"Uh oh," Rebecca said. "Is awkward silence starting already?"

"Oh shit. Favorite color? Favorite movie? Favorite food?"

She laughed. "Blue, *The 'Burbs*, and pizza."

"Excellent answers. Love *The 'Burbs*."

"You?"

"*Jaws*, steak, and I don't really have a favorite color. Black, I guess."

"Love *Jaws*. Still have a problem going in the ocean. But I burn easy, so I use that excuse."

Ryan smiled. "Irish?"

She shrugged. "I'm a mutt. But I definitely have Irish skin. What about you?"

Now Ryan shrugged. "Mutt. I tan pretty well though."

"Jerk."

They shared a laugh and drank.

"So what is your fifth-grade team like?" she asked. "You met all of them already, yeah?"

Ryan nodded. "I like them. All girls, though. It would have been nice to have another guy."

Rebecca felt a twinge of jealousy in spite of herself. "Oh, I'm sure you'll *hate* that."

Ryan smiled and took another swig from his beer. "It's okay, I guess. I was just hoping for a male ally to do battle with the lovely ladies of the school such as yourself—" He tapped the top of her hand.

Ah, flirting was officially served. She ate his offering greedily.

"Poor Ryan," she said with a coquettish smile.

"Yeah, yeah. One girl on my team is pretty cool. Trish. Talks a million miles an hour, but is actually more amusing than annoying."

Another twinge of jealousy in spite of herself. She pried subtly. "Oh yeah? What's she look like? I may have seen her."

"Tiny little thing. I'd say barely five feet. Round face with curly dark hair. Reminds me of one of those Cabbage Patch Dolls. You remember them?"

Rebecca nodded and felt better. She could compete with a Cabbage Patch Doll.

"What about the others on your team?" she asked.

"They seem nice. Kind of kept to themselves. I guess I'll get to know them better next week during orientation. Trish was the one I spoke to the most. She helped me with my room a lot."

I can compete with a Cabbage Patch Doll, she reminded herself.

"What about you?" Ryan asked. "What's your first-grade team like?"

"Very nice. They're all about my age except for one. She's a bit older. Still sweet, though. Kind of like a mom to all of us, I guess you could say, although I doubt she'd like us referring to her as such."

Ryan mimed locking his lips.

Rebecca smiled. *I like him*, she thought.

They were three rounds deep, Rebecca sporting a healthy buzz, Ryan fine. Rebecca had taken the risk of asking Ryan whether he minded if she had a cigarette. He'd said he didn't mind, even adding that he too was guilty of bumming a smoke or two over a few drinks, although truth be told, it had been years since he'd done so. Still, he wanted her to feel at ease and went as far as to bum one from her tonight.

"My mom would kill me," she said as she lit his first and then her own. "She spent all this money on those patches for me so I could quit."

"You're a stealth smoker," Ryan said.

She exhaled and laughed.

Ryan exhaled and fought the urge to cough.

"So do you think you might ever take me out on a date-date?" she asked.

"A *date-date*?"

"Like an official date. You know, picking me up for dinner and a movie and stuff."

And stuff. Woohoo, baby.

"I drove you here, didn't I?" he joked.

She wrinkled her nose. "That doesn't count."

Ryan took one last drag from his cigarette, then put it out prematurely, the cigarette buzzing him more than the beer. He took a swig from his beer and said: "I think a date-date might be fun."

"Great-great," Rebecca said. "When-when?"

Ryan smiled. "I don't know. Tomorrow night? Dinner. Then maybe *Jaws* after? Followed by a late-night dip in the ocean, of course."

She laughed again.

"I'll tell you what," Ryan went on, "I'll take you back to your car now. We can go home, get some well-deserved sleep, and then I'll call you tomorrow—after you give me your number, that is."

She grinned. "Deal."

"And of course I'll pick you up," he added.

"Who said chivalry was dead?"

He laughed, took her hand, and gave it a little squeeze. Rebecca grinned again.

21

Rebecca kissed *him*.

When Ryan pulled up alongside her car in the school's lot, she immediately leaned over and planted a big one on him. It took him off guard, but he liked it. Liked it a lot. He kissed her back, this one longer, a little tongue action.

"You okay to drive?" he asked when they pulled away from one another.

"I'm fine. Thanks for the drinks. You sure you don't want any money?"

"Shut up."

"*You* shut up," she said, and kissed him again.

They kissed a final time before Rebecca exited his car and drove off in her own, waving goodbye as she pulled away.

————————◆————————

Rebecca drove home on a cloud. She felt an immediate connection with Ryan. Nothing felt labored or routine. Sure, the wine helped, and it certainly helped her attack him in his car (something she would maybe feel silly about in the morning), but the booze certainly did not affect his behavior, and she'd sensed a reciprocal connection. She had, hadn't she? Or had the wine affected her *perception* of that reciprocal connection?

Just shut the hell up and enjoy the moment, girl.

———————— ✦ ————————

Rebecca gone, Ryan stood by his car for a spell, both arms resting on the roof, chin resting on his arms. He could not see the school sign from where he stood, but it had since been fixed and now read "Pinewood Elementary" once again. For now.

A part of Ryan told himself to get into his car and drive home. To savor the feeling of a successful first date (*but not a "date-date,"* he thought, and immediately smiled) and call it a night.

Another part told him to head towards the school. He had a key now and could be inside the building in a matter of moments. But why would he?

Digging. Karl's words in his head as clearly as if the old man was standing next to him. Then his own words countering right back: *Digging got those people killed, didn't it?* Ryan shook his head. *No. Nobody killed those people. They killed themselves.*

Ryan started towards the school, stopped, and stared. It stood dark and ominous in the distance. A freaking elementary school dark and ominous. Absurd.

He took a few more steps forward—casual, probing steps. And those steps continued to accumulate, almost without his say. He felt like a kid creeping up on the spooky house in the neighborhood, friends behind him, goading him on. Only there weren't any friends to goad him on. Something inside him was doing the job just fine, something he couldn't quite comprehend.

Whatever it is that lives here was brought *here.* Karl's words again, now like a whisper in his ear.

Ryan now stood before the school's main entrance. He felt eyes on him and turned. Dusk had left. His vision was becoming impaired with the growing night, yet he spotted no one. He was alone. He wasn't sure whether that was a good thing. He turned back towards the entrance.

What the hell would I do in there anyway? Where would I dig? How would I dig? Would I visit the teachers' lounge and hope to see my three friends seated at the table again?

A feeling of silliness came over him. The silliness brushing aside the invisible hand that had inexplicably carried him to this spot, the precise way one inexplicably does things in the dream world against better judgment. And Lord knows he'd become an expert in that bastard world this past week. Was he dreaming now? No. No, he was sure he wasn't. He could still taste the beer. Still taste Rebecca.

"I am *not* dreaming," he said aloud. "*I* am in control. And this…this is utterly ridiculous."

His own voice sounded good in the dark quiet, his convictions in his voice even better. He turned and headed back towards his car, refusing to give the school a final glance.

Ryan got maybe ten yards when he spotted two large silhouettes in the distance, hovering around his car, the lot's street lamps telling the story. *I'm not dreaming*, he told himself again. *Whoever those two people are, they* are *people*. Yet his convictions this time offered fleeting comfort, only served to remind him of the crazy lady who'd been waiting for him by his car when he'd left the human resources building that morning. Only served to raise a question that he felt, in his gut, held no good answer: *Who* were these two guys waiting for him by his car? Better yet, why?

Rebecca had turned the car around. The wine had persuaded her to go back and see Ryan. She knew it was stupid, and she knew it was taking things a bit too far too soon, but her buzz, both from the wine and from Ryan himself, were making her choices for her now, and heading back to see Ryan for perhaps one more kiss seemed like a damn good idea. She only hoped her mission wasn't a futile one. Probably, it was. He would almost assuredly have gone by now, but then she'd only been on the road less than a minute when she'd decided to pull a U-ey and head back to the school. Again, likely a fool's errand, but she hoped otherwise.

Rolling up towards the school, Rebecca felt the now familiar tingle in her belly when she spotted Ryan's car in the distance, still parked in the lot. Her tingle growing that much stronger when she spotted Ryan himself. Only…he wasn't alone? Two men surrounded him, their body language aggressive. She rolled down her window and killed the engine by the main entrance, hoping she wouldn't be spotted. She could hear the men shouting at Ryan.

Just what the hell was going on?

————— ◆ —————

"So, you're gonna be teaching here, huh?" the first of the two men had asked. He was a big man in jeans and a tight tee to show off his powerful torso. He also appeared drunk.

"That's right," Ryan said, extending his hand. "Ryan Herb. Nice to meet you."

The man ignored Ryan's hand. The second man, shorter, but even broader than the first, spoke next. He too was wearing jeans and a tight tee to display his physique. Unlike the first man, whose head was shaved, the second had wings of black hair poking out of the sides of his backwards baseball cap.

"Don't you know about this place?" the second asked, a distinct slur to his voice. No surprise that he too appeared drunk.

Ryan searched for the right words, if they even existed. More a peacemaker than a fighter, Ryan had still had his share of stupid scraps with drunken idiots during a night on the town with his buddies. He knew damn well that reasoning with a drunk was the very definition of futility.

"Yes, I do. It's a tragedy what happened at Highland," he said.

Shaved head took a step forward. "What happened *here*," he said. "It's the same fucking place. Just cuz they call it Pinewood now doesn't change a fucking thing."

Ryan felt adrenaline tickle his gut and add weight to his limbs.

"You know what happened to my buddy's daughter in this place?" shaved head asked, pointing to baseball cap.

Ryan feared the worst. And a part of him, if the worst truly was the worst, could actually sympathize with their anger. He only wished he wasn't the current recipient of it. He played dumb anyway.

"No, I'm sorry, I don't," he said.

"She was killed," shaved head said. "*Stabbed* by another fucking kid in the building *you* want to work in."

The worst was the worst.

Both men inched closer. Ryan took a step back. He had the sickening feeling that a physical encounter was imminent.

"Jesus, man, I am so sorry," he said to baseball cap.

Baseball cap lowered his head for a moment, looking as though he may cry. Ryan felt a tug at his heart. He went to say something else—again, the right words elusive—but would never get the chance. Baseball cap's head snapped upright and he lunged forward, lifting Ryan off his feet with an almighty shove, Ryan landing hard on the unforgiving concrete butt-first.

Ryan did not attempt to find his feet right away. He wanted to, wanted to scramble to his feet and start swinging, but it would be wrong. Still, he would not be a soccer ball for these two guys as he sat on the ground, so he scooted backwards before getting to his feet, making sure to keep both men in his sights as he did so.

"*You took my baby girl from me!*" baseball cap spat at Ryan. The man was crying now.

Ryan held up his hands in a pleading manner. "I didn't take—"

Shaved head cut him off. "It's fucks like you that want to start things up again! *You want to kill more children?! Huh?! Is that it, motherfucker?!*"

Ryan shook his head. "Of course not—"

Shaved head reached forward to grab hold of Ryan. Ryan slapped his hand away, instantly regretted doing it, and braced himself for the inevitable.

Baseball cap dove at Ryan's waist, tackling him to the ground, Ryan's head whiplashing back against the concrete. The man straddled Ryan's chest. Heavily dazed, Ryan instinctively brought his hands up to protect his face for the punches that were sure to follow.

Ryan felt no such punches. Did, though, feel the weight of the man on his chest vanish. He rolled to one side, vision wavering. He heard grunts and shouts, saw legs—three pairs now—shuffling violently around his head as the evident struggle above him ensued. Then the fast, retreating sounds of footsteps on concrete, warning shouts—growing distant—accompanying them and threatening reprisal. A short moment later, and there was only one pair of legs next to his prone body. One pair of legs with two exceptionally large feet. A deep voice boomed from above.

"You all right?"

Ryan looked up. A black man, one hell of a big one at that, was extending his hand down towards him. Ryan took it. The man lifted Ryan to his feet with little effort. "Yeah," Ryan managed, still dazed. "I think so."

Ryan cleared the cobwebs, dusted himself off. He took in his savior, marveling at his size. Ryan was six feet tall. This man had a good four inches on him. He was also twice as wide.

"Stew," Ryan said. "You're Stew, right?"

The man frowned. "How did you know that?"

"Karl said you looked like Denzel Washington. He was right; you do. Denzel Washington on steroids."

22

Rebecca had watched the confrontation and the brief scuffle from her car. She felt helpless from where she sat. Even had her cell phone out at one point to call for help. The numbers were pressed and "send" was about to be pushed when Rebecca saw the big man step in and save Ryan. However, any relief she felt for Ryan's safety, and it was considerate, was transient in the face of a new mystery: the identity of Ryan's savior.

Rebecca contemplated getting out of her car and running towards Ryan and the man who'd helped him, but the wine had not dulled *all* her senses; that of self-preservation was still strong, and although the two men who were fighting with Ryan had run off, they could still easily be close by, could even be coming back with more allies.

And so she felt content to stay put and watch from the safety of her car; however, she would soon discover that she would not be able to watch for very long. Ryan and the big man soon entered the school and were gone.

Rebecca cursed, started her engine, and drove off.

———— ✦ ————

Ryan and Stew headed down the first- and second-grade hallway, the school dark and quiet, their footsteps the only sound. As they walked, Ryan explained who he was and why he was there. In fact, he told Stew *everything* that had occurred to him in the past week; it seemed to have just spilled out with no second-guessing, and to Ryan's surprise, Stew seemed unfazed by it all.

"So, you've been talking to old Karl, have you?" Stew said.

"Yeah—well, more like *he's* the one who's been doing all the talking."

Stew gave a hearty laugh that echoed throughout the empty halls. "Yeah, once he gets going…"

Ryan had so many questions, yet top priority went to: *How did you happen to show up at such an opportune time in such an inopportune place to bail me out?* And so he'd asked it.

"I live close by," Stew began. "I was on my way home when I saw two cars in the school lot. After what happened to the sign out front the other day, I slowed down and parked far enough away to keep an eye out, making sure those two cars didn't contain vandals with a new can of paint.

"I saw you with a young lady and then watched the lady leave. I was about to leave myself when I saw you start to wander. I thought that was a little odd for a young fella like you to be doing on a Friday night, so I have to admit, I followed you. I guess you know the rest after that. I have a feeling we're gonna be getting a lot of heat from some folks around here."

Ryan grunted in agreement. He then froze. Stew walked a few steps ahead before realizing Ryan had stopped. He turned and faced him.

"Wait a minute," Ryan said. "I don't wanna go in there." They were in the cafeteria. Dead ahead was the teachers' lounge.

Stew gave Ryan a curious look. "I was thinking we could have a soda. Sit and chat for a bit," he said.

"The soda machine doesn't work," Ryan said. "Besides, I just told you what I saw in there the other day."

Stew put a hand on Ryan's shoulder. "The soda machine *does* work, and I promise the only person you're gonna see in there is me."

"So, you don't believe me then?"

Stew opened the door for Ryan. "I didn't say that. Come on."

23

Ryan reluctantly entered the lounge. It looked exactly as he remembered, sans three dead teachers sitting at the table. The soda machine *was* up and running. Ryan silently cursed it.

"What do you want?" Stew asked as he pulled two one-dollar bills from his wallet and fed them into the machine.

"Whatever you're having is fine."

The machine gave definitive *kerchunk*s as their bottles arrived in the rectangular mouth below. Stew handed one to Ryan and motioned for him to take a seat. They sat across from one another, and Ryan appreciated something in Stew that became apparent after a short moment. The man was not one for small talk.

"There *is* something here, Ryan," he said. "Karl might be older than dirt, but he's right. There is definitely something in this school with bad intentions."

Ryan unscrewed his soda carefully to allow the fizz to slowly escape. "I'll tell you what I told Karl, Stew. What I told Jerry Hansen. I don't believe in ghosts or curses or voodoo or whatever the hell you want to call it. What happened here? Children murdering children? Teachers taking their own lives? Those are things people did on their own accord. Nobody *made* them do it. How could they?"

"You really believe that? You really believe that children—*babies*—took the lives of other babies on their own accord? You tell me it happened once and that one child was unstable, and I'll buy it. But you try to tell me that after *three* incidents with three *different* children years apart, and I'm afraid I'm not buying anything. Never mind the suicides."

"So why did they do it?"

"I don't think there's a man or woman on this earth that knows." Stew sipped his soda.

Ryan sat quiet for a minute. He thought about John Gray. About the boiler room he'd apparently investigated. How everyone who had ever claimed to have seen something here had wound up taking their own lives in horrific fashion.

"John Gray was your friend," he finally said. He hoped it wasn't too abrupt, that it didn't require further prompts.

Stew nodded and sipped his soda again. The fluorescent lighting overhead hummed like a busy hive. And of course the stupid soda machine did, too. Ryan was not ready to forgive the bastard machine just yet.

"He was my *best* friend," Stew said.

"Did he tell you he saw something? That he saw a child? That the child told him to dig around in the boiler room?"

"Yeah, he told me."

"Did you believe him?"

Ryan was stunned that Stew did not immediately answer in the affirmative. Instead, he dropped his head and fiddled with his bottle cap. It was an odd sight. Such an imposing man, now looking ashamed, almost childlike.

"No," was all he said.

"Why not?"

Stew continued fiddling with the cap as he spoke.

"John was going through a divorce at the time. He was drinking too much. Caught his wife in bed with another man. Each day I saw him it was obvious his situation was taking its toll. Maybe some couldn't see it in him, but I could. He was my boy, you know? I could see it in his eyes. Each day that passed, the light in those eyes would get dimmer and dimmer. I offered all the support I could. When he mentioned seeing the little boy in the school, what that boy had said, I just…I don't know…"

"You didn't believe him."

"Maybe I misspoke. I believe he saw a boy. A student. I can even believe that the boy said something about the boiler room. But the reasons John was going on about? That the boy was some kind of ghost telling him something bad was in that boiler room?" He splayed his big hands. "Can you blame me for doubting? Especially given his addled state of mind at the time?"

"Not at all." And it was true. Even after what Ryan had seen, he himself still doubted. He sipped his soda. "He went back to that boiler room the following night," he prompted again.

"Yeah. God knows what he found or what happened, but the next day was when we found...when we found him in the gym." Stew had tears in his eyes. Ryan's heart sank. He admired an imposing man like Stew showing such vulnerability. It was an impressive show of character.

Ryan waited a few moments for Stew to collect himself. He sipped quietly from his soda.

"What do you believe now, Stew?" Ryan eventually asked.

Stew wiped away the last of his tears. "Everybody thought John did what he did because of his divorce. It made sense to most, and with a school like this, the less unexplained stuff the better, right? Far easier to blame his suicide on divorce than some malevolent force, you know?"

Ryan nodded.

"But I know my friend," Stew went on. "He was depressed and devastated about what happened with his wife, but I know—I know it in my heart—that he would never have taken his own life. Not John. Not unless someone made him."

Stew's last words dropped the temperature in the room. At least for Ryan, they did. "Karl told me that everyone who had taken their own lives at Highland had claimed to see something," he said. "He then said the reason that photo was left on my car was because someone was trying to help me—to get me to start digging. I definitely saw something that day in this lounge and will swear to that until the day I die. But I have to confess that if 'digging' is going to end up getting me killed, well, then you can count me—"

Stew held up a hand. "I can't speak for Karl. And I can't tell you about who left you that photo on your car, but the truth is, you *did* see something. And my guess is you're gonna keep on seeing things until something is done."

"You sure as hell sound like Karl."

Stew offered up a mollifying little smile. "I'm a God-fearing man, Ryan. And I think God chooses those he wants to protect. John—given what was happening in his life at the time—likely wasn't strong enough. Mr. Johnson or Miss Ballentine probably weren't either. But maybe you've been chosen because you *are*."

"I'm not a religious man, Stew."

Stew did not seem offended or deterred.

"That's okay. I don't think faith in God can help us anyway. His will can guide us, but it won't help us."

"So what *will* help us?" Ryan asked.

Stew splayed his big hands again. "If I knew, we wouldn't be having this conversation."

Ryan rolled his eyes. "Great."

24

Rebecca's headlights washed over Carol Lawrence's den as she pulled into the driveway. Carol sat up from her spot on the couch and greeted her daughter at the door. Rebecca entered, looking upset.

"Uh oh—I'm taking it the date didn't go so well?" Carol asked.

"No. I mean, yes—yes, it went well. It went really well, but…something weird happened after."

"Tell me." Carol guided her into the den.

Rebecca flopped on the sofa and sighed. Carol took a spot next to her daughter, both women doing a quarter turn to face one another.

"So, tell me what happened," Carol said again.

"Happy hour was great. We got along really well and just had an amazing time. He's awesome."

"But?"

"But then later I saw him outside the school, and it looked like he got into a fight with these two guys."

"*What?*"

Rebecca nodded.

Carol then frowned. "Wait—why were you at the school after you went to the bar?"

"He offered to drive. We left my car in the school lot. He was taking me back to get it after our date was over."

"So, he got into a fight with two guys when he was dropping you off?"

"No—it was after I had left."

"You're confusing me, Becks. Are you saying he got into a fight *after* you had already left the school?"

Rebecca nodded.

"Well, then how do you know he was in a fight?"

"I guess I was still kind of smitten from the date. I turned around real quick after I had left, hoping I'd catch him before he'd gone. Sounds kinda corny, but I was hoping for one more goodnight kiss."

Carol smiled and rubbed her daughter's knee. "Not corny at all."

Rebecca went on. "Anyway, I pull in, and he *was* still there, but he wasn't alone. The two guys were there with him. I was confused, so I parked on the road to watch and listen. The two guys were really angry with Ryan about something."

"Angry about what? Could you hear anything?"

"Not much. I did hear one of them accuse Ryan of wanting to kill more children."

"*What*?"

"I know, right? Anyway, they started fighting, but then some big black guy showed up and pulled the two guys off of Ryan. The two guys took off after, and Ryan and the big black guy went inside."

"Went inside the school?"

Rebecca nodded.

"That must have been Stew Taylor. He's the gym teacher there."

"He sure saved Ryan's butt."

Carol grunted. "I wonder what Stew was doing there. Lucky break he just happened to be there at that precise moment to save Ryan's butt."

Rebecca shrugged again. "Got me there. Are you suggesting that Stew the gym teacher might have been *following* Ryan?"

"No idea. It sure doesn't make a heck of a lot of sense. Chances are you were right in that Stew just happened to be in the right place at the right time, and let's be grateful for that."

Rebecca nodded again. An emphatic one.

"So, with the exception of the weirdness at the end of the night, all else went well?" Carol asked.

"It really did. I like him a lot."

"Are you going to see him again?"

She smiled. "Yup. In fact, we already made plans for another date tomorrow night."

Carol rubbed her daughter's knee again. "I'm happy for you, sweetheart. I really hope it turns out to be something."

A thought hit Rebecca. She stopped smiling. "Should I mention what I saw tonight?"

"I wouldn't," Carol said. "See whether he mentions it first. If he doesn't say anything, then maybe he's got something to hide."

Rebecca looked upset by her mother's comment. "What would he have to hide?"

"I'm not trying to be a downer, Becks. But this is twice now you've said he's acted strange."

"But this time was different. The first time was just—" She shook her head, not wanting to believe her potential knight had a chink in his armor. "This was different than the first time."

Carol rubbed her daughter's knee once again. "Okay, okay…"

"Oh God, please don't let there be anything wrong with him. We had such a great time."

"I'm glad," Carol said, but her reply sounded hollow.

Rebeca gave a dry chuckle. "Knowing my luck, he'll be the next teacher at that stupid school to commit suicide."

"*Rebecca.*"

25

Stew and Ryan, still seated across from one another in the teachers' lounge, sat in silence for a spell. There seemed nothing else to say. Ryan felt a kind of protection in Stew's presence. Not for his size, but because...

(*because what?*)

because the man was still alive? Whatever it was that lived in this school—and Ryan was shocked at how easily he was now considering such absurdities, because he *still* considered such paranormal notions absurd; he did, dammit...didn't he?—clearly hadn't been able to claim Stew. And it was this shield the man possessed that gave Ryan his temporary sense of comfort, as though he was sharing that shield. Unless...

(*unless what?*)

unless Stew was the one who had, as Karl had so delightfully put it, brought *it* here.

And what else was it that old Karl had said? *I don't trust a single one of 'em.*

(*Well, if Stew* was *the one who brought* it *here, then he's got more in common with Denzel Washington than just looks. Guy's got his acting chops as well; he seemed genuinely distraught when discussing John Gray.*)

As a great actor should. And how about his just happening to be in the neighborhood when you were getting your ass kicked?

(*Saving my ass just to kill it later?*)

To make you *kill it later.*

(*Absurd.* All of it. *Absurd, absurd, absurd.*)

"You about ready?" Stew asked.

Ryan jumped. The break in silence, the break in his train of thought; he couldn't help it.

Stew gave a little laugh. "You all right?"

"I'm fine. Yeah, I'm ready."

Stew leaned across the table, grabbed Ryan's empty soda bottle, stood, and dumped it into the trash can in the corner along with his own.

"Wait," Ryan said. "I'm actually not ready."

Stew glanced back at Ryan. "Something wrong?"

Let me count the ways…

Ryan decided to just come out with it. "Karl told me about the veterans of Highland. You, him, Carol Lawrence, and…shit, I can't remember her name. The head secretary?"

Stew took his seat again. "Barbara."

"Right. Barbara. He told me the four of you were there from day one, from the very first tragedy."

Stew nodded. "That's true."

"Karl also told me that he didn't trust any of you. According to Karl's logic, whatever was 'brought here' must have been brought by one of you four. Well, according to Karl, you three."

"You believe that?"

"My belief system has been on the fritz lately."

Stew smiled. "Understandable." He stood again. "Come on, we'll talk along the way."

Ryan stood and followed Stew out of the lounge.

◆

"It was nice to meet you, Ryan," Stew said as they headed back towards the main entrance. "You're an easy guy to talk to. Can't remember the last time I cried in front of another man."

Them Denzel acting chops?

(*Shut up.*)

"You're an easy guy to talk to as well," Ryan said. "And thank you for the help earlier. I'd probably be in the ER right now if it wasn't for you."

"Yeah—I'm sorry you had to deal with that. I'd love to say it was a onetime thing, but the locals around here…"

"So I've noticed."

"Can't really blame some of them—there's a lot of heartache in this town. Some folks moved on or moved out, but some just can't let go, I guess."

"I get it," Ryan said. And a part of him truly did. To lose a child was unimaginable.

"As far as your other concern, or should I say, Karl's concern, his lack of trust, I wouldn't entirely chalk it up to an old man's paranoia. When you've experienced the things we have, it can make you a little batty. But Karl means well. I expect it's why he encouraged you to go digging around. He wants your help. *We* want your help—the four of us."

"So Carol and Barbara know about what I saw too?"

"No. Not sure if I plan on telling them just yet, either."

"I'd rather you didn't."

"All right. But I *can* tell you that if you somehow have the ability to…" He searched for the right words. "Find a thing out or two, then I'd be keen on telling them then."

"Assuming one of you four aren't responsible for bringing the devil here." His sarcasm was out before he could pull it back.

Stew stopped and faced Ryan.

"I'm sorry," Ryan said.

Stew ignored his apology. "You say you saw my dead friend."

"I think I did."

"Earlier, you swore on it."

Ryan dropped his head and sighed. "I did."

"That means you have the ability to see things we can't."

"I know. Karl already told me all—"

"It means you may have the ability to fix things. Put them right."

"How the hell am I—?"

"I don't know. Like I said in the lounge, if any of us knew, then we wouldn't be having this conversation. And if we don't know, then how the heck are you supposed to know?"

"Exactly, Stew. I don't want to get—"

"But I'm asking you to *try*. To not shy away from anything that may come your way. Please, Ryan."

Just placate the guy. Tell him what he wants to hear, however insane it sounds.

(*And yet you* did *see his dead friend...*)

"Fine," he said. How he'd love to be back at West Chester right now with his grumpy old academic advisor. *Now suppose I get a job in a haunted fucking school...?*

Stew placed one of those large hands on Ryan's shoulder. "Thank you."

Ryan grunted.

They headed out to their cars, said their goodbyes, and left.

———— ♦ ————

Three hours have passed since Pinewood Elementary has had a visitor. Now, at half past midnight, it is occupied again. The footsteps are neither hurried nor slow; they are patient and methodical, knowing exactly where they are going throughout the dark halls, knowing the precise location where they will soon stop before the steel door that leads below ground, into the boiler room.

Down the stairs, below the earth, and into complete darkness, the blackness of the boiler room's surroundings no impediment for the footsteps that know their way as footsteps do when strode thousands of times.

Light does eventually appear, but it is minimal, all that is necessary. A flashlight, its small circular beam in the blackness soon settling on a section of wall behind the great boiler, the section of wall unremarkable. A steel panel on that wall, a few feet high, a few feet wide, it too unremarkable, no different than the myriad of steel panels throughout the four walls of the boiler's dungeony home. That dungeony home one of the few places unaffected by the great fire, needing no renovation, much to the current occupant's exceptional delight.

A sizable canvas bag hits the floor, its contents clanking slightly on concrete. Also...moving? Something in the bag moves when it hits the ground. Something alive inside.

Hands withdraw a large screwdriver from the bag, one of the remaining contents of the bag moving again, stirred by the act, perhaps wishing the rummaging hands would soon set it free from the confines of the canvas bag.

The tip of the big screwdriver is worked into an edge of the panel, popping it free with a wavering clang. The panel is then carefully removed and set aside, the sole occupant of the boiler room then crawling their way inside, canvas bag with them, crawling deep inside the concrete wall, the narrow passage long since chipped away by deliberate hands, akin to an inmate's life's work.

The narrow passage ends, opening up to a makeshift chamber no bigger than a prison cell. The ceiling is low, allowing kneeling only. Another click of the flashlight and the beam settles on a large ring of thick candles. Into the canvas bag again, and out comes the lighter, the hands promptly lighting the large circle of candles. The flashlight now tucked back into the canvas bag, the flickering glow from the ring of candles sufficient lighting for the job ahead.

Back into the canvas bag. Out comes a square of cloth, a piece of charcoal. The hands begin to work with the charcoal and the cloth. Before long, the cloth reads *Ryan Herb*, the cloth then delicately placed within the large ring of candles.

The canvas bag, its lively contents still moving, finally clucks. Hands remove a chicken, the chicken then cradled into a pair of arms, hands stroking it lovingly until its fidgeting subsides.

The hands stop stroking, one of them reaching for the final item in the canvas bag. A scalpel. The chicken's throat is slashed; the arms immediately drop the scalpel and hold the chicken tight, waiting for its death spasms to play out. They soon do, and the hands hold the chicken over the piece of cloth, working the lifeless animal in small circles across the cloth within the ring of candles, deliberate spiral patterns in the medium of the chicken's blood covering the charcoal work that reads *Ryan Herb*.

The chicken is placed back into the canvas bag, along with the scalpel that took its life. The busy hands are not quite done; the remainder of its ritual will need to wait. It cannot be finished tonight, as a more personal item of Ryan Herb needs to be obtained to do so.

But there would be compensations until the ritual was complete. The animal sacrifice would achieve a probing effect that would jab at the delicate walls of Ryan Herb's psyche until something personal could be acquired, something that would ultimately drive the young man over the edge. And how fun it would be to see those walls slowly crumble during the interim. Compensations indeed.

Before leaving, the visitor gazes adoringly towards the other items that adorn the perimeter of the chamber, the candlelight seemingly sharing the visitor's adoration as it caresses each item with its wavering glow.

All is how it had been originally left before the fire, again, unaffected by the vigilante act, to the great delight of the chamber's current occupant. And that occupant's gaze now settles on John Gray's framed picture in the corner, a silver gym whistle—a treasured gift from his ex-wife, his initials carved into the silver, the whistle mysteriously vanishing the day before he took his life—hanging from the corner of the picture frame. The picture itself? A noose around the man's neck, inked in blood that is long caked and a reddish brown, is still ever present.

Also ever present are the dozens of other personal items and photographs that once belonged to those who died within the walls of Highland Elementary, teachers and students alike.

26

Two things happened during the next five days. Ryan and Rebecca had seen each other every day and night since they'd shared their first drink together on Friday. And Ryan had struck up a great friendship with his fellow first-year and fifth-grade teacher, Trish, the five-foot, motor-mouthed Cabbage Patch Doll.

"Did you get it up yet?" Trish asked.

"I beg your pardon," Ryan replied in a lousy British accent.

Trish punched him in the arm. "Perv. Do you want me to send you an email to see whether it's up and running yet?"

They sat side by side, each in front of a laptop trying to set up their school email accounts. It was close to noon; the third day of orientation had ended early, and the instructors had encouraged them to return to their classrooms to practice the internet skills they had learned earlier that morning. Trish and Ryan had chosen the latter's room to practice, which realistically consisted of ten minutes of computer time and forty-five minutes of Pinewood gossip: which teachers seemed cool, which seemed a headache, and, of course, the lovely Rebecca Lawrence.

"Send it," Ryan said. A short moment later and the number one appeared next to the inbox on Ryan's screen. "Booyah."

"It came through?"

"It did."

"Awesome. What are you doing for lunch? I mean besides Rebecca."

"You flatter me. Like I could last that long during a lunch break. I'm more of a water break guy."

Trish let loose her trademark laugh—a machine gun loaded with helium. Nails on a chalkboard to some; adorable to Ryan.

"Seriously, what are you doing for food?" Trish asked when her laughter died.

"Brought a hoagie. I told Rebecca I'd meet her in the cafeteria. You wanna come along?"

"Nah—third wheel."

"That's dumb."

"Your mom's dumb."

"She's actually quite smart."

"Sometimes the apple does fall far…"

"I'll hit a girl."

"Probably punch like one too."

They shared a grin.

———————◆———————

Happy with her email progress, Trish got up and wandered around Ryan's room.

"You ended up doing a good job in here," she said.

"*You* ended up doing a good job."

"Meh. I just pointed. You did all the labor."

"My little foreman," Ryan said, still staring at his computer screen.

She bopped him on the back of the head. "I'm five-two in heels."

"I'm six-two in them."

She laughed and continued to wander. The rest of the fifth-grade wing was empty. Everyone had indeed gone to lunch. Ryan hit one last button, and his screen went black. In fact, the whole room shut down. Lights, air-conditioning (the school had mercifully turned it on a few days ago), everything.

"What the hell?" Ryan said, quickly taking his hands away from his laptop as though he might have caused it all.

"What happened?" Trish walked over to her own laptop. It too was dead.

"Must be a power failure or something," Ryan said.

"Then why did our laptops go out, dummy? They're on batteries."

Ryan felt a familiar touch of fear. He flashed on the teachers' lounge, the brief power failure therein, the three dead teachers staring at him with their barren faces.

"Hey—*Hey!*" Trish called out. She was standing at Ryan's classroom door now, looking out into the hallway. She spun back towards Ryan. "Did you see that? A little boy just ran by your room."

"What?"

"A little boy just ran by your room," she said again. "I saw him."

"One of the teachers must have brought their kid."

"Not dressed like that, they didn't."

Ryan frowned. "Dressed like what?"

"I don't know. Weird. Like a pilgrim or Amish kid or something."

Ryan stood. "What the hell are you talking about?"

Trish seemed more excited than rattled. "I shit you not—he looked like one of those little Amish kids. All in black. Black wide-brimmed hat too. Be right back."

"No, Trish—*wait.*" Ryan did not follow her. He stayed put. Called after her again, but she was already gone. A strong beat of silence followed.

It was a teacher's child. A teacher brought their kid. That's all.

(*And the way Trish claims he was dressed?*)

She was mistaken. She'll show up here at any moment with the kid, and it'll explain everything.

What came next was a scream, its pitch so high it could only have come from Trish.

———————— ✦ ————————

Trish turned the corner of the fifth-grade wing and watched the child in black disappear into the boys' room.

Quick little bugger, she thought.

She stood outside the boys' room door and contemplated entering. What if Ryan had been correct? Maybe a teacher *had* brought their kid here, and the poor bugger just needed to take a whizz something fierce. *You go in and catch him at a urinal midstream and you might scar the poor little guy for life.*

But his clothing. It was so odd. Yes, the boy had run by Ryan's classroom quickly, but she had still managed a decent look at him. The boy was even wearing one of those wide-rimmed black hats, the kind she'd seen the Amish, adults *and* children, wearing during the few times she'd visited Lancaster.

So, what did that leave? An Amish kid hiked all the way from freaking Lancaster to pop into Pinewood Elementary and take that whizz he so desperately needed? Of course not. There were plenty of other possibilities; however, right now Trish's curiosity was getting the better of her.

She decided to enter.

The boy was there. He was not using one of the urinals on the right, nor was he in one of the stalls on the left. He sat on the floor, far back against the wall, beneath a small square window overhead, the window doing a modest job showing all in the dimly lit bathroom that was not immune to the recent power outage.

The boy's outfit confirmed what she'd seen, right down to the black, wide-brimmed hat. The boy's head was down, the top of the hat resembling an old record to Trish. If the boy heard Trish's entrance, he did not show it. He just sat against the tiled wall, legs out in front, head down. He was humming to himself.

"Hello?" she called to the boy.

The boy lifted his head and looked at Trish. His face was round; his cheeks, cherub red. His eyes—black, too black, crowlike—fixed on Trish. He continued to hum.

Trish inched forward. She squatted before the boy. "Are you okay?"

The boy stopped humming. "You wanna see something?" His tone was pleasant.

"Okay."

"This is what it made us do," the boy said.

The boy slowly began to tilt his head backwards. A long gash appeared across his throat, thin at first, then widening like a mouth the further back the boy's head went. When the boy's head could go back no further, a waterfall of red gushed from the wound, soaking the boy's front.

Trish slapped a hand over her mouth. Tried to scream, but managed nothing.

The boy's head pitched forward, his eyes no longer a crow's eyes, but rolled back white. His skin was the color of ash. He grinned at Trish with a mouth that seemed impossibly wide.

"See?" the boy said with that grin. Those white eyes. "*See?*"

The boy spat a mouthful of blood into Trish's face and giggled.

Trish found her voice and screamed.

<hr />

Ryan bolted from his classroom and followed Trish's scream into the boys' room. He did not notice Trish right away. He couldn't. Instead, his eyes were on the little boy in black, the boy now on his feet, capering about the room, eyes white, grin his whole face, his tiny black shoes tracking his own blood along the bathroom tile underfoot. "*See?*" the boy sang over and over as he danced. "*See? See? See…?*"

"*Jesus Christ!*" Ryan hollered.

Trish, cowering in the corner, hands covering her face, shielding her eyes from the atrocity, dropped her hands and raised her head towards Ryan's shouts. She sprinted into his arms. Ryan literally picked her up and carried her out of the boys' room.

27

Trish and Ryan's scene had attracted those who had not left the building for lunch. Those who were just as concerned about the recent power outage as any, and then, of course, by the chaos that had echoed throughout the once quiet building shortly after.

"*In there!*" Ryan cried out, pointing his chin towards the boys' room, Trish sobbing in his arms.

Alex Barnett and Nora Haywood—second-grade teachers—cautiously opened the boys' room door and went inside. Ryan held Trish tighter. For a moment, her sobs were the only sound.

The bathroom door opened. Alex Barnett poked his head out. "Ryan?"

Ryan looked at him. Alex motioned for Ryan, and Ryan alone, to join him and Nora inside. He nodded back and held Trish at arm's length. "I'll be right back," he said to her. "Stay here." He followed Alex into the bathroom.

"What happened here, man?" Alex asked once they were inside. He was a young teacher, younger than Ryan. And right now he appeared flummoxed, trying to comprehend why Ryan and Trish had lost it in the boys' room in the fifth-grade wing. Trying to figure it out because there *was* nothing in the bathroom. No bloody little footprints on the floor, no blood anywhere. More importantly, no trace of a little boy in black capering about the damn bathroom with maniacal glee as he chanted "*see?*" over and over again. Nothing.

Ryan could only stare in disbelief. He'd seen it. He had, he fucking *had*. He quickly flashed on his conversation with Karl:

> *"I believe you, son…I believe every word you just said."*
> *And then Ryan's fleeting sense of relief over Karl's words:*
> *The old janitor believed him. Hurray. Who the hell would believe them?*

Trish. That's who. Because *she* had seen it—

(*see? see?*)

saints be praised (and this feeling of relief was just as fleeting as it had been with Karl, more so even; he did *not* want Trish involved in this madness), Trish could see too.

Ryan bolted from the bathroom without a word to either teacher. They followed cautiously behind him.

Rebecca was now on the scene, trying to console Trish, to ask what had happened. Ryan did not acknowledge her. Instead, he immediately fronted Trish. "He's not in there, Trish. *Nothing* is in there."

Trish looked up at Ryan with disbelieving eyes. She then looked down at hands that had wiped away blood that had been spat in her face only moments before. They were clean. She shouldered Ryan out of the way and rushed towards the bathroom, needing to see for herself.

No scream echoing out from the bathroom this time. Just Trish's incredulous cry: "*No fucking way!*"

28

Trish and Ryan sat alone in the teachers' lounge, each gripping a Styrofoam cup of coffee, each wishing the coffee was very Irish.

They had told their story to everyone in the building and were now content to be left alone. Fitting; after their story was told, everyone in that building was likely more than content to leave *them* alone.

But not for reasons born from fear, but for the simple fact that no one appeared to believe them. Despite Trish's hysteria and Ryan's palpable angst, despite the sympathy offered, it was clear not a one was buying it. Ryan knew placation when he saw it.

And why the hell *should* they believe the story? Ryan would have done the same if the shoe had been on the other foot, if someone else had claimed to have seen what they saw. Even the principal, Miss Gates, appeared to be among the disbelievers. Ryan flashed back on Hansen telling him that many had been spooked by their interview with him alone, had chosen not to take the job. How long, Ryan wondered, would it take for a sort of converse to come true? For he and Trish to be let go for spooking others? Perhaps let go for concocting some sort of sick practical joke?

"Trish," Ryan said.

Trish did not look up right away. She was staring into her coffee, seeing something else. Almost assuredly seeing the boy in black.

"*Trish,*" he said again.

She finally looked up.

"What we just saw was real," he said.

Trish lowered her head again and spoke into her coffee. "No one else saw it."

"But *we* did. We *both* saw it. Are you telling me that two different people imagined the exact same thing?"

"I don't know," she said.

"You *do* know about this school, right? You know the shit that happened here?"

Trish nodded. "Doesn't everyone?"

"Yeah, well, what we just saw? That wasn't the first time for me."

Trish frowned, her expression clear. *Elaborate*, it said.

And so Ryan did.

Ryan told her everything. What he'd seen and experienced in the lounge they were currently seated in (and Trish had given an understandably wary look around the lounge immediately after), Hansen's tale about the former principal and the boy *he'd* encountered, the photo on his car, the fight in the lot, Karl, Stew, Carol, Barbara, even his dreams.

"You can *see* it, Trish," Ryan said. "Just like me, you can *see* it."

"I think I've had enough of that word for the day."

Ryan offered a thin, understanding smile.

"So, what does this mean?" she asked.

"Well, first, it means I'm not crazy. Much as I hate to have you as an ally in all of this right now, I *do* take comfort in that." He finished the last of his coffee in a gulp. "And second, it means that we *are* allies in this. We can help each other."

"Help with what? After what I just saw today, I'm not even sure I want to work here anymore."

"No, no, no—don't say that."

"Why not? Whatever the hell was in that bathroom clearly doesn't want us here."

"I don't think that's right. I think that whatever's here wants our help."

Trish scoffed, "It's got a funny way of showing it."

"That's not what I—I'm not sure how to explain it."

"Try."

Ryan fiddled with his Styrofoam cup for a moment. Then: "There are two...*things* in this school. One bad, the other victims of that bad. The bad wants to keep it bad. Make it worse, even. The victims of that bad want us to stop it, make sure it never happens again. I told you what Karl and Stew said: something in this building needs to be found and put right, whatever the hell that might be."

Trish dropped her head again and shook it. "This is insane."

"You're preaching to the head of the fucking choir, sister."

29

"I don't know what you want me to say, Rebecca," Ryan said.

"I want you to tell me exactly what happened this afternoon. The truth."

It was after four. Most were gone for the day, Trish included. Rebecca and Ryan had stayed. They now stood in the school's lot by Rebecca's car.

"I told you what happened," Ryan said. "The truth."

"That's ridiculous, Ryan. Nobody else saw it."

"Trish did."

"Oh, of course *Trish* saw it."

"Please don't tell me you're starting with some jealousy bullshit."

"I'm not," she lied. "But give me a little break, will you? This isn't the first time you've acted like this. You're making it all so difficult for me."

"Making what difficult?"

"Us."

Ryan nodded quickly. "Okay, okay—I get it. And I don't blame you one bit for feeling the way you do. I don't. But you need to know a few things. First is that I am not lying about what I saw today. I'm *not*. I wish I had a decent explanation for what I saw, but I don't. I'm sure Trish feels the same."

Rebecca rolled her eyes at the mention of Trish's name.

"*Second*," Ryan said quickly when Rebecca rolled her eyes at Trish's name, "is that I really like you. It would kill me if my behavior deterred you from wanting to see seeing me again."

Rebecca considered him. He looked so sincere. If he was crazy or just an attention whore who liked to stir things up, he was damned good at projecting otherwise.

"I *do* want to see you again," she decided to say.

"Promise?"

"Yes." *Screw it.* "Is there anything between you and Trish?"

"Not at all," Ryan said immediately. "She is a friend; that's all. You're…"

"A what?"

"Someone more than a friend."

Her belly gave its familiar swirl. Crazy? Attention whore? Her belly just didn't seem to care.

"You do make it very difficult for me, you know," she said with a little smile.

"At least it's not boring."

"I would welcome boring right about now."

"You say that now…"

She succumbed to a small laugh. "Do you want me to come over this weekend? I could stay the night."

Up until now she had stayed a few nights at Ryan's place. They had not had sex yet. They had come close—*very* close—but it still hadn't happened. Both of them wanted it more than oxygen.

"If you'd like," he said.

"Would *you* like?"

"I would like," he said. Then: "No—wait. Can't. My mom is having company. Relatives from out of town. Christ, a thirty-year-old man just said he couldn't have his girl stay over because his mommy was having company."

Big-time swirl. "Your girl?"

Ryan groaned. "Someone more than a friend."

She grinned.

"What about your place?" he asked.

"My mom has that rule about boys spending the night…"

Ryan puffed out his chest. "What about men?"

"Men who still live with their mommy?"

"Cheeky bitch."

No succumbing this time. A genuine laugh. Oh, how she wanted to punch him one minute and kiss him the next.

"We'll see," she said. "I'm still a little creeped out by you."

"But still not bored."

"No." She kissed him. "Something tells me I'll never be bored around you."

30

"Are you prepared to be shocked?" Trish said a second after Ryan answered his cell.

"Bring it on," he said. "At this point, I'd say I'm fairly shock-proof."

"I did some digging today and found out an interesting thing or two about our beloved school."

"Trish, I promise you; whatever you unearthed is not news. The school's history is not exactly a closed book."

"Unless you're reading from a different book."

"Come again?"

"My uncle. He's got *all* the books."

"What books?"

"It's a figure of speech, dummy. I mean he knows everything about anything. Or at least he can find everything about anything. The internet is his bitch. Guy rocks like five generators just in case his power goes out. I'm not even sure he remembers how to walk, he's on his computer—or should I say *computers*—so much."

"I'm not following you, Trish."

"I know you're not, my dim-witted friend. What I was getting to was our school's history. The *real* history."

"And?"

"Do you know what happened there over two hundred years ago?"

"I do not."

"Murder. Slaughter. Suicide. Turns out there was an old schoolhouse from way, way back. Built on the same grounds that you and I walk on today."

"And?"

"And some Satan-loving teacher made all her students commit suicide."

"*What?* Where did you hear this?"

"I just told you."

"Bullshit. You're telling me that something like that was kept secret from everyone *but* your uncle?"

"Oh no—it was buried miles deep. My uncle just has a hell of a long shovel."

"Why was it buried?"

"A ritual suicide involving over twenty children? A benevolent—well, *seemingly* benevolent—teacher the culprit? Gee, I wonder."

"Wait, wait, wait—I still can't buy that this is not common knowledge. Something like this—"

"It *isn't* common knowledge because officially it *didn't* happen. The town buried the whole thing. Think about it, Ryan: It's the good old days; somebody farts and it's a big deal, right?"

"Yeah, but come on, Trish."

"'Yeah, but come on, Trish' nuthin. This was a time when religion meant a hell of a lot more than it does today. People believed in witches and demons as much as they believed in their own reflections. The town was still growing, and if word of a supposed theological disaster like that got out, it would have crippled it."

"So, who was the teacher?" Ryan asked.

"Some lady named Tarver. Helen Tarver. Apparently, her curriculum was a wee bit out of the norm."

"What do you mean?"

"I mean while the kids *should* have been learning math and grammar, she was teaching them incantations and ritual chants. Plus performing acts of possession and whatnot."

"And these children never told their parents about their 'curriculum'?"

"Apparently not. Makes sense, though, when you think about it. The sway she had over them. She *literally* convinced every child in her class to slit their own throats."

"*Jesus*...and no other teachers in the school ever suspected?"

"There *were* no other teachers. This is *Little House on the Prairie* times, remember? One schoolhouse, one teacher."

Ryan grunted.

"Sadly, that's not the sickest part," Trish went on. "On that final day, when all the kids...you know...a townsperson happened to drop by the schoolhouse and stumble on to what Helen Tarver was up to. Apparently, Miss Tarver was in the process of...*collecting* things from her dead students."

"*What?*"

"Like I said, a townsperson dropped on by after the children were all dead. Tarver had already gathered jars of their blood—they were sitting on her desk—and she was in the process of removing certain *body parts* from some of the children. Apparently, a boy's penis was already removed and floating in a jar next to the jars of blood on her desk."

"*What the fuc—?*"

"Naturally, the townsperson freaked and ran for help. By the time she came back with that help, Tarver was gone."

"They never caught her?"

"Oh, they caught her. Hard to hide in a small town like that. They caught her and then some."

"They killed her."

"Bingo. Literally tore her to bits. It's rumored that one person ripped her heart right out of her chest and gave it to a local priest so he could cast her soul into the bowels of hell."

"You made that last bit up, didn't you?"

"I did say it was a rumor."

"I meant the 'bowels of hell' part."

"Oh. Yeah. That was for flair."

"Well done."

"So, what do you think?" she asked.

"What happened to the schoolhouse?"

"Burnt to the ground. Ironic, huh?"

"That's not irony, Miss Morissette."

Trish's groan was audible. "So what is it, then?"

"A creepy fucking coincidence. I still can't believe nobody knew about any of this."

"Oh, I'm sure some people do, but I would wager enough time has gone by where the word 'legend' is thrown around more often than not. You gotta remember: no internet; no TV; no radio; hell—no phones! Small town like that back then? Once that school turned to ash, the secret was as good as sealed. Still, any remaining members of the Tarver family apparently moved far away. Changed their name to Moyer. Can't say I blame them. You know how creepy people were back in the day. Just having that same name would have probably gotten them burned at the stake with no trial."

Ryan grunted in agreement. "Still, taking into account your 'legend' comment, we should consider that much of the story has been embellished over the years. It can't *all* be true."

"I'd agree," Trish replied. "But I certainly didn't imagine what I saw in that bathroom today, and neither did you. You told me that your buddy Karl felt that someone brought something bad to this school. I'd say it's more likely that someone brought something *back*."

31

The following day, Trish unwittingly discovered a small razor blade between a stack of papers she'd been photocopying. Or more aptly put: the palm of her hand had unwittingly discovered the small blade. The cut was deep, spattering a good number of the papers, and anything else close by, with a generous amount of her blood.

There were several witnesses in the copy room at the time, the majority rushing to her aid when she'd cried out, the majority wanting to help, but wanting nothing to do with the cleanup. Not for blood. Enter Karl, who was on the scene a short while later to do the deed.

With the exception of the cut—and the mystery as to why a razor blade was hiding in between her stack of papers—Trish's day had gone fairly well. Orientation was cut short once again, and she found herself in Ryan's company for the remainder of the day, rehashing *the* topic from their phone call the night before.

"Talk about history repeating itself," Trish said. They were alone in Trish's room this time. "Hundreds of years ago right back to us in one big creepy circle."

"Yeah, but *why* is it repeating itself? And are we actually admitting now that we both believe in ghosts and witchcraft and whatever?"

Trish checked the bandage on her palm when she replied: "Who knows what to call it? But wouldn't you say it's safe to assume now that all of those children *did* in fact commit those murders of their fellow students against their will? The suicides too? If this Helen Tarver whacko can persuade a group of children to cut their own throats back in the day, then I don't see why someone else with her same knowledge and...*desires* couldn't persuade others to do similar sick deeds today."

"Assuming the history is accurate."

"Never let the truth get in the way of a good story, my friend."

Ryan grunted. "I'm not particularly digging the story."

"Me neither. But it appears to be required reading—at least for us."

Ryan grunted again. Then: "Remember when I told you about Jerry Hansen's story with the principal and the kid with the chants and the white eyes? The kid that stabbed the principal in his foot?"

"I remember."

"They claim that kid had no recollection of anything. They claim none of the kids who committed the murders did either. So I guess it sort of makes sense: they were in some kind of trance or something."

Despite the occasional wince, Trish kept fiddling with her bandage as though it helped her think. "You know what I don't get? This stuff that happened back in the day happened over two hundred years ago. Highland was built in what? The fifties?"

"I think so."

"But all the murders and suicides didn't happen until the eighties, right?"

"Right."

"So what the hell took so long? Were the naughty spirits just biding their time for thirty years before deciding to start some shit?"

"Well, maybe it's like you said on the phone—maybe something *wasn't* here all this time; maybe something was brought *back*."

Trish nodded. "And logic would indicate that it was someone who came on board shortly before the first tragedy."

Ryan made a face as though finding a hole in the logic. "That could be *dozens* of people. Plus, if this person—or *persons*—has been managing to do this crazy shit for the past twenty years and is *still* capable of doing it today, then wouldn't you think they'd be clever enough not to have gone cooking shit up shortly after their arrival? They would have bided their time so as not to draw any parallels; it wouldn't take a genius to figure out that bad shit started going down shortly after so-and-so arrived."

"That's a good point, I guess."

"Karl says he doesn't trust anyone here except me," Ryan said.

"Why you?"

"Because he was there when I freaked out in the teachers' lounge. Karl seems to have a lot of respect for the remaining employees from Highland—the ones who were there from the very first tragedy—but he told me he believes he's still alive today because he doesn't trust any of them. That he looks out for number one."

"Isn't Karl one of those original four?" Trish asked.

"Yeah."

"So, it could be him. Maybe his paranoid spiel is to throw us off his scent."

"Very possible."

"Do you think it could be one of those four who's responsible for it all? Maybe *all* four?"

"No idea."

"What if it was someone who already left Highland? Someone who still holds the ability to do what they do from—I don't know—remote control?"

"Remote control?"

She made a face. "You know what I mean."

"I'm still not sure it's as easy as pointing a finger at a man or a woman. After what I've seen the past couple of weeks—after what *you've* seen—I wouldn't be surprised if the school *itself* was somehow running the show."

Trish shook her head. "Then why did it lie dormant for those years from the fifties to the eighties? No—it's somebody. Somebody who knows the same buried history about this town that we now know. Somebody who wants to get the ball rolling again now that the school is back up and running. I mean, when you think about it, the suicides make sense. If they were all people who claimed to see things, then maybe they could have ultimately exposed the person or persons responsible through the visions they were having. The person or persons responsible would need to dispose of those who could see sooner than later to keep such an eventuality from ever happening. Protect his or her identity. Keep things running smoothly."

"Keep murdering children," Ryan said.

"Which raises yet another question. Why children? The teacher suicides make sense if you buy my theory about the evildoer covering their ass, but why children?"

"Who knows? Maybe it's some kind of sacrificial thing. Like some cults do with virgins or whatever."

"Oh, now you're really screwed."

"And you're really safe."

She laughed and punched him. "Speaking of which, have you and Miss Rebecca Lawrence done the deed yet?"

"A gentleman never talks."

Trish looked at her classroom door. "Who came in?"

Ryan burst out laughing. A diehard Three Stooges fan, Ryan instantly got Trish's joke: whenever someone referred to the Stooges as gentlemen, they would, without fail, spin towards the door and ask: *Who came in?*

"A Stooge fan…" he said. "I'm now certain we were separated at birth."

She extended two fingers and went for his eyes. He did the classic block with the vertical flat of his hand.

When their shared laughter died, Ryan added: "I'll tell you one thing: I'd sure as hell like to know who left that photo for me on my car."

"Yet *another* mystery," she said. "Was it a threat, or was it someone trying to help like your buddy Karl suggested? Or was it Karl himself?"

"Karl thinks it was planted there to get me to start snooping around. So, yeah—help, I guess. What it did was scare the freaking crap out of me. Not everyday someone leaves you a photo of three dead people you actually saw the day before. Still can't believe it's gotten to the point that I can say that with a straight face."

Trish smiled and fiddled with her bandage again. Winced again.

"How's your hand?" Ryan asked.

"Hurts. You'd like to know who left you the photo; I'd like to know how a stupid razor blade wound up in a stack of papers."

"Let me see."

Trish showed him. The white dressing was soaked through with red. She peeled back the tape and showed him the wound underneath.

"That looks pretty bad, Trish."

"Can you go and get me another bandage from the nurse's office before this one is completely soaked too?"

"You need to get it checked out, Trish. Seriously. It looks bad. You can't just keep wrapping it. You might need stitches."

"You might need to just do what you're told."

"Pain in my ass." Ryan bonked her head lightly and left her classroom for the nurse's office.

When he came back ten minutes later, Trish was sprawled out on her classroom floor, a lake of blood around her head, her throat slashed from ear to ear. In her open right hand was a razor blade. Her eyes were open, and she was very dead.

<hr />

It was not long before a crowd had gathered around Trish's body. Some screamed; some cried; some turned away and left the room covering their mouths, afraid they may soon see everything they'd eaten that day.

If you were one of the individuals in the building who knew where to look, you would have found a piece of canvas with Trish's name inscribed on it, tucked far away within a hidden chamber in the boiler room, behind the great boiler. On this canvas you would have found the bloodied bandages Trish had been discarding in the nurse's office throughout the day, meticulously placed in precise positions around her name, several razor blades entwined within.

32

Trish Cooke's post-funeral reception. Ryan was seated at the small bar in the banquet hall the Cooke family had reserved for the occasion. He was on his third scotch. Trish's funeral had gone about as well as funerals go. Ryan had cried, but the tears were born from equal parts sorrow and rage. And so here now, Ryan was content to drink, mourn, and figure out who was

(*because according to Trish, it is a who. Not a what, a WHO. And so it now IS*)

responsible for Trish committing suicide.

"Hello, my friend." Stew appeared to Ryan's right. "How you holding up?"

"I'm not," Ryan replied, looking at the bottom of his glass.

"You two were close?"

"Yeah. She was such a wonderful—" Ryan stopped, his throat tightening.

Stew put his hand on Ryan's shoulder. The big man's touch had the cathartic result it was meant to, and Ryan wiped away tears. He drained the remainder of his scotch and signaled the bartender. Then to Stew: "You want a drink?"

"Never touch the stuff."

"You mind watching *me* drink?"

"Knock yourself out."

Ryan ordered a fourth scotch and took a healthy pull from it the moment it arrived. He looked to his left and saw Rebecca and her mother in the distance. They were at the Cooke table, offering condolences. Rebecca made eye contact with Ryan and gave a quick, thin smile; the only type of smile appropriate for such an affair. Ryan returned the same smile and turned back to Stew.

"Jesus, Stew. I mean, *Jesus Christ*."

Stew didn't say anything. He seemed to know Ryan was not finished.

"You should have seen her, man," Ryan went on. He spoke in hushed tones. "Lying there like some kind of fucking rag doll, staring up at the ceiling. Her throat was cut so bad it looked like she had two mouths, for Christ's sake. How can you do that to yourself? How is it possible? She had a tiny little razor blade in her hand. How can you slice that deep with something so small—" His throat tightened up again, and he stopped.

"My guess—and I know you're already thinking it—is that she wasn't exactly herself when she did it, Ryan. Just like all the others."

"But it's all hearsay, isn't it, Stew? What can we prove? We can't prove dick."

Stew put his hand on Ryan's shoulder and squeezed it again. Ryan turned and looked towards the array of banquet tables. He spotted the principal, Miss Gates, waiting behind Rebecca and her mother, waiting to offer condolences to the Cookes. He flicked his chin her way and said: "Maybe I should pull her aside and tell her I quit."

"That won't bring Trish back."

Ryan hung his head and nodded, acknowledging his empty threat. He sipped his scotch and looked at Stew with clear, helpless anger.

"What do we do, Stew?" he asked. "I mean, what the actual *fuck* do we do?"

Stew leaned in close and told Ryan to watch his language. Nearly four scotches deep, his anger on equal footing with his sorrow, Ryan might have offered up some resistance to such a suggestion. But when a man Stew's size tells you to watch your language, you watch your fucking language.

"I'm sorry," Ryan said. "I'm just…"

A third pat on Ryan's shoulder. "I know."

Ryan finished his fourth drink in a gulp and looked around the room in an attempt to clear his head. He locked eyes with Barbara. He gave her the funeral-appropriate smile he and Rebecca had shared. She did not return it.

"Miserable old cow," he muttered.

"Come again?" Stew said.

"Barbara. I just smiled her way, and she blanked me."

Stew said nothing.

"You ever wonder about her?" Ryan asked.

"Barbara?"

Ryan nodded.

"How so?"

"You know what I mean."

"Barbara's old and grumpy, but that's all."

"She's one of the original four, Stew." He looked away and added: "Just like you." He looked back. To his surprise, Stew did not seem offended.

"Maybe you've had enough to drink, Ryan," was all he said.

Ryan's reply was to drain his scotch and order a fifth. Stew gave Ryan a final pat on the shoulder before heading over to the Cooke table to pay his respects. Rebecca and her mother appeared at Ryan's side shortly after.

"How are you doing, Ryan?" Carol Lawrence asked.

Ryan was buzzed, but still clear-headed enough to know better than to be belligerent to his love interest's mother, member of the original four that she was.

"Good as I can be under the circumstances, I suppose," he replied.

"Rebecca tells me you and Trish were close?"

"Yes."

"I'm sorry."

Rebecca leaned in and kissed Ryan on the cheek.

"Where are you two headed after?" Carol asked Ryan and her daughter.

Rebecca and Ryan exchanged a look. Rebecca said: "We haven't really discussed anything yet."

"Why don't you go somewhere quiet for a few drinks after?" Carol said to Rebecca. Then to Ryan: "Rebecca can give you a lift back to our place after. You can stay the night, if you like."

Rebecca and Ryan exchanged another look, this one far different than the previous.

"You sure?" Rebecca asked her mother.

"Just use good judgment and don't stay out too late. Watch the drinking and driving."

"We will. Thanks, Mom," Rebecca said.

"Yeah—thank you, Mrs. Lawrence," Ryan said, the notion that he was thanking the woman for giving him the opportunity to finally have sex with her daughter not escaping him.

"Carol," she corrected him. Then, with a wink: "If I'm granting you the courtesy of being adults in my home this evening, you can knock off all this 'Mrs. Lawrence' stuff."

Ryan smiled and looked away. Rebecca blushed.

Carol went to turn and leave. Just then, the scotch overrode Ryan's better judgment.

"Carol?" he said.

She stopped and faced him.

"What are they going to do?" he asked.

"I'm sorry?"

"The school. How will they explain the suicide? It's what everyone in this town has been waiting for, isn't it? For history to repeat itself?"

Ryan could feel Rebecca's stare. Knew it was an incredulous one. Yet he kept his eyes fixed on Carol.

Carol sighed. "I can't say."

"How would *you* explain it?" Ryan asked.

"It was a suicide, Ryan."

"No. How would *you* explain it?" he asked again. "A veteran of Highland like you."

And one of the original four…

(*Won't stop you from spending the night at her house and screwing her daughter, though, will it?*)

Ryan could feel Rebecca's stare now boring a hole into the side of his head. He still kept his gaze on Carol.

"I can't explain it," she said. "If I could—if I could explain any of it—then I don't think we'd be having this conversation right now."

Jesus, Stew had said the exact same thing, almost verbatim.

Ryan finally broke his gaze, dropped his head, and nodded.

Carol stepped forward and gave Ryan a hug. "I'm very sorry for your loss, Ryan." Her face held genuine warmth. She then hugged her daughter and gave her a light kiss on the cheek. "Don't be out too late, you two." She left.

"What the hell was *that*?" Rebecca asked.

Ryan shook his head. "Nothing. Forget it." He tried on a smile that felt weird. "You want a drink?"

33

They'd ended up staying at the restaurant where Trish's post-funeral reception was held, moving from the small bar in the banquet hall to the main bar in the heart of the restaurant.

When the bartender approached them for last call, Ryan suggested hitting up a bar-bar, not a restaurant that gave last call at eleven o'clock.

"Actually, I was thinking we should head home," Rebecca replied.

Ryan was at first disappointed. He was just drunk enough to want to keep drinking. Nothing else seemed to matter. When Rebecca reminded him that something else far greater mattered—and this reminder was accompanied by a wandering hand below the bar ledge—Ryan was suddenly content to never touch a drop again.

And then the metaphorical angel and devil on each shoulder:

Angel: Sex only hours after your friend's funeral. Very classy.

Devil: Trish would have approved. Downright insisted.

The devil's reasoning brought on instant sorrow. Yes, Trish would have insisted. How he wished she was here now. Ryan could envision her teasing him in her way, telling him to beware of whiskey dick after all the damn scotch he drank tonight.

Angel: Still, you really want your first time with Rebecca to be the day of your friend's funeral? Not cool, man.

The devil then had an ally. Trish's voice loud and clear: *Would you get going already, dummy? I will NOT have you missing out on a chance to get laid because of me.*

Ryan: I miss you so much.

Trish: And I miss you too. Now please go and curl that girl's toes before she realizes what a pussy you're being.

Ryan laughed.

Rebecca gave him a curious look. "What?"

He shook his head. "Nothing." He leaned in and kissed her. "I'm definitely ready to go."

She grinned, her wandering hand brushing his groin below the bar.

Ryan plunked four twenties on the bar. They did not wait for the change.

----------◆----------

The transition from the bar to the bedroom felt instantaneous, anticipation a time machine. Only one obstacle remained. The fucking condom.

"Do you need any help?" Rebecca asked as he fiddled with the wrapper. His fingers were slippery after recently being inside her.

"Fuck it," he said, and used his teeth to tear the wrapper, the condom springing free, Ryan scrambling after the damn thing like it was ticking.

Rebecca laughed.

Make that two obstacles, the second being the dreaded interval. The part all men feared. If you asked Ryan, he would tell you there is that moment when a man is truly aroused and absolutely incapable of conducting a fine motor skill. Then the condom is asked to be opened and placed onto the penis, a fine motor skill, and the blood leaves one organ—*the organ*—to assist other organs in order to achieve said task. Most men can manage it, because, well, most men are men. But when a half gallon of scotch is flowing through your veins…

"Everything okay?" Rebecca asked.

It was the question from hell. Two simple words that really meant something far direr. Loosely translated, something like: *Is there a problem down there, stud?*

He flashed back on the moment in the bar, the one where he imagined Trish still alive and warning him about the pitfalls of whiskey dick.

Oh, no. No, no, no, no, no.

And just then, as if he needed yet another reason to like the girl, Rebecca purred in his ear, "Maybe I can help," and began sliding her tongue down his torso.

No more obstacles. Ryan was soon suited up and very ready.

34

Ryan was pretty sure Rebecca came. He knew he sure as hell had. And after a fairly impressive display of staying power, if he did say so himself. There was always the fear of coming too soon the first time, especially with someone you really liked. But the alcohol, the very thing that had threatened to keep him from rising to the occasion, had ended up his savior in the endurance department, the fickle bastard. And when Rebecca had expressed her admiration for this endurance after, he was only too keen to give zero credit to that fickle bastard. Something borderline cheesy that went: "Hey, when I'm with the perfect girl…"

And she had greedily eaten up his response—dripping with cheese or no—planting a big kiss on him before laying her head on his bare chest and adding: "I would kill for a smoke right now."

"Won't mommy get mad?"

"She's asleep."

"Won't she smell it?"

"Not if we sneak out onto the deck."

"Such a naughty girl."

She tweaked his nipple. "You telling me naughty is a bad thing?"

"I am assuredly not."

She laughed.

The two of them slinked out of Rebecca's bedroom and out onto the deck for an after-sex smoke.

———————— ✦ ————————

Ryan dreamt of spirals. They floated in front of him like incessant gnats, some big, some small. Some spun slowly, and some spun fast. He tried running from them, but they followed as though they were his helmet.

At times he would briefly surrender to them, finding their twirling hypnotic and enticing, like a pleasant trip on some drug. And yet, despite such an intoxicating sense of euphoria, something always stopped Ryan from succumbing completely, something always willing him to look away, to abort the trip. And, furthering the parallels to a drug, with resistance came sickness. A feeling of withdrawal. Disorientation. Nausea. The resolute feeling that the drug would ultimately win. Would prey on his will until it was broken. Own his body and soul complete.

"Leave me alone…"

The spirals were…laughing now? How could they laugh? And yet he heard it all the same, echoing all around as though carried on gusts from unseen winds. No—it was not the spirals laughing; it was the hands working the spirals that were laughing,

(*whose hands?*)

and as the laughter grew, so too did the intensity of the spirals' rapidity grow,

(*whose fucking hands?*)

with it the intensity of Ryan's nausea, the dreaded feeling of certainty that the spirals would soon win, bore themselves into his skull where they would dig their way into the darkest corners of his mind, the corners most susceptible to trauma and manipulation—

(*WHOSE FUCKING HANDS??!!*)

"Ryan, wake up!"

Ryan sat bolt upright in bed. For a fleeting moment, the spirals were still there, the laughter was still there, echoing all around him in Rebecca's bedroom. He looked at her with wild, irrational eyes.

She placed a tentative hand on his shoulder, almost as though she feared he may lash out at her touch.

"It's okay…" she said. "It's okay…"

The spirals were gone. The laughter was gone. Just Rebecca's face before his now, a picture of concern and not a little fear of her own.

Ryan shut his eyes tight. Opened them again, expecting the clichéd scene of dreams thought to be over to be anything but, for the spirals to be back, for the laughter to resume as loud and wicked as ever, for Rebecca herself to maybe be the one laughing, eyes rolled back white, mouth too big, hands working in ritualistic circles, drawing spirals before his very eyes.

But of course it was only Rebecca, her face no less concerned, no less frightened. "Jesus…" he muttered. "I had a nightmare."

Rebecca risked touching him again. "*You think?* You were thrashing and yelling something I couldn't—my God, you're soaking wet."

"I had a nightmare," he said again for some reason.

Her tentative hand on his shoulder felt safer now. It began to massage his arm. "What about?"

He shook his head and breathed deep. "I have absolutely no idea." He ran a hand through his hair. Ran a hand across his bare chest. Felt the sheets by his legs. "Jesus, I *am* really soaked." He flashed back on the dream he'd had about the old principal Mr. James, the classroom of children with their white eyes and evil grins and their scissors ready to launch at his head. How he'd woken up soaked from that dream as well, fearing he might have pissed the bed. That fear was no less now, but he would soon discover, with fleeting consolation in the wake of far more disturbing matters, that he again had *not* pissed the bed. That he was soaked only with sweat. Night sweats. Fucking *terror* sweats.

"Why don't you go to the bathroom and splash some cold water on your face?" she suggested.

He nodded and threw his legs over the side of the bed, sitting there a moment, collecting himself. Realizing he was nude, he then began searching the floor for his boxer shorts. He found them, slipped them on, and stood. He then paused a moment, his gaze dropping to the bedroom floor, landing on the condom wrapper. He did not stop there, though; he continued searching the bedroom floor.

"What are you looking for?" Rebecca asked.

Ryan felt a twinge of embarrassment. "I can't, uh…I can't find the condom."

"What?"

"The condom we used…I can't find it." He bent and snatched up the wrapper. "Here's the wrapper, but I can't find the actual condom."

Rebecca sat up.

"You didn't flush it?"

"Not exactly." His face grew hot. "I kinda just dropped it on the rug after. I was going to flush it after we came in from outside, but I guess I forgot. I'm sorry."

"Well, it's got to be there," she said.

Ryan was now on all fours, searching. "I'm not seeing it," he said. "Where the hell could it be?"

"Just leave it," she said. "We'll spot it in the morning when the sun is up."

Ryan was relieved. He feared she might have been grossed out at the prospect of a used condom hiding somewhere on her rug. "You sure?" he double-checked anyway.

She smiled. "No biggie."

Yet another reason to like the girl so damn much. He kissed her and crept into the hallway, glancing down the end of the hall where Carol's bedroom door was. It was closed, the light underneath it out. Thank God his dream hadn't woken her—

WHOSE FUCKING HANDS??!!

These words from his dream, hitting him in the dark hallway like a sucker punch.

Ryan closed his eyes tight, shook his head in a bid to regain his wits as though he *had* been punched.

He opened his eyes and looked at Carol's door at the end of the hall again.

(*She's one of the original four…*)

And?

(*The dream felt different this time, didn't it? Stronger. Could it be because you're sleeping in the very house of those hands?*)

Ryan crept towards Carol's bedroom door. He could hear light snores from within.

It was her idea I sleep here. If I was some kind of threat to her, then why would she invite me to stay the night?

(*…keep your enemies closer?*)

Ryan shoved away the thought. He'd had enough trauma for one night, thank you. He went into the bathroom for that much needed splash of cold water on the face, and rejoined Rebecca in bed. Much as he thought it would never come, he was pleased to find sleep soon after.

But still no damn condom.

35

When Ryan and Rebecca woke the next morning the first thing Ryan did was look on the floor for the condom. He found it almost instantly.

"Here it is," he said. "How the hell did I miss it last night?"

Rebecca shrugged. "It was the middle of the night. We'd been drinking."

"Yeah, but it's *right here*," he said, pointing down at it.

"Who cares? Pick it up and flush it."

He bent and picked it up, shielding Rebecca from the act with a slight turn of his body. Strange thing, condoms, he thought. Their ability to go from yeah to yuck in seconds.

He poked his head out of the bedroom and checked Carol's room at the end of the hall. He didn't want any surprise encounters on the way to the bathroom. *Morning, Carol. Oh, this? Just the condom I used on your daughter last night. All about safe sex, me.* Fortunately, the coast was clear—Carol's door was closed. He hurried to the bathroom, shut and locked the door behind him, and was about to flush the thing when he noticed something unusual. There was barely any semen in the condom. A drop, if that.

Did I shoot a blank? Or nearly a blank? How is that possible? I haven't come in days. He dropped the condom into the toilet where it floated pathetically on the surface. *One second, yeah; the next, yuck.*

Ryan flushed the toilet and watched the condom spiral

(*spirals…*)

in the bowl. He stood transfixed on the spiraling pool of water, unable to look away. When he did, his head began to throb. His previously forgotten nightmare now coming back to him in fragmented pulses of light, the flashes hammering the nerve endings behind his eyes, even when he shut them tight.

And then it was gone. Quiet in the bathroom now. Only the sound of the toilet's tank filling back up.

What the hell *is wrong with me?*

And this brought forth the original question. The used condom. Its lack of…content. What was wrong with him? Why had he failed to produce anything substantial? He sure as hell climaxed—of that he was certain.

Had it dried up overnight? No. With no great pride in recall, this was not the first time Ryan had tossed a condom aside to be picked up and discarded the morning after. He remembered no shortage of semen those times.

Had he…oh God, had he *spilled* some on the rug when he so carelessly dropped it to the floor?

Ryan hurried back to the bedroom. Returned immediately to the spot where he had found the condom. He noticed no whitish spot on her dark rug. Still, he began nonchalantly dabbing his foot around the area, looking for any section of rug that might be…crusty? *All class, dude. You're all class.*

Rebecca, who was getting dressed, spotted his try at casual foot archeology.

"What are you doing?"

Finding nothing of note, Ryan looked up and forced a smile. "Nothing," he said, a little too quickly.

"Did you flush your little friend?"

"He is no more."

She smiled back and finished dressing. A pair of shorts and a tee. Blonde hair pulled back into a ponytail. She was beautiful. First thing in the morning, no less.

He approached her. "How do you feel about morning-breath kisses?"

"I can deal with yours if you can deal with mine."

They kissed.

"Not too bad," she said. "How was I?"

"I held my breath."

She laughed and slapped his still bare chest.

"I better get dressed," he said, and began performing a new type of archeology: morning-after dress clothes archeology, typically followed by the ever popular walk of shame home. Only there was no shame here. No way. He would be proudly taking that walk home.

"How are you feeling?" she asked as he dressed.

"Sad," he replied.

"That's understandable. But I was kind of referring to your dream."

Ryan did not mention the incident just now in the bathroom. The incident last night when he'd gone into the bathroom to splash water on his face, only to stare at Carol's bedroom door and consider her a possible culprit in all this insanity.

"I'm okay," he lied. "It was just one hell of a nightmare."

"Do you remember any of it?"

"Not really." *Two lies now. This relationship is off to a lovely start.*

"Good. It's probably better that you don't. You seemed really upset."

Dressed now, he waved a dismissive hand at her. "I'm fine. The events preceding the dream more than compensate." He winked at her.

She grinned. "You know, today is our last day of freedom."

He nodded. Tomorrow was Labor Day. The kids officially arrived the day after. If they wanted one last hurrah before their worlds became chaos, it should be tonight.

"What were you thinking?" he asked.

"A repeat of last night works for me," she said with another sexy little grin.

Ryan knew exactly what she meant, but his smile dropped before he could help it. He thought of Trish.

Rebecca immediately went to him. "Oh God—that came out so wrong. You know I didn't mean—"

He cut her off with a hug. "Stop," he said. "I know exactly what you meant. It's okay. Yes—I would love a repeat of last night, all things considered."

She sighed in relief and hugged him tight. "If you want time to mourn..." she said into his shoulder.

He thought of Trish. Her joining the devil on his shoulder, insisting that he not pass up another chance to get laid on her account. His heart both swelled and ached.

Ryan held Rebecca back at arm's length. "I'm fine," he said. "So, just a repeat of last night? No dinner or a movie beforehand? Just right to sex?"

She laughed and sighed with more relief. Then: "I'm thinking sex, dinner, movie, and then more sex. Thoughts?"

"I'm thinking I'm very lucky it was my shoe you chose to spit gum on that day."

36

Ryan had driven only a few minutes before he had to pull over and throw up. The sickness he felt was not unlike the aftermath of a dizzying ride at the amusement park. One that spirals and spirals and spirals...

He puked again, his head hanging out the driver's side door.

Something is...something is very *wrong with me.*

Cynthia Herb met her son at the front door. He'd called ahead to say he was on his way home. He'd also said he was very sick.

She was ready at the door with all things mother and registered nurse. Ryan wanted none of them. He pushed past her, muttering, "I just need to lay down," and stumbled down the basement stairs towards his bedroom.

She followed close behind. Took his temperature the moment he flopped onto his bed fully clothed and passed out. Curiously, he had no fever, yet his complexion was pallid, and he was sweating profusely. She wondered whether he'd drank too much the night before and failed to mention it. His symptoms *were* typical of that of a major hangover, and considering he had just come from a funeral, one for someone Cynthia knew her son cared deeply about, imbibing heavily afterwards wouldn't have been unheard of.

She brought him a cool cloth for his head and fixed the fan on his nightstand to stay directly on him as opposed to letting it oscillate, as usual. She then placed a trash can next to his bed, just in case, before retiring back upstairs.

A deep sleep took hold of Ryan. Even the incessant vibrating of his cell phone on the pillow next to him—Rebecca calling—failed to wake him.

37

"Should I call his house, you think?" Rebecca asked her mother. "The landline?"

"He's still not answering his cell?" Carol replied.

"No." A look at the clock on her cell. "It's after nine."

Carol gave her daughter a look.

Rebecca batted it away instantly with an adamant shake of the head. "No. No, no, no. He wouldn't do that. You know I'm the queen of pessimism, Mom, but even *I'm* sure he wouldn't do that."

Carol showed her daughter her palms. "Okay…okay…"

"I think something's wrong. I don't think he was feeling well when he left."

"Maybe he's asleep then. If he's not feeling well…"

Rebecca nodded. "Yeah. I am going to try his landline."

Cynthia Herb answered on the second ring. She and Rebecca exchanged brief pleasantries before Rebecca got to the point.

"I tried his cell a bunch of times, but he never answered."

"He's probably still asleep," Cynthia said. "He wasn't feeling well when he got home. He went right to bed."

"Would you mind checking on him?" Rebecca asked. "I'm worried about him."

"Of course. He has been asleep awhile. Hold on a sec; I'll go check."

"Thank you." Rebecca looked at her mother. "You were right. He's asleep. She's checking on him."

Carol smiled back.

A lengthy pause. Then the sound of Cynthia's voice echoing in the background, calling her son's name.

"Rebecca?" Cynthia said when she came back on the line. She sounded concerned.

"Yeah?"

"He's not here. And his car is gone."

38

Pinewood Elementary might've been brand new, but decades of custodial work had taught Karl nothing if not that kids were hard—brutal—on a building. So he'd continued his Labor Day tradition of sneaking in while the school was empty to handle the last-minute preparations. Except this year, to his surprise, he heard someone enter through the side entrance of the building.

He called out for a reply and got nothing in return but the sound of casual footsteps getting closer. He called again. Warning whoever had entered—*how the hell* did *they enter? The door was locked, wasn't it?*—that the building was closed. That whoever they were, they were trespassing.

The only reply Karl received was more footsteps creeping closer in their lazy, unhurried way. He called out yet again, demanding an answer.

Ryan emerged from the shadows. Karl sighed in relief.

"Dammit, son, you gave me one hell of a—" but he got no further. Ryan was present in body only. The boy's eyes were closed, his continuous steps forward blind but not blind as he strolled right on past Karl as though he wasn't there, heading somewhere particular, heading towards, Karl would soon find out, the teachers' lounge.

Ryan sat alone at the big faculty table in the lounge. He'd entered the pitch-dark room and taken his seat with no trouble. It was Karl, following close behind, who'd flicked on the overhead lights, worrying for a moment that it might disturb Ryan's trance, but no such occurrence had taken place. Ryan remained seated at the table, face blank and undisturbed. His eyes were no longer closed, but only just. They were fluttering slits, his lips not unlike his eyes, opening and closing but only just, muttering softly, producing nothing Karl could understand. To Karl, it looked as though the boy was having a conversation with someone seated across from him. Only it was just the two of them in the lounge. At least as far as Karl could see.

<hr />

Across from Ryan sat John Gray.

"Do you know who I am?"

"Yes. You're John Gray."

"And you're Ryan Herb."

"How do you know me?"

"We all know you. We've all been waiting for you."

"We?"

"Those of us who can't leave here."

"Why are you waiting for me?"

"Because you can see it and you're still alive."

"I don't know what I see."

"It will become clearer as you get closer. You just can't allow it to claim you as it did us."

"Why did you hang yourself?"

"I did no such thing."

"You don't remember doing it?"

"No."

"I see children too. Children died here—long ago."

"I know."

"And children are still dying. Why?"

"We believe it's their purity. That their essence is being fed to a higher power."

"What higher power? Is this why you were killed? Is this the information you found out?"

"Yes."

"Then tell me more. Tell me everything I need to know."

"I can't. The power that inhabits this building is too strong. It has given us glimpses in moments of carelessness, but it is far too cautious most of the time. We know a little, and that's all."

"What did you find in the boiler room?"

"Nothing significant, I'm afraid. But I was led there by a murdered child. We believe it's the source."

"The source of all that goes on here?"

"Yes."

"So you know all about Helen Tarver and what she did years ago?"

"Yes."

"And is someone here trying to carry on her work?"

"Yes."

"Who?"

"We don't know—it's kept from us. But it's someone who is rewarded for the sacrifices they are giving to that higher power."

"Rewarded how?"

"Something beyond our means of comprehension."

"The photo. The staff photo from Highland. Karl the janitor believes it was left on my car to help me. To help me recognize you and the others so I would start digging around for a way to stop all this."

"Yes, it was given to you to help you start searching, but the giver's motive was not one of help—it was one of malice."

"Malice?"

"Someone suspected you had the ability to see. The photo was a ploy to see how you might respond to it. A way to confirm their suspicions if you responded to that ploy in exactly the way you did. To confirm whether you were someone who needed to be dealt with. Someone has been keeping a very close eye on you, Ryan."

"Who?"

"We don't know."

"I was sick today. Very sick. Like nothing I'd ever experienced. I dreamt of these…spirals last night. I don't know how to explain it. I mean, I've had dreams since coming here, quite a few actually, and none of them pleasant, but never anything like this. This dream was…this dream felt like…"

"A means to possession. An attempt to own your mind."

"Yes! How tempting it felt to just submit…"

"And yet you fought."

"Yes."

"Which is why you're on that side of the table and not here next to me. Not here with all of us. You have an inner strength that all of us lacked."

"Stew said the same thing."

"He was right."

"How do you know your buddy Stew isn't the one keeping a close eye on me? That Stew isn't responsible for it all?"

"I don't."

"Comforting."

"If your dream felt like a try at possession, then it's already begun. Someone has already managed to take something from you."

"Take something from me?"

"Your friend Trish was forced to take her own life because her blood was spilled earlier in the day and used."

"So that razor blade in the stack of papers…that was placed there on purpose. It was no accident."

"Yes."

"Placed by someone who knew Trish could see."

"Yes."

"I haven't spilled any blood."

"Neither did I. My urine was used."

"Your urine?"

"My erratic behavior following my divorce led some to believe I was using drugs. I was made to take a urine test once a day. On one particular day, twice."

"Twice in one day?"

"Yes."

"Why?"

"Because the first sample was misplaced."

"Not misplaced, though, right? It was stolen."

"Yes."

"By whom?"

"I don't know."

"Of course you don't. Are you here to help me or—"

"I don't think you have much time, Ryan. If the attempt at possession has already begun, then it means someone has taken something from you."

"Like what??? Never mind—forget it."

A pause.

"What does this asshole want, John? I mean seriously—what the fuck do they want?"

"We believe the children are sacrificed because of their purity. It is the ultimate spit in God's face. To offer the blood of one who possesses the free will he gave them before that will can be tested—"

"I'm not a religious man, John—"

"—against the evil that inhabits this world. Claiming innocence in its purest form. Untainted and true. A pre-emptive attack on God's children."

"Only the children were tainted by evil. They were tainted by the crazy fucker who occupied their bodies when they were carrying out those horrific attacks on each other."

"Clearly, such a thing is not an obstacle. Otherwise, we would not be having this conversation."

"Jesus, how many fucking times am I going to hear that?"

"Sorry?"

"Never mind."

"As you already know, Ryan, those who are a threat to this liturgy are dealt with. I wasn't strong enough, and neither were the others."

"A woman claimed her son's IQ dropped fifty points. The former principal was stabbed in the foot by a child who doesn't remember doing it. What were these incidents?"

"My guess? Unfortunate recipients of experimentation before the hands responsible

(WHOSE FUCKING HANDS??!!)

honed their craft. And those hands will only get better, Ryan. Their craft stronger."

"How do you know that I'm strong enough to deal with this?"

"We don't. We can only hope. Follow me to the boiler room. I will do my best to lead you as far as I can, but I cannot guarantee that my strength will hold out. I may fade, and if I do, then you're on your own."

39

"He's not there?" Carol asked her daughter.

"No," Rebecca said as she laced up her shoes. "His mother claimed he came home and went right to sleep. Now he's gone."

"She never saw him leave?"

"Of course she didn't. Why would she go check on him if she did?"

"So where are you going?" Carol asked.

Rebecca grabbed her car keys from the kitchen counter. "I'm going to go meet Mrs. Herb at her house, and then we're going to go look for him."

Carol stopped her daughter at the door. "Wait a minute, sweetheart. Don't you think you might be overreacting a little bit?"

"No," Rebecca said flatly. "His mother said he left his cell phone behind, but his car is gone."

"Where will you look?"

"I have a funny feeling he may be at the school."

"At the school? Why on Earth would he be there?"

"I don't know. A feeling. Something's not right, though." Rebecca nudged her mother aside and opened the door.

"Rebecca…"

Rebecca was already getting into her car.

40

Karl watched Ryan for a long time in the teachers' lounge. Watched him sit perfectly upright at that lounge table even though it was clear the boy was either asleep or in some type of trance. When Ryan finally stood, Karl flinched and took a step back.

Ryan turned and faced Karl but never saw him. In fact, as Ryan began to move, he would have collided with Karl had the old man not backed up flat against the soda machine like a convict caught in a searchlight.

Ryan exited the lounge. Karl followed close behind. The school was dark, Ryan's eyes still fluttering slits, but just as before, the boy seemed to have no trouble finding his way.

He's being guided, Karl thought to himself, patting the hairs now standing up on the back of his neck. *Someone's guiding him.*

Ryan followed John Gray, John's image occasionally flickering like a shoddy projection of the man. The closer they got to their destination, the more John flickered, his image often disappearing entirely for a second or two.

"*Down there*," John said.

They were standing outside the door to the boiler room. Ryan tried the knob, expecting it to be locked. It was not. He peered down into

(*the abyss*)

complete blackness. Stood there for a moment, unable to look away.

("*…if you gaze long into an abyss, the abyss also gazes into you.*")

Nietzsche's words, filling him with dread. Was someone or something from that abyss staring back now? And though no great dissector of philosophy, Ryan was learned enough to know that if the abyss *was* staring back, it was one of his own making.

Nietzsche's quote whole now, bringing an even greater—and far more frightening clarity—to his situation: "*He who fights with monsters should look to it that he himself does not become a monster. And if you gaze long into an abyss, the abyss also gazes into you.*"

Only he hadn't picked this fight. The fight had picked him, and now he had no choice but to become someone who might never be the same.

Scratch that: *I will never be the same.*

Fear gripped him whole. He looked at John.

"*I'm afraid.*"

"*So am I,*" John said.

"*What the hell do you have to be afraid of? You're already dead.*"

John Gray said nothing.

"*Sorry. Are you coming?*"

"*I will try.*"

Karl watched Ryan open the door to the boiler room and head down the stairs. The boy did not even hit the light switch on the wall to his left before descending into the blackness below. And why should he? He hadn't turned on the light when he'd entered the teachers' lounge, and the boy had made his way just fine. Karl had hit the light in the lounge, of course, and the boy hadn't stirred. Should he risk doing the same now?

No. The lounge had been different. Karl wasn't entirely sure whether the boy had been just sleepwalking. Now he knew better. He knew the boy's journey held some sort of purpose, that someone or something was guiding him. To risk disturbing his trance now would be foolish. He wanted to see it through, watch how it all played out. Unsure of his elderly feet that he was,

(*feet don't fail me now*)

Karl would follow the boy down into the dark. And, after all, he had his flashlight on him—just in case.

Karl followed Ryan, a death grip on the handrail to his right. He was thankful Ryan had not bothered to close the door behind him; it offered some light to trickle below. Karl only hoped that what consolatory light it did offer would be sufficient for him to see.

See what? *is the question.*

Feet? Karl was now unsure of his heart.

———— ✦ ————

Ryan and John stood next to the giant boiler.

"Can you see it?" John asked. An absurd question considering the surrounding darkness, but like the inexplicable hand that guided him blind to and inside the teachers' lounge, so too had something navigated Ryan here without his conventional means of seeing.

"What is it that I'm looking for?"

John's visage was flickering uncontrollably now, an image on a shit TV seconds from shorting out.

"We must *be close,"* John said. *"I feel weak. I feel I'll be gone at any moment. You have to hurry."*

Ryan searched.

He was behind the boiler now, inches from the panel on the wall that led to something deep within.

Led to a sacrificial chamber that contained countless photographs of men, women, and children, unknown substances, instruments, and symbols carefully smeared, placed and drawn onto the photos that required them.

Contained John Gray's photo, soaked through with his own urine, a noose drawn with chicken's blood long caked over around the man's neck.

Contained a canvas scribbled with Trish Cooke's name, the canvas adorned in the bloodied bandages she'd been repeatedly discarding on the day she died, a multitude of razor blades entwined within.

Contained a canvas with Ryan's full name scrawled onto it, endless spirals covering his name in the medium of dried chicken's blood, dried semen. His semen.

Ryan knew this because he saw it, the images coming all at once and without pity, a flash flood of atrocity that attempted to drown his mind as it tried to swim towards sanity.

And then instantly the flood relented, allowing his mind to break the surface and gasp a breath of control back into its gray, the things he'd seen still ever present, circling his battered mind in the ocean of horror the flood had created.

Ryan spun towards John, frenzied in his desire to tell him what he'd seen.

John was gone.

Worse still, whatever ability had been granted to Ryan to find his way was gone too. He stood alone in complete darkness.

And yet not alone. Something was here with him. He felt it in his bones. And his bones also knew with certainty that this something was well aware of what Ryan had just seen. And that this something was very…displeased.

He thought again, *I will never be the same*, and this harrowing truth did not exclude death. After all, one could certainly argue that being dead was not the same as being fucking alive.

Ryan's next thought was: *I wonder how it'll have me kill myself.*

41

Karl watched Ryan gaze unblinking at the wall behind the boiler for close to a minute before he turned and looked directly at Karl.

"Ryan?" Karl risked.

Ryan said nothing in return. Did not even blink when Karl spoke his name. Whatever trance held the boy was clearly still in effect.

"Ryan?" Karl tried again.

Ryan spoke, low, almost in a whisper. "I'll never be the same," he said.

"Ryan, can you hear me?"

Ryan still looked through Karl as though he wasn't there; the trance had its hooks in damned good.

"I wonder how it'll have me kill myself," Ryan said.

"Jesus, son; *wake up.*"

Ryan dropped to the floor as though shot from above. He gripped the sides of his head and cried out.

Karl no longer cared if he broke the boy's trance; the boy's words, what was happening to him now, proved he needed saving.

Karl ran to Ryan and shined his flashlight down into Ryan's face, taking him by the shoulder, shaking him, calling out his name repeatedly.

Ryan rolled onto all fours and promptly vomited on Karl's shoes. Crumpled onto his stomach and then rolled onto his back again. Vomited again. Unrelenting streams of black bile that were now choking the boy on his upturned position on the floor.

Karl immediately dropped to his knees, attempted to roll the boy back to his side to keep him from choking on his own vomit. Ryan wouldn't budge. His weight was unnaturally heavy,

(*something is pinning him down, holding him in place, watching him choke*)

far greater than Karl's old muscles—*hell, probably even Stew's muscles*—could move.

Karl scrambled to his feet, began frantically waving his flashlight throughout the boiler room's interior, looking for something, anything as Ryan continued to choke to death at his feet, the black bile unrelenting

(*so much! So fucking much!!!*)

as the boy fought to expel it.

Karl's flashlight caught the sink in the far corner of the boiler room. Next to that sink, a large white bucket. Karl ran to it. Began filling the bucket, periodically glancing back at Ryan, urging him to hold on.

Ryan had stopped moving, the bile unrelenting still as it continued to ooze from his open mouth.

Karl hoisted the giant bucket of water, felt his back cry out in protest, ignored it and hurried back towards Ryan, nearly tumbling before arrival from the cumbersome act of carrying the bucket of water's substantial and uneven weight.

And then panic gripped Karl further still. The boy was choking. *Had* choked. Was currently without breath. The bucket of water had been a desperate attempt to rouse the boy from his trance. Pouring water on him now would be akin to throwing gasoline on a damn fire.

Mouth-to-mouth. Gotta give the boy mouth-to-mouth.

The thought was revolting. All that bile, still inexplicably oozing its way out of Ryan's now unresisting mouth.

You want the boy to die? Do it now!!!

Karl did, wiping as much of the bile from Ryan's mouth as he could, bent and pressed his lips to Ryan's, attempting to breathe life into him. Stopped instantly and withdrew, his lips on fire. His hands too.

The bile BURNED? What in the name of all that's holy…???

The bucket was now a godsend. Karl reached into it and splashed water over his mouth, wiping furiously, the water ridding his lips and hands of the burning. Scooped more water and wiped the remaining bile from Ryan's lips, bent to the boy again and resumed.

Now CPR. Karl's hands on Ryan's chest, compressing accordingly and steadily. Back to mouth-to-mouth. Then more compressions on Ryan's chest. Then more mouth-to-mouth.

Ryan came to life, expelling a generous amount of bile into Karl's face, the bile singeing Karl's cheeks and eyes, Karl crying out, blindly groping for the bucket to cleanse his face, Ryan still coughing his way back to life before him.

His face now clean, Karl immediately attempted to roll Ryan onto his side again.

This time he budged.

Ryan now lay on his side, coughing and sputtering the last of it, his breath labored but now approaching normalcy. He made his way back onto all fours.

Karl, vision still blurred from the bile, was nevertheless able to locate the flashlight from its solitary glow in the blackness of the boiler room. He snatched it at once and shined it on Ryan, blinking away the burn that still lingered.

"Ryan? Ryan, you with me?"

Ryan turned towards Karl's voice. He was still on all fours, his eyes wide and wild in the flashlight's beam; a frightened animal caught in a hunter's sights. "*Where…?*" he managed, his voice rough from the incessant vomiting, his choking.

"It's okay, son." Karl placed a hand on Ryan's back and began to rub it. "It's okay."

"Where?" Ryan asked again.

"You're in the school. In the boiler room. Are you all right?"

Ryan attempted to find his feet, stumbled, and fell back down to all fours.

"I feel sick," he said.

"It's okay now, son—"

(*is it?*)

"—let's get you on your feet and get the hell out of here."

"Why I am here?" Ryan asked. "How did I get here?"

"Ryan, I really think we should leave first."

Ryan was suddenly aware that his hands were in vomit. Was suddenly aware that vomit was everywhere.

"I think…I think I might have thrown up a little."

Karl flopped onto his butt and sighed. "I know."

42

Three people watched Cynthia Herb and Rebecca Lawrence hurry towards the front entrance of Pinewood Elementary: Stew Taylor, Barbara Forsythe, and Carol Lawrence.

Stew and Barbara were together, waiting. They were in Stew's car, ignition off and parked far enough away on school grounds to stay out of sight, yet close enough to see. They were there because Karl had phoned them privately after leaving Ryan briefly for what he described as a much-needed cleaning up in the boys' room. Karl had told Stew and Barbara everything. He had told Rebecca and Cynthia just enough: that the boy must have been sleepwalking, and that Karl, working late, had found Ryan unconscious in the school's boiler room, of all places. Karl told them that the boy was clearly sick; he had thrown up.

Carol Lawrence was not in her car. She had parked a block away and had made the rest of her way on foot. She was now crouched behind one of many low walls near the main entrance, hidden. She too was waiting. Watching. There to see whether her daughter's hunch about Ryan being at the school and in trouble had been correct. When she saw Ryan—looking very much the worse for wear—being led out of the front entrance with Rebecca on one arm and Ryan's mother on the other, she felt conflicted. There was immense joy for Ryan's condition, and there was concern for her daughter's growing attachment to Ryan. It was going to complicate things.

43

Karl wished Ryan well and accepted the many thanks from Cynthia, Rebecca, and Ryan himself.

Once the women had gotten Ryan safely into Rebecca's car and were gone, Karl pulled out his cell phone to dial the same number he had dialed only moments before. Stew answered on the first ring.

"Where are you?" Karl asked.

"Here. West end of the building."

"Is Barbara with you?"

"Yeah."

"Okay. I'll be there in five. I think we should go somewhere else to talk."

***

Carol was just about to head back to her car when she spotted Karl the janitor leave the building. She did not know he was inside with Ryan, Rebecca, and Mrs. Herb. Had he been there the whole time?

Karl made his way down the front steps of the main entrance and headed, not towards his truck in the school lot, but towards the west end of the building. Curious.

Follow him? Rebecca would undoubtedly be at Cynthia Herb's house, helping her tend to Ryan. Likely, she would even be staying the night.

She had time to follow.

Stew rolled down his window as Karl approached.

"This is wrong," Karl said.

Barbara leaned across Stew's lap, her trademark scowl ever present. "What is?" she said.

"We're *using* that poor boy. He almost died in there tonight."

Stew nudged Barbara off his lap, back into her seat. "How bad was it?" he asked.

"*Bad.*"

Stew unlocked the doors. "Get in. We'll go somewhere and talk."

Carol watched them drive off. She did not know what was going on, but she suspected the worst. Was their little meeting about her? Maybe. It may not have been directly *about* her, but it was certainly about what she'd been *doing.* And her experience up until now had always told her that any potential obstacle needed to be dealt with.

All three were as good as dead.

44

Cynthia Herb headed straight for the teakettle as Rebecca helped Ryan into the den and onto the sofa. Cynthia made mint tea in an effort to settle her son's stomach and placed it on the coffee table before him. Ryan never acknowledged it. He just lay on the sofa with his eyes closed, breathing slowly and deeply through his nose in a bid to stem his nausea.

Cynthia retrieved her nursing equipment. She took Ryan's blood pressure. The sharp, unmistakable sound of Velcro tearing as she removed the pressure cuff from her son's arm was as dramatic as the look on her face.

"I think we should get you to the hospital."

"Is it that bad?" he asked.

"Not if you just had fifty cups of coffee."

"I'm fine, Ma. I don't need to go to the hospital. I just want to rest."

Cynthia and Rebecca exchanged a look.

"What happened tonight, sweetheart?" Cynthia asked.

Ryan closed his eyes again and kept them closed as he spoke. "I have no idea, Ma. I went to sleep here and woke up at the school. That's all I remember."

"Karl said he found you in the school's basement. In the boiler room," Rebecca said. "Do you remember that?"

The words "boiler room" resonated instantly with Ryan. He was well aware of their significance, yet chose not to share that significance with Rebecca or his mother.

"I remember waking up down there. That's all."

"He said you threw up," Cynthia said.

"I didn't feel well earlier. You know that."

"You don't remember *anything*?" Rebecca asked again.

Ryan strained to recall. It was not unlike the day after a hard night on the town. Brief flashes here and there, all of them hazy and fragmented, all of them causing deeper nausea the more he tried to get them to coalesce.

"No—not right now," he said. "I just need to rest. Maybe I'll remember more in the morning. Right now I just want to rest. Please."

Cynthia kissed her son's forehead. Rebecca kissed his cheek. Ryan offered a weak smile to both and fell asleep almost instantly. Cynthia motioned for Rebecca to follow her to the front door. They stepped outside, Cynthia closing the door gently behind them. "He's never had a sleep-walking episode in the thirty years I raised him," Cynthia said. "And, my God, he managed to *drive a car*." Cynthia closed her eyes and shook her head, clearly envisioning her son behind the wheel in his state. "He hasn't been himself lately. His dreams, his bouts of sickness, and now this. Please don't take this the wrong way, but as a mother, I have to ask. Are the two of you using any sort of recreational drugs?"

Rebecca's face popped with surprise. She placed a hand on her chest and shook her head adamantly. "Mrs. Herb, no—*God*, no. I've never touched a drug in my life."

Cynthia hung her head, nodded, and sighed deeply. "Okay, I'm sorry. I had to ask."

Rebecca placed a hand on Cynthia's shoulder, hoping her touch was mollifying. "It's okay…"

Cynthia went in for a hug. Rebecca hugged her back.

"What's wrong with my son?" Cynthia said into Rebecca's shoulder, and started to cry.

Rebecca held her tight. "I don't know."

45

Three of the last four remaining employees from Highland Elementary sat at a local diner. None of the three had food in front of them. Just plenty of coffee.

"We're using that poor boy," Karl said for the second time this evening.

Both Barbara and Stew looked at their coffee cups.

"We're following him like hawks, hoping that he leads us to something we can't figure out on our damn own," Karl went on. "You should have seen him tonight. The trance he was under; his episode in the boiler room. I'm telling you, that stuff that came out of his mouth was like nothing I ever seen. It *burned* me, for Christ's sake."

Stew kept his head down. Barbara lifted hers.

"We didn't *choose* Ryan, Karl," she said. "We never chose *any* of them. Ryan went to that school tonight on his own accord."

"But we can't *keep* the boy there, Barbara. She *knows* that he can see. She *knows* that he can expose her. We've got to get him out. Tell him to leave."

"Seems to me like it's too late for that," Barbara said. "It's obvious she's already got her hooks in the boy. You think his leaving the school is going to change that? He's a threat to her no matter where he goes. He can expose her from the moon if he wants."

"The boy doesn't know she's responsible."

"You think that matters to her?"

Karl shook his head. "Got to get the boy out."

"But if he can *give* us something, Karl," Barbara insisted.

"That poor boy won't give us nothing but another dead body to explain and another notch on Carol Lawrence's belt."

"If it *is* Carol," Stew said.

"You're doubting now?" Barbara asked.

Stew sipped his coffee. "After all this time, all we really have is conjecture. We don't have anything tangible."

"Which is *exactly* why we need the kid," Barbara said. "He can see; great. The others could see. Unless he gives us something concrete, then he'll just be lumped in with the others, rubber-stamped as a loony."

"John was *not* a loony."

"*We* know that."

A pause in the conversation. Everyone sipped from their cups.

"I told Ryan in the beginning that I didn't trust any of you," Karl said. "I wanted him to figure it out for himself." Karl's face was all regret.

"And he's gotten nothing thus far," Barbara said. "Which is once again the precise reason why we need to keep him in the school. Keep him close so he *can* find something."

"Is it possible he *did* find something?" Stew said.

"And what? He's keeping it a secret?" Barbara mocked.

Stew frowned at her. "I meant that Ryan claims he doesn't remember anything that happened tonight. Maybe we *get* him to remember. Let's face it, if Karl wasn't there tonight, Ryan would be dead. Karl put one hell of a wrench in Carol's plan."

"Plan?"

"Perhaps Carol suspected that Ryan did or would find something incriminating tonight. Don't ask me how, but just suppose she did. She would need him out of the way ASAP."

Karl looked up slowly from his coffee, his old face alive with revelation. "I think I know how Carol might have known what Ryan was up to tonight."

Stew and Barbara just stared at Karl, urging him to go on.

"It makes a heck of a lot of sense when you think about it too. Kind of stupid we didn't put the pieces together already."

"Karl…" Stew said impatiently.

"Who came and picked up Ryan tonight?"

"His mother and Rebecca—*ohhh…*" Stew said.

"*What?*" Barbara said. "Ohhh what?"

"Rebecca is Carol's daughter," Stew said. "She's also Ryan's girlfriend."

Karl pointed at Stew. "Ryan's mother told me she called Rebecca when she couldn't find her son. Said that Rebecca had a 'hunch' that Ryan was at the school, what with all his odd behavior there lately. How much do you want to bet that Rebecca told her mother every damn bit of that?"

Their shared glance was one of great discovery.

"It would sure as hell explain why Carol didn't come along," Barbara said.

"Sure," Karl said. "She needed to stay behind and, I don't know"—he waved his hands about, a feeble attempt at miming black magic—"do her thing."

"Still not sure it's Carol, Stew?" Barbara said.

46

Rebecca and Cynthia drank tea while Ryan slept on the sofa, periodically checking on him to make sure he didn't perform another disappearing act.

Confident he was down for the night, Cynthia urged Rebecca to head home and get some sleep of her own. Rebecca reluctantly agreed, insisting Cynthia call her if anything should happen. Cynthia of course agreed, and they hugged goodbye. Rebecca barely remembered the drive home.

———— ◆ ————

"So what happened?" Carol Lawrence asked as she met her daughter at the front door.

"I don't know, Mom. I honestly don't know."

"You don't know?"

"I can't think right now, Mom. Please."

Carol patted the air. "Okay, okay…" Then: "You *did* find him, though."

"Yes."

"And he was at the school like you thought?"

"Yes."

"Did he say *anything*? Anything at all? How he got there? Who was with him? Why he was there?"

Rebecca sighed, exhausted. "He managed to drive himself there while asleep, if you can believe that. The janitor found him, but there was no one else in the building that I know of. He can't remember what happened. He went right to sleep as soon as his mother and I got him home. He was really sick."

Carol Lawrence hugged her daughter, then ushered her upstairs with a loving smile, urging her to get some sleep. When she heard her daughter's bedroom door close, Carol's smile dropped like a stone, the fingernails on her right hand—the hand now a fist at her side—digging deep into her palm, drawing blood.

47

"It's almost too perfect," Barbara said without joy as Stew drove them back to the school to retrieve Karl's truck. "I mean, she's got him. She can track every move he makes through her own damn daughter. Which begs another question: is the daughter involved somehow?"

"Doubtful," Karl said.

"We need to talk with Ryan," Stew said. "And I mean *really* talk with him. Tell him who we suspect and what kind of danger he's in, and, most importantly, try to get him to remember what happened tonight."

"He knows what kind of danger he's in," Karl said.

"He doesn't know about Carol, though," Stew said.

"Does it matter? We still can't prove anything."

"But if we can get him to remember."

"And if we can't?"

"John remembered," Barbara said. "The others too."

"John and the others remembered seeing a few things; so what?" Karl said. "Ryan remembered seeing a few things as well. This is completely different. Carol has already made her move on the boy."

"And he survived, thanks to you," Barbara said. "And you're right; it *is* completely different. Carol sent that boy on a one-way trip to hell, never thinking for a moment that the boy might return. His returning is our chance to find out what he discovered on that trip. We've never been so close."

Karl snorted at her metaphors. "Again, suppose we can't get the boy to remember? Suppose there *is* nothing to remember? Stew, how long did we search that boiler room before the fire? What did we find? A big fat goose egg, is what."

"You were there tonight, Karl," Stew said. "First John's claims, and now what you witnessed with Ryan? Are you honestly going to tell me that the boiler room doesn't hold some sort of significance? That there might be something down there we were simply unable to find? What's going on with you? Why are you fighting this all of a sudden?"

"I'm just worried about the boy, is all."

"All the more reason we need to get him to remember," Barbara said. "And soon. As you said, Carol already made a move on the boy."

"Why don't we just kill her?" Karl said.

"Come again?" Stew said.

"Kill Carol. Hell, I'll do it myself. I'm old. I've lived a good—well, I've lived a life."

"And all your years going on about wanting to live long enough to see whatever evil inhabits the school die before you do?" Stew said.

"If I kill the bitch, then it *will* die before I do."

Stew bit back a smile. "Sorry, Karl. Not an option."

"You say that now…"

48

Ryan sat alone in the auditorium, dead center, several rows back. On stage, before the great red curtains, was an easel, the easel supporting a sign. "Pinewood Elementary Talent Show," it read.

The lights dimmed. Complete darkness for a moment. Then a solitary beam of light from overhead, illuminating a lone stool on stage, a microphone on its stand before the stool, the red curtains now drawn. Inexplicable applause in the empty auditorium as a woman took center stage. She was dressed in black. Her hair, long and full, was black. All of this in stark contrast to her ghostly white face; her ghostly white face in stark contrast to her piercing black eyes. The woman carried a large suitcase, this too black. The initials "HT & TC" were clearly evident in red lettering on the case.

The woman took the stool. The inexplicable applause from the empty auditorium died down to a low hush, then total silence.

"Good evening," the woman said. Her smile was enormous. She bent and opened the suitcase and pulled a large ventriloquist's puppet from it. The puppet's attire was identical to that of the ventriloquist's. Only the head was different. It was Trish's head. And it was no toy copy. It was Trish's real head, gray and lifeless, dead eyes fogged over into a milky white, absurdly disproportionate to the rest of the puppet's body.

"My name is Helen Tarver. My friend Trish and I would like to give you a little show tonight. Would that be all right?"

Another round of applause.

"Say hello to the nice people, Trish." Helen Tarver's hand did not reach behind Trish's back to operate her the way a traditional ventriloquist would its puppet, but instead balanced the puppet's body on one knee, using both her hands to work the slack flesh on Trish's full face.

"Hello, nice people," Helen Tarver said out of the corner of her mouth, working Trish's jaw and lips, her voice high and playful as Trish's had been.

"Tell the nice people what we have in store for them tonight, Trish."

Again, Helen attempted to operate Trish's lifeless mouth. And Trish's head promptly rolled off the doll's shoulders, Helen failing to catch it in time, the head hitting the stage and rolling to a stop on one side, milky dead eyes staring at nothing.

"*Whoops!*" Helen Tarver exclaimed.

The crowd roared.

"All part of the show, folks," Helen said with that enormous smile.

The crowd roared some more.

Helen Tarver stood and snatched Trish's head by her curly mop of dark hair. Returned to her stool and placed the head back onto the doll's shoulders. A definitive *click!* and the head was reattached. But different now. Trish's face came alive. Her ashen tone was now pink and healthy. Her milky dead eyes were now wide and brown and bright, brimming with life. Her eager smile bunched her cherub cheeks just as they always had.

The doll with Trish's head jumped off of Helen Tarver's lap and began to walk towards the end of the stage. It teetered absurdly from side to side as it did so, the weight of its human head on its plastic frame making the job a grotesque chore.

It reached the end of the stage, fixed on Ryan, and grinned at him. "*I see you, Ryan,*" it sang in Trish's voice.

The auditorium went black, the sound of something small hitting the floor with a grunt right after. Footsteps now—tiny clacks from plastic feet on concrete, the clacks broken and awkward in rhythm, likely continuing to struggle remaining upright while wearing Trish's head.

So—a pause.

No more footsteps. But something. A shuffling. A scuttling. Definitely more than just two feet working together.

Crawling.

Yes. It was crawling now, and quickly, perhaps realizing it had better mobility this way, the rows of chairs in front of Ryan being bumped and jostled as it scuttled closer.

He heard labored breathing one, maybe two rows away.

Ryan picked up his feet and hugged his knees. Shut his eyes tight in spite of the surrounding black. "Please go away," he begged. "*Please…*"

Something reached up and touched his foot.

Ryan screamed and leapt from his seat, tumbling backwards into the row of bolted-down seats behind him before hitting the floor. He immediately went to get up, but his right leg had become wedged between two of those seats behind him. He lay trapped and blind on the auditorium floor.

"Please…" he begged again, all but wept. "…just go away…"

Something licked his ear.

He screeched and jerked his head away. Tried to pull his leg free to no avail, resorted to swatting blindly in the dark, hitting nothing.

Lips at his ear again, so close he could feel and smell its breath, hot and foul.

"*Miss me?*"

"Trish, please…"

"*Let me in.*" It stuck its tongue in his ear.

He went to jerk his head away again but could not. His body was suddenly useless.

The tongue burrowed its way in, its impossible length pushing through his ear canal, entering his mind, probing inquisitively and with oh-so-ill intent as a snake might when happening upon an unattended nest.

"*Mine…*" These words, hissing inside his skull, no longer Trish's voice.

"*Mine…*" These words, spoken by Carol Lawrence, who was reclined comfortably in her chair at home, eyes closed, directing Ryan's dream while her daughter slept, her daughter perhaps dreaming herself. Dreaming about the well-being of the boy.

Such a thought tickled Carol.

It did not, however, tickle her as delightfully as the fact that she had been able to enter the boy's dream, a feat she had never managed before. Either she was becoming more powerful, or the boy's psyche was becoming that much more fragile. Either prospect was just fine, the latter perhaps the better of the two; her strength had plenty of time to grow. Ryan needed to be taken care of sooner than later. The boy had proved to be durable—and damned lucky. She told him so:

"*No Karl to help you this time, Ryan...*"

Trish's tongue continued encircling the nest of Ryan's mind, growing satisfied that the nest was indeed unattended, telling him so in the same detached voice that was no longer Trish's,

("*No Karl to help you this time, Ryan...*")

its ill intent pulsating, keen to strike and latch on and not let go until Ryan was all but—

Gone?

Ryan had vanished from the auditorium.

Carol sat upright in her recliner. "*No!*"

Sounds of Rebecca waking, her bedroom door opening, hurried footsteps into the den to check on her mother.

"Mom?"

Carol's angst was very real, and her explanation for this angst was technically accurate.

"It's okay, sweetheart," she said. "Just a bad dream."

"Oh, don't you start now," Rebecca said, clearly referring to Ryan.

Carol forced a smile.

"You sure you're okay?" Rebecca asked.

"Fine," she lied.

"You coming to bed? You're not gonna sleep in your chair all night, are you?"

Carol flirted with the idea of staying put, making some sort of excuse about wanting to sleep in the den tonight, and then attempting to enter Ryan's dream again. Only she wasn't sure she'd be able to. Something had broken the connection. The lucky little bastard had slipped away from her yet again. How? Had her bravado about entering Ryan's dream state been premature? Did it require more time, more work?

"Yes," she finally said. "I mean, no—I'm not going to sleep in my chair all night. Yes—I'm coming to bed."

Rebecca waited for her mother to gather herself, then saw her off to her bedroom. They hugged goodnight, and Carol closed her bedroom door behind her.

The lucky little bastard. What saved his ass this time?

Sebastian the cat had saved Ryan's ass. He did not, however, save Ryan's balls.

Asleep on the sofa, in the throes of his nightmare, Ryan—his lap in particular—had apparently looked like a damn fine place for Sebastian to settle in for his fiftieth nap of the day.

Unfortunately—no, *quite fortunately*—Sebastian did not stick the landing quite right, and landed not on Ryan's lap, but smack on his groin, jerking Ryan awake with a groan.

He had never been so grateful to be hit in the balls.

Ryan sat up. He was soaked. His head throbbed, even more than his nuts. "Jesus…" he muttered.

He went to the kitchen, stuck his head under the sink's faucet, toweled off, and then filled a glass of water that he downed in two gulps.

Sebastian leapt onto the countertop, keen to once again allow Ryan to give him an early jump on breakfast, please.

Ryan stared at the orange tabby, the tabby staring back with his yellow eyes. He recalled his comment to the cat the first time he'd given him that early breakfast: *You owe me one, buddy.*

"I'd say we were even," he told Sebastian, "but something tells me you hooked me up a *hell* of a lot more than I hooked you up."

Ryan fed him again. Gave him the whole damn can.

49

Ryan's cell phone woke him. He had made his way downstairs to his bedroom after waking from his nightmare in an attempt to grab more sleep—a laughable task at the time—and actually did manage to find some. And with nary a nightmare to be had, no less.

"Hello?" His voice was raspy from sleep.

"Hi. It's Rebecca."

"Hi."

"How are you feeling? You sound tired."

"I didn't sleep well." He chose not to tell her about his nightmare, the savage intensity of it, unlike any of the ones that had preceded it.

There was a pause. Ryan envisioned Rebecca choosing her words.

"Last night was kind of…spooky," she finally said. Her tone was cautious, not particularly warm.

"Ya think?" He plucked a sleep crumb from the corner of his eye.

"Do you remember anything yet?"

"No."

"How are you feeling physically?"

"I feel okay. Bit of a headache."

"I was thinking: your car is still at the school."

Ryan had forgotten he had somehow managed to drive to the school in his sleep. This sobering truth made him miss her next words.

"Say that again?" he asked.

"I was thinking I could come pick you up and we could do a late lunch or something. Go get your car after." Her tone still seemed off.

(*Can you blame the girl?*)

"This lunch," he said, "is it something I should be worried about?"

"What do you mean?"

No sense in beating around the bush. Out with it. "I mean, is this a breakup lunch?"

"No—why? Is it for you?"

"You invited *me.*"

She chuckled. A little warmer, but only just. "True. How about I come to your place at four?"

"What time is it now?"

"It's two. I tried calling you earlier."

He sat up. "*Two?* Jesus, I really slept late."

"Something tells me you needed it."

A-fucking-men to that.

"I guess I did."

"See you at four?" Her tone was still cautiously warm.

"See you then."

"You won't pull another disappearing act on me?"

Well, at least she's joking about it.

(If *she's joking.*)

He wanted to believe she was and thus replied with what he hoped was equal levity. "Car's at the school. And I'm awake. I'm not going any-where."

"Touché. See you soon."

Ryan hung up. His phone rang immediately after.

"Hello?"

"Ryan?"

"Yeah?"

"It's Stew."

"Hey, man. What's up?"

"All right if we drop by?"

"Who's we?"

"Karl and I."

"What for?"

"It's important."

Ryan frowned. "Can't you just tell me over the phone?"

"We'd rather talk to you in person. Are you alone?"

"Yeah—my mother's at work."

"Good."

Ryan's frown remained. "Seriously, Stew; what's this about?"

"You'll find out soon."

Ryan sighed. "Fine. Just know that Rebecca's coming to get me at four."

"Be there in twenty."

Stew hung up.

Ryan dropped his phone hand and sighed again. "Any more drama, anyone?" he asked the empty house.

50

"You sure you know where he lives?" Stew asked the second Karl was in his car.

"I'm sure. I got it from the office directory."

They backed out of Karl's driveway.

"We going to pick up Barbara first?" Karl asked.

"She's not answering her phone. No big deal—we can handle it."

"What are we gonna tell him?"

"Everything we know."

"You know, something just occurred to me," Karl said.

"What?"

"Well, we've been keeping quiet about what we suspect for a long time now. We tell Ryan everything we know, there's a good chance he's going to tell Rebecca. Good chance she's going to—you're gonna want to make a left up here—good chance she's going to tell her mother. That'll be putting us in Carol's line of fire."

"Yeah, I thought of that," Stew said. "But those who died were those who could see."

"They died because they were a threat to her. Now, we're making ourselves a threat."

Stew glanced over at Karl. "So be it."

51

Carol Lawrence stood in the doorway of her daughter's room. She had a cup of tea in her hands.

"I'm not sure it's such a good idea that you see him anymore, Becks," she said.

Rebecca was putting away some clothes. She stopped midway when her mother's words hit. Turned and faced her mother with clothes in hand, drawer hanging open on a slight angle behind her.

"What? *Why?*"

Carol entered her daughter's room and took a seat on her bed. She patted a spot next to her. Rebecca took it. Carol handed her the cup of tea.

"Have some—it's really good."

Rebecca took the tea but did not drink it. "Why shouldn't I see him anymore?"

Carol gestured towards the tea in her daughter's hands. "Have some, Becks. It'll soothe you."

Rebecca rolled her eyes and sipped the tea. "Yummy. Now tell me why."

"I know you like him, sweetheart. I like him too. But he doesn't seem very stable to me. His behavior is very erratic."

"I'll admit he's had a rough couple of weeks, but you don't see the stuff I see when we're together."

Carol nodded and gave a small smile, a placating smile. "I know I don't. But I do see things *in* him."

"Like what?"

"His behavior sounds like he may need some medical help. Especially after what happened last night. There could be something seriously wrong with that poor boy, Becks. I don't want you getting hurt in the long run."

"Medical help?"

Carol gestured towards the tea again, and again Rebecca drank quickly from the cup to appease her mother, to hurry the conversation along.

"Becks, think with your head and not with your heart. Hallucinations? Sleepwalking? Sleep-*driving*? My goodness, Becks…please just think about it for a minute."

She did. And it killed her to find little to no flaws in her mother's logic. Was she setting herself up for a potential disaster? Her feelings for him were very strong, despite their short time together, but how well did she really know Ryan?

Rebecca took another healthy sip of tea, wishing it was wine. Then another, polishing it off. Carol took the empty mug from her, set it aside, and then placed a hand on her daughter's knee.

"Look at me, Becks."

Rebecca did.

Carol patted her daughter's knee five times, an odd rhythm to her pats—one; one, two, three; one. Then: "I think you should end this now before you get hurt, Rebecca. Ryan is very unstable, and I don't want something bad to happen to you." A pause, and then: "I want you to end this now."

Rebecca's gaze on her mother was unblinking. "Okay, Mom. I will."

"That's my good girl." Carol patted her daughter's knee again, the same odd rhythm as before—one; one, two, three; one.

Rebecca blinked, stood, and went back to putting away her clothes. Carol left with the empty teacup.

⎯⎯⎯⎯ ◆ ⎯⎯⎯⎯

Carol rinsed the teacup well before putting it away. She was pleased its contents had placed her daughter in such a highly suggestive state, allowing her to do her thing. She could not help but smile at her accomplishment. A twinge of guilt over doing such a thing to her daughter, yes, but all done out of love. Done to help cushion the blow when she finally killed the little fucker.

52

As Stew and Karl drove to Ryan's house, they passed the school and saw a group of picketers outside. One particular picket sign sported a large photograph of Trish Cooke. Above the photo, it asked: *How many more have to die?*

"Looks like word about the Cooke girl got out after all," Karl said. "Twenty-to-one classes get cancelled tomorrow."

Stew grunted.

They arrived at Ryan's.

"No car in the driveway," Karl said.

"It's still at the school, remember?"

"Oh right. The mother?"

"Ryan said she was at work. She's a nurse. No holidays for those poor people."

They parked in the driveway. Stew killed the ignition and looked at Karl. "You ready?"

"As I'll ever be. Sure we shouldn't try Barbara one more time?"

"Ryan said Rebecca was coming by at four. We go back to get Barbara and we're eating up precious time."

"We should at least tell her where we are, what we're doing."

Stew agreed and tried Barbara again. He got her answering machine and hung up without leaving a message. "Still not answering. Maybe she's with family for Labor Day."

"Maybe."

Barbara Forsythe sat in her armchair facing the television in her den. Her cat, Chester, periodically jumped onto the armrest of the chair and pawed at his owner's face, wondering why she was not showing him the affection she usually gave him.

Eventually, the coroner would classify Barbara's death as a heart attack. A strong family history of heart problems helped solidify this cause of death.

Carol Lawrence knew Barbara's family's medical history quite well. She also knew that three messy suicides over twenty years could be a horrible coincidence, but several over a period of a few days was downright unbelievable.

And this was where her ingenuity kicked in. She did not have to dispose of her recent obstacles in a public display of brutality as she'd previously done; she could dispose of them with a hand of subtlety that would ultimately achieve the same result. In fact, due to Barbara's age and weak heart, Carol was quite pleased to discover that a personal substance of Barbara's was not required for the end result.

Carol had not gone back to sleep after her unsuccessful attempt on Ryan via his dreams, as Rebecca thought she had, but instead waited until her daughter was asleep, and then headed to the school. Her ego demanded compensation. Self-preservation demanded Barbara, Karl, and Stew needed to die, and soon. She chose Barbara first.

If one were to visit Carol's altar now, they would find a photograph of Barbara taped to the wall. On that photo they would find a valentine's-shaped heart drawn in goat's blood. Stuck directly in the center of that heart they would find a small dagger.

Next to Barbara's photo on that wall? Nothing yet. But soon it would contain photographs of both Karl and Stew. Karl, Carol had decided, would be the next to go. While no prior health problems existed that she knew of, what Carol did know was that Karl was quite old, his immune system assuredly compromised. And it was this truth that filled Carol with optimism that no personal item from Karl would be needed to take his life as well. If there was any pessimism among that optimism, it was that Carol was not sure she would be able to make Karl suffer sufficiently before he died. Barbara had likely died quickly. She wanted Karl's death to be hell itself. He was, after all, the one who had saved Ryan, impeded her work.

Stew? Such a strong man would be a challenge. She was up for it, though. School would be starting soon. She needed her obstacles out of the way so she could begin harvesting the exquisite souls of children anew.

53

Ryan answered his front door looking rough as ever.

"Hi, Ryan," Stew said.

Again Ryan asked, in the doorway, "What's this about, guys?"

"Can we come in?" Stew asked.

Ryan stepped aside and waved them in. He gestured towards the sofa. Stew and Karl took a seat.

"You guys want anything to drink? Coffee or tea or something?"

Both men held up their hands and mumbled a "no thanks."

"Good. I don't feel like making anything."

Both men accommodated Ryan's wit with smiles.

"How are you feeling?" Stew asked.

"Better. My dreams, though. Jesus, my dreams…"

"What about them?" Stew asked.

"They're getting worse. Like *way* worse. The one I had last night…" He shook his head as though unable to believe it himself.

"What was it about?" Stew asked.

Instead of telling them, Ryan decided to ask a question he had neglected to ask anyone since discussing it with Trish. "Have either of you guys ever heard about a woman named Helen Tarver?"

Stew looked at Karl. Karl shrugged. Stew looked back at Ryan. "Can't say we do. Who is she?"

"Before Trish died she had her uncle—some super sleuth computer geek—do some digging around. Turns out that around two hundred years ago, some nutty schoolteacher was into all this evil hocus-pocus and whatnot. Apparently, she made all of her students perform a ritual suicide."

Stew raised his eyebrows. Karl had no eyebrows. He raised what he did have.

"I know, right? It gets better, though. Apparently the schoolhouse where this Helen Tarver lady taught was on the *exact* spot where Highland—or Pinewood or whatever—is now. Apparently our locals weren't the only people fond of arson; the folks back then burned the schoolhouse to the ground as well. Not before tracking Helen Tarver down and killing her crazy ass first, of course."

Stew leaned in. "Why don't more people know about this?"

"I said the exact same thing. Apparently the town buried it well. I mean, come on, you guys have been on top of this thing since day one. If you never heard about it…"

"So what are we saying here then?" Karl asked.

Ryan shrugged. "Maybe someone who is still very much alive today knows all about Helen Tarver. Began studying her. Resurrected her work and has been implementing it for their own sick reasons for the past twenty years. At least that's what Trish suspected."

Karl and Stew exchanged a look.

"Ryan, how do you feel about Rebecca?" Stew asked.

The sudden change in topic paused Ryan a moment. "Huh?"

"Rebecca. How do you feel about her?" Stew asked again.

"Why?"

Both Stew and Karl said nothing.

"I like her," Ryan finally said, and then again asked: "Why?"

"What about her mother?" Karl asked.

"Her *mother*? Did we just change topics without my—?"

"This is very much on topic, Ryan," Stew said.

"Well, then, any chance you can just come out with it, please? I'm a big boy."

Stew held up an apologetic hand. "We believe Carol Lawrence is the one who is responsible for what's been happening at the school."

"*Carol?*"

"I wasn't exactly honest with you when we first met, Ryan," Karl said. "I told you I didn't trust anyone. Well, I do trust Stew and Barbara."

"But not Carol."

Karl nodded.

"Why?"

"We've suspected her for a long time," Stew said. "We just couldn't prove it."

"Can you prove it now?"

"We're hoping you can."

"*Me?*"

"You need to remember what happened last night."

"I don't."

"Everyone who could see is dead because they were a threat to Carol," Stew went on. "*You're* a threat to Carol. She tried to kill you last night. You're only alive because Karl was there to save you—don't you understand that?"

"I *do* understand that. What I *don't* understand is why Carol Lawrence is responsible."

"Who knew you were at the school last night?" Stew asked.

"I don't know."

"Sure you do. Stop and think for a minute, Ryan. Who came looking for you at the school?"

"Rebecca and my mother."

"Right. Do you suspect your mother?"

Ryan made a face.

"Okay then. Do you suspect Rebecca?"

"She's twenty-three. Unless she was pulling this voodoo shit off when she was an infant, then I would have to say no, I don't suspect her."

"Good, good…" Stew looked pleased with where his line of questioning was going—a suspect falling into his trap. "Now, what are the odds that Rebecca told her mother where she was going last night and why?"

"Strong, I guess."

"And did Carol come along with her daughter and your mother to help?"

"No."

"Strange, don't you think?"

"Maybe."

"No—not 'maybe.' Strange."

"It's still pretty flimsy, Stew."

"So help us then. You're different than all the others who died before you. They could see, like you; however, they never lived long enough to see more. Carol saw to that. But you…"

"I live to tell the tale."

"Are you mocking us?"

"Can you blame me? You're accusing my girlfriend's mother without any real proof."

"*Yes*. Yes, I can blame you. Whether or not you want to point the finger at Carol, can you deny what's been happening to you thus far? Is that a laughing matter? All the people who've died—all the *children* who've died? Is that a laughing matter?"

"Whoa, whoa—I am *not* making light of those tragedies one bit. I'm just saying your evidence towards Carol is—"

"How about your friend Trish, son?" Karl said. "She seem the type to slash her own throat with a razor blade to you?"

"Of course not. But it still doesn't prove—"

"Hell," Karl went on, "after the accident she had earlier in the day, you'd think she'd never want to even *look* at another one of the damn things again, never mind taking one to her own throat."

Ryan flashed on the cut Trish had received the day of her death. How bizarre the accident was. And then Trish's words: "*I'd like to know how a stupid razor blade wound up in a stack of papers.*" And then her need to constantly change her bandaged hand, the bleeding had been so bad. *If* Carol was responsible for Trish's death, had she been the one who'd slipped the razor blade in between those stack of papers, cutting Trish's hand prior to her death? What possible reason could she have had for doing such a thing? The cut was hardly fatal. If it had intended on being so, it was ridiculous in its design.

(*If your dream felt like a try at possession, then it's already begun. Someone has already managed to take something from you.*)

Take *something from me*?

(*Your friend Trish was forced to take her own life because her blood was spilled earlier in the day and used.*)

"Ryan," Stew said, "we need you to trust—"

"*Shut up!*" Ryan slapped both hands over his ears. Shut his eyes tight. "*Don't talk to me!*"

Neither Stew nor Karl spoke. It was clear that Ryan was not resorting to childish behavior, physically attempting to block out words he didn't want to hear. On the contrary; it seemed clear Ryan was trying to listen:

> *So that razor blade in the stack of papers…that was placed there on purpose. It was no accident.*
>
> *Yes.*
>
> *Placed by someone who knew Trish could see.*
>
> *Yes.*
>
> *I haven't spilled any blood.*
>
> *Neither did I. My urine was used.*
>
> *Your urine?*
>
> *My erratic behavior following my divorce led some to believe I was using drugs. I was made to take a urine test once a day. On one particular day, twice.*
>
> *Twice in one day?*
>
> *Yes.*
>
> *Why?*
>
> *Because the first sample was misplaced.*
>
> *Not misplaced, though, right? It was stolen.*
>
> *Yes.*
>
> *By whom?*
>
> *I don't know.*

Ryan spun away from Stew and Karl, hands still pressed tight to both ears, eyes still shut tight. He was back at the school, sitting at the table in the faculty lounge. Sitting across from John Gray.

Stew and Karl looked on, not daring to interrupt.

> *The photo. The staff photo from Highland. Karl the janitor believes it was left on my car to help me. To help me recognize you and the others so I would start digging around for a way to stop all this.*

Yes, it was given to you to help you start searching, but the giver's motive was not one of help—it was one of malice.

Malice?

Someone suspected you had the ability to see. The photo was a ploy to see how you might respond to it. A way to confirm their suspicions if you responded to that ploy in exactly the way you did. To confirm whether you were someone who needed to be dealt with. Someone has been keeping a very close eye on you, Ryan.

Ryan broke away from the scene with John and thought back to Trish's post-funeral reception, the conversation he'd had with Rebecca and Carol Lawrence:

Well, why don't you and Rebecca have a few more drinks, and then she can give you a lift back to our place? You can stay the night.

Back to him and John again. Certain phrases being played over again:

Someone has been keeping a very close eye on you, Ryan.

I haven't spilled any blood.

Neither did I. My urine was used.

In Rebecca's bedroom now after they made love:

What are you looking for?

I can't, uh…I can't find the condom.

What?

The condom we used…I can't find it. Here's the wrapper, but I can't find the actual condom.

You didn't flush it?

Not exactly. I kinda just dropped it on the rug after. I was going to flush it after we came in from outside, but I guess I forgot. I'm sorry.

Well, it's got to be there.

I'm not seeing it… Where the hell could it be?

Just leave it. We'll spot it in the morning when the sun is up.

And then the next morning when the condom was found, practically in plain sight:

> *Here it is…How the hell did I miss it last night?*
> *It was the middle of the night. We'd been drinking.*
> *Yeah, but it's right here.*
> *Who cares? Pick it up and flush it.*

And when he had gone to flush it, how there had been hardly any semen in the condom, his thoughts at the time:

> *Did I shoot a blank? Or nearly a blank? How is that possible? I haven't come in days.*

Recalling the moment intently now, wondering whether the semen in the condom had dried overnight. Quickly dismissing the idea as it had shamefully not been the first time he'd tossed a used condom on the floor to be discarded the morning after. How there had been no shortage of semen those times. Worrying then, again with not a little shame, whether he'd actually spilled some on the rug when he'd so carelessly tossed it to the floor. Only to re-enter Rebecca's bedroom and check the rug, finding no such spot on her dark rug, no dried substance beneath his feet when he'd nonchalantly tried to check with his toes.

John Gray's words now for a final time:

> *If your dream felt like a try at possession, then it's already begun. Someone has already managed to take something from you.*

Ryan turned back slowly towards Stew and Karl. Opened his eyes and lowered his hands from his ears. His face was lost.

"Ryan…?" Stew said.

"I spoke to John last night."

"John? John *Gray*?"

Ryan nodded. "He told me everything but who it was. But…"

"But what? Christ, Ryan, *what*?"

"My God, it makes sense…" Ryan said in barely a whisper. "It makes sense…the photograph. The condom. Trish. It all makes sense."

"*You're* not making any sense," Stew said. "Tell us what the hell you're—"

"She's got me," Ryan said, still distant, almost trance-like. "She's got what she needs. I'm as good as dead."

"Ryan, what did you see in that boiler room?" Karl asked.

Ryan's behavior now was almost the total antithesis of his recall just prior. He did not suddenly spin away from Stew and Karl. He did not slap both hands over his ears in a bid to exclude all noise. Instead, he merely closed his eyes and remembered. And much like his behavior now, so too was his recall of the boiler room altar and the contents therein the total antithesis of when he'd first glimpsed it. There was no flash flood of atrocity to overload his senses. No fear or pain. Just simple recall, as though remembering a scene in a film.

Better yet, Ryan recalled the altar's location. "I know where it is," he said, opening his eyes.

"Where *what* is?" Stew said, all but begging.

The words left Ryan's mouth without pause, surprising even him. "Where Carol Lawrence carries on Helen Tarver's work."

"And that is?"

Ryan looked at them as if they should already know. "The boiler room."

"Impossible," Karl said. "We searched for *years*."

"It's there," Ryan merely said.

"What's the connection with this Helen Tarver lady?" Stew asked. "How did Carol find out about this woman from over two hundred years ago when an entire town had no knowledge of her or what happened? How is she able to do what she's capable of doing now?"

"Maybe they're related?" Ryan said.

"Her last name is Lawrence," Karl said.

"She could have easily changed it," Ryan suggested.

"She used to be married," Stew said. "Lawrence is her married name."

"Well, what's her maiden name then?" Karl asked.

"It couldn't be Tarver," Ryan said. "That would be too easy."

"Where's her husband now?" Stew asked.

"Dead. Died of a stroke several years ago," Ryan said.

"Well, how do we find something like this out?" Stew began. "Her real name, I mean. If the whole Helen Tarver thing was buried and nobody knows about it—"

"*Wait,*" Ryan said, closing his eyes again. "Wait, wait, wait, wait…" He was back at the tavern with Rebecca, having their first drink together:

> *How did he die?*
> *Massive stroke. I was in middle school.*
> *I'm sorry. Must have been hard on you guys.*
> *It was. To be honest, I think my mom is still in denial about it, even after all these years. She doesn't like to keep photos of him around or anything. Just his ashes in a big urn in her bedroom. I have a picture, though. Wanna see?*
> *Sure.*

Ryan remembered the photograph well. Even remembered commenting on what a good-looking guy her father had been. That photo came back to him now, not as the one Rebecca slid across the bar table towards him to see, but as one that had been hanging on the altar room wall. He had absorbed it last night, but had not recalled it until just now. Mike Lawrence, Rebecca's father, with a necklace of small needles lining the perimeter of the man's throat, below the necklace of needles the word "stroke" written in something red.

Ryan opened his eyes again. His look of revelation showed no satisfaction whatsoever, for there was no longer any lingering doubt in his mind—his girlfriend's mother was the one.

"She killed him," he said at last. "Carol Lawrence killed her husband."

"You said he died of a stroke," Stew said.

Ryan shot Stew a disappointed look. "And John willfully hanged himself. Trish voluntarily cut her own throat."

Stew conceded Ryan's point with a nod.

"Why would she kill her husband?" Karl asked.

"Why did she kill everyone else?" Ryan asked.

"They were a threat," Stew said.

"Exactly."

"And the children?" Karl asked.

"No threat there," Ryan said, "she's just an evil fucking woman who wants children to kill children for her own sick needs."

54

Ryan had changed his mind about making coffee; he felt all three of them deserved a hearty cup. They sipped periodically as they spoke.

"So why was Carol's husband a threat?" Stew asked.

"Maybe he could see things too," Karl suggested.

"That doesn't make sense," Ryan said. "The people who claimed to see things saw them in the school only."

"You don't know that for sure," Karl said.

"Okay, fine—but Rebecca said her father died when she was in middle school. That was what? Ten years ago, give or take? Carol's been doing her voodoo shit twice as long as that. If this guy started seeing things, Carol would have sniffed him out immediately. I mean, she was *married* to the guy. If there's one thing we know, it's that Carol doesn't take chances—she thinks you're a threat; you're dead."

"That means he was a threat in some other way," Stew said.

"Most likely. My guess is he found out what his wife was up to."

"Well, then, using your own logic back at you, Ryan, how could he be married to Carol for all those years and not suspect something sooner?" Stew asked.

"No idea. As we well know, Carol's not exactly blatant about what she gets up to."

"Maybe the husband was into all this crazy stuff *with* her," Karl offered. "Maybe after a while he had a change of heart. Wanted to stop or something."

Stew and Ryan looked at each other and shared a shrug. Stew said: "That could make sense."

"I'll call Rebecca," Ryan said. "She's supposed to be here at four. I'll tell her to come now so we can talk to her."

"Whoa, whoa, Ryan—slow down," Stew said. "You can't do that to the girl."

"Do what?"

"Sit her down with the three of us and tell her we suspect her mother is responsible for mass murder. That she killed her own father."

"Fair point. Suppose we don't say anything about Carol then? We just ask about her father."

"Ask what? If our theory about her father being in on everything with Carol is true, there's simply no way that child would know anything about it."

Ryan splayed a hand. "I'm open to suggestions."

Ryan's cell phone vibrated on the coffee table. Ryan snatched it and checked the incoming call.

"Speak of the devil," he said. "It's Rebecca."

55

Rebecca had held her cell phone in her hand so long before dialing that her palm was now sweaty. Was she really going to call someone she liked so much and tell him she didn't want to see him again?

She played her mother's words over and over again in her head. The more they played, the more they continued to make sense. He was prone to hallucinations. He sleepwalked. Check that—sleep-*drove*. He was unstable. She would only be hurt in the long run. It made sense. Her mother was right. But over the phone? Tell him over the phone? What would school be like, seeing him every day? It would be so hard. So awkward.

Should she go over as she had planned? Tell him face to face? Her mother's words continued to echo inside her head, frustrating her. Such an impact those words had. Why? Past words of advice over questionable men weren't regarded this intently. Hell, often she ignored them completely, preferring the classic thrill of defying her mother in favor of the "bad boy." Why did it all feel so different now?

Don't think, just dial. Don't think, just dial.

She dialed.

56

"Hey," Ryan answered his phone, "I was just thinking about you."

Stew and Karl listened intently from their spots on the sofa.

"Hey," Rebecca said.

"You still coming over?"

"I don't think so."

"What? Why?"

Stew and Karl leaned forward.

"I don't know, Ryan...after what's been going on lately...I don't know—I think maybe we should just lay low for a while."

"*Lay low*? What does that mean?"

"I don't know...the school incident last night, your behavior in the past—you just seem so...*out there* sometimes. I don't want to end up getting hurt, you know?"

This isn't her, Ryan instantly thought. *This isn't her decision.*

"I don't believe you, Rebecca. I don't believe you mean that. Are you all right?"

"I'm fine," she said. "I think I better go."

I'm going to lose her. I can't let her hang up.

"*Wait!* Please don't hang up just yet."

A pause.

"Hello?" Ryan said.

"I'm here."

Just ask it. You can win her back later, but not if you're dead. Just fucking ask.

"Tell me about your father," he said.

Karl leaned into Stew's ear. "*Boy's not one for foreplay, is he?*" he whispered.

Stew hushed Karl with tight lips and a frown.

"*What?*" Rebecca asked.

"I know it sounds random, and if you really want to stop seeing me, then I have no choice but to accept that. But I want to know about your father."

Rebecca seemed at a loss for words, and Ryan bet it was only her curiosity towards his odd questioning that kept her on the line.

"What do you want to know?" she finally said.

Ryan closed his eyes. *Thank you.*

"What was he like?"

"This is weird, Ryan. Why do you want to know?"

How to sell this? She wants to break up. Can't exactly say I want to know more about her to further the relationship, et cetera. Go for the cryptic angle and hope her curiosity keeps her on the line? "Just some stuff I'm trying to work out."

"What stuff?"

"I'll tell you in a minute. What was he like?"

He could hear her sigh. Whether it was from Ryan's insistence or her having to recall the loss of her father, he couldn't be sure. Nor did he care, to be honest. As long as he kept her talking.

"He was great," she finally said. "I loved him a lot."

"You mentioned he passed away from a stroke, right?"

"Yes."

"Had he had any strokes leading up to the one that took his life?"

"No—just the one."

"Did his behavior change at all leading up to his death?"

"What do you mean?"

"I don't know—was he acting unusual in any way before he died? Did he ever say anything to you that you felt was out of the ordinary? Do anything out of the ordinary?"

"Ryan, this is really—"

"Come on, Rebecca; it's just a question."

Another sigh. "He became born again. I guess that was a little un-usual."

"*Born again?*"

Stew and Karl looked at each other.

"Yeah."

"Why?"

"I'm not really sure; he didn't talk about it much with me. If I had to guess, I would say it was because of his sister. She became born again shortly before he did. Maybe she talked him into it."

"Did she pass away too? His sister?"

"As far as I know, she's still alive. My mom and I haven't seen her in years. I think she went a little loopy after my dad died. She's kind of a recluse now."

"Does she still live in the area?"

"No idea. Their family had a house they shared for generations in the area, but I'm not sure what the status of that is today. To be honest, I wouldn't be surprised if she was committed to an asylum by now. At least that's what my mother says. Again, she kinda went loopy after my dad died."

"What was her name?"

"Samantha Lawrence."

"Your mom ever consider changing back to her maiden name?"

"Doubt it. I think she keeps the name out of respect for my dad. Plus, she told me she was never fond of her maiden name."

"Which is?"

"Moyer."

(*Even the remaining members of the Tarver family moved far, far away and changed their name to Moyer. And can you blame them? Having a whacko like that in their family?*)

Trish's words coming back to him, as though she was next to him now, whispering them in his ear.

"Hello? Ryan, are you still there?"

Ryan's mind was on fire with discovery. He went to answer, but doubted his own tongue.

"I'm here," he managed. "I've got to go now, Rebecca."

So, that's it? You're just gonna let her go?

Yes… His previous thought—*You can win her back later, but not if you're dead*—now had a firm ally that was, …*for now. Can't necessarily try to win her back when I'm in the middle of trying to expose her crazy fucking mother, can I?*

"Are you all right?" Rebecca asked.

Such a loaded question. He knew she was referring to the breakup, but oh, if she only knew.

"Fine," he lied. "I guess I'll see you around."

Ryan hung up just as she went to respond.

What was she going to say?

Does it matter right now?

He turned off his phone in case she decided to call back. And that was okay, he supposed. Better to think he was sulking rather than playing *Scooby Doo* with Stew and Karl.

"Well?" Stew said.

Ryan faced them. "We need to go find a woman by the name of Samantha Lawrence right now."

"A relative?" Stew said.

Ryan nodded. Then: "Speaking of relatives, it appears that Carol Lawrence is related to one Miss Helen Tarver after all."

57

Finding Samantha Lawrence was no easy task. Even excessive digging on the internet revealed very little. Ryan's solution? Trish's uncle.

Ryan had met the man briefly at Trish's funeral, a fortunate thing as no introduction was needed over the phone, just a reminder as to who Ryan was.

Trish's uncle was happy to help; he too simply could not believe Trish had taken her life on her own accord. Ryan did not bog the man down with specifics as to *why* they were looking for Samantha Lawrence—Carol; black magic; the works—for fear of scaring the man away (although Trish had told Ryan that her uncle was into all kinds of conspiracy theories and would have likely digested such outlandish claims). Ryan had just stated that they needed to find the woman to help bring closure to Trish's death and to please take his word for it. And again, Trish's uncle was happy to help, on the condition that Ryan would keep him in the loop with whatever they found.

Ryan of course promised, and before long, Samantha Lawrence had an address. The name tied to that address, however, was not Samantha Lawrence (which came as no great surprise to any of them), but to one Karen Webster. And they were headed east on Route 76 towards Philadelphia now, to pay "Karen Webster" a visit.

"God bless the man," Stew said, referring to Trish's uncle. Stew was driving. Ryan rode shotgun. Karl was in back.

"Don't get too excited just yet," Ryan said. "Just because we found out where she lives doesn't mean she's still there, or that she's going to even talk to us."

"She'll talk to us," Stew said. "If it's about her brother and the woman who murdered him?"

"Rebecca said she was a little loopy," Ryan said. "She might not have a clue what we're talking about, or even what planet she's on."

"What we need to do is get back to the school as soon as possible and put an end to all of this," Karl said.

"How, Karl?" Ryan said mockingly. "Please tell me how."

"What do you mean *how*?"

"Even if we go back to the school and I take you to the precise spot in the boiler room where I found her altar, what then?"

"We call the police is 'what then.' We have her ass arrested."

"Are you honestly going to tell me that the police can help us in a situation like this? Whatever the hell Carol Lawrence or Moyer or whatever the fuck her name is has started, how can the police stop it? They can arrest her, sure, but that won't change what she's done to *me*. Her psycho fucking wheels involving yours truly are already well in motion, and we need to find a way to reverse the fuckers before you guys are attending *my* funeral next."

"No need for such language, Ryan," Stew said.

Ryan said nothing.

Stew then said: "So your hope is that Samantha Lawrence can somehow help us with all that? Reverse what's been done to you?"

"No, Stew, we're just dropping by to say hello."

58

Rebecca sat on the edge of her bed, cell phone in hand. She had tried calling Ryan back a number of times but got his voicemail immediately, no ring. He'd clearly turned it off.

Her mind raced. She couldn't make sense of his earlier questioning. Why did he want to know about her father? Was this the odd behavior her mother was referring to? *Was* Ryan mentally ill? She definitely felt something for him. Damn the risk of entering the world of cheese—she had felt a "spark" between them. But spark or no spark, wasn't it all ultimately irrelevant? If the guy was mentally unstable...

"Hi, Becks." Her mother stood in the doorway. Rebecca wondered whether she'd listened to their conversation. "Everything okay?"

Rebecca looked down at her phone and then back up at her mother. "I spoke to Ryan. I told him it was over."

Carol took a seat next to her daughter on the bed. "I'm sorry, sweetheart; I know that must have been hard." A pause and then: "How did he take it?"

"He was upset, I guess."

"You guess?"

"He seemed upset at first—" She sighed. "But then he got weird again."

"You see? You made the right choice." She began rubbing Rebecca's back.

"Yeah…"

Another pause. Carol then asked: "What did he do that was so weird this time?" "He started asking me questions about Dad."

Carol stopped rubbing her daughter's back. "Your father? Why was he asking questions about your father?"

Rebecca shrugged, her head down, turning her phone over and over in her hand. "No idea. Who knows why he does any of the things he does."

"What kind of questions did he ask?"

"How he died. What he was like. He even asked about Aunt Samantha."

Carol's posture changed, her back stiffening. "Samantha? Why would he ask about her? How would he even *know* about her?"

"I told him Dad had become born again, and that Aunt Samantha might have been an influence."

"I see."

Rebecca lifted her head and looked at her mother. "Why do you think he would ask all those things? It was all so random."

Carol placed a hand on her daughter's knee and patted it five times—one; one, two, three; one. "I wouldn't worry about it, sweetheart. Like I said, the boy is unstable. You did the right thing ending it when you did. You've got a huge day ahead of you tomorrow—kids arriving and all. This is the last thing you need to worry about."

Rebecca nodded and leaned into her mother for a hug.

"I love you, Mom."

"I love you too, Becks."

59

"Yeesh," Ryan said as the three men pulled up to the home of Samantha Lawrence—aka Karen Webster. "You think Lurch will answer when we ring the bell?"

"Apparently not a *Better Homes and Gardens* subscriber," Karl said.

The house, detached and located in a quiet town on the outskirts of the city, was a picture of neglect. The surrounding lawn and foliage, or lack thereof, had Ryan concerned that while they may have located the home, it would be as he feared: unoccupied. Unless it was all by design.

Ryan led the way to the front door, countless shin-high weeds and thick grass predominating the stones underfoot that once made a path.

Stew voiced Ryan's fear. "Can anyone actually live here?"

And Ryan voiced the logic he hoped countered such a notion: "Maybe it's like this on purpose."

Stew looked at Ryan.

"Well, would *you* voluntarily drop in a place like this?" Ryan said.

Stew nodded. "Let's hope you're right."

Ryan knocked lightly. Nothing. He knocked again. Still nothing.

Stew nudged Ryan aside and rapped his meaty fist on the wood hard enough to make Ryan flinch.

"You're gonna knock the damn door down, Hercules," Ryan muttered.

The blinds to the windows adjacent to the front door were drawn, but they too suffered from neglect, and Ryan saw a shadow of movement through a gap in one set.

"I see someone," he said.

Eyes on them now through that slit, vanishing as quickly as they'd arrived.

"Hello?" Ryan called to the window, and then moving back towards the front door, louder now: "*Hello? Samantha Lawrence?*"

"No one here by that name," a female voice behind the door replied.

"Karen Webster then," Ryan said.

"I don't want to be bothered."

Ryan raised his voice more so. "Please, Karen—we *need* to talk to you."

"I don't want to be bothered," the voice said again.

"It's about your brother—"

"Please leave—"

"—and his wife, Carol Lawrence. We know all about her, Karen. *All* about her."

A pause and a click, the door then opening as far as the security chain would allow. A sliver of a woman's face appeared, her wary eye dominating it.

"What do you know about Carol?" she asked.

"We know she murdered your brother," Ryan said. "Along with countless others."

"I don't want to get involved."

"Please," Stew spoke up. "Children are dying. More will die…"

Her wary eye fixed on Stew, looked him up and down. Then on Karl. "Who are you people?"

"Desperate," Stew said. "Please."

The door closed. Sound of the chain sliding, and then the door opened completely. There stood the woman they all hoped was indeed Samantha Lawrence, looking exceptionally tired and unkempt. "If you're here on Carol's behalf, I only ask that you do it quickly," she said.

"I promise you," Stew said, "we're here to do no such thing."

Samantha Lawrence's living room reminded Ryan of a museum that had long been closed to the public. It smelled of old wood and mold. Dust swirled in what few beams of sunlight she allowed from the outside world. Sheets covered most of the furniture.

She encouraged Ryan, Stew, and Karl to take a seat on the sofa, it too covered in a large white sheet. She took her seat next to them in a battered green armchair, no sheet for the chair. A crossword puzzle book lay on the arm, a pencil holding her spot.

"How did you find me?" she asked.

Ryan told her about Trish's uncle. About Trish herself.

She seemed to accept this answer. "Well, I guess we can stop with the whole Karen Webster thing, then. You can call me Samantha."

"Samantha," Stew began, "what can you tell us about your brother's wife?"

Samantha looked away, as though considering her words. She then did something unexpected so soon into the visit. She started to cry.

"We were all into it," she said. "*All* of us. It was like a drug. You have no idea the power it can hold over you. The power it can *give* you."

She appeared to be asking for forgiveness. They were not, however, there to put her conscience at ease. Stew's questioning was firm.

"Samantha, are you aware of all the lives that have been lost?" he said. "The lives of children?"

Samantha only cried harder. "Of course I am. Mike and I never wanted to harm children. To harm *anyone*. We only wanted the…advantages it could give us."

"Advantages?"

"To attain things in life that seemed unattainable to us by conventional means. Money, status, you get the idea. Like I said, it was like a drug. My brother and I just wanted a few hits. And then a few hits more, but never at the expense of lives."

"But not Carol," Stew said.

"No—not Carol. Her goals were…*different* than ours."

"And they were?"

"I honestly don't know. Something that goes beyond my level of comprehension. Likely beyond *all* our levels of comprehension. Evil operates in ways that only evil understands."

"Does any of this really matter?" Ryan asked Stew sharply. "The *whys*?"

Stew went to reply, but Ryan cut him off, turning his attention back to Samantha. "I don't have much time left, Samantha. Carol has seen to that. And once she's done with me, I would wager these guys I'm with are next—"

Karl's lack of eyebrows jumped.

"—and then after them, more *children* will be next. So, I am only going to ask you one question. If you know, please tell me, otherwise don't waste my time." Ryan paused deliberately for effect. Then: "Do you know how to stop her?"

Samantha Lawrence wiped away the last of her tears. "Yes," she said. "Only I don't know where she keeps it. She would never tell Mike and me."

"Keeps what?"

"The heart of Helen Tarver."

60

Carol Lawrence hummed the *Jeopardy!* theme song as she cut the photo of Karl the janitor out of an old Highland Elementary yearbook. She was in her bedroom with the door locked. Seconds later she had the photo of Karl at hand.

"Good old Karl," she said as she held the picture up to the light. "You had a good run."

She reached into the cardboard shoebox at her feet and pulled out a large white rat, wood chips sticking to its feet and fur. She plucked off the chips and stroked the rat gently before kissing it on the nose, its whiskers tickling her. "Such an appropriate offering for someone like you, eh, Karl? Though I suppose a snake would have been equally as appropriate. Perhaps for Stew." She kissed the rat again and let the animal's whiskers tickle her nose some more. She then reached into the shoebox at her feet again and withdrew a scalpel.

Finished, she placed the blood-soaked photo of Karl aside and held the dead rat to her lips, whispering into its ear: "I'm sorry, little guy. But please take comfort in the fact that with your sacrifice comes great reward. Karl will soon become one of the very things you like to nosh: a vegetable."

She giggled faintly at her own wit, resumed humming the *Jeopardy!* song, and kissed the rat a final time before placing it back in the box.

61

"The *heart* of Helen Tarver?" Ryan asked. "Are you fucking *kidding* me?"

"Ryan…" Stew said.

"*What?* It's like something out of a stupid horror movie." Back to Samantha: "How is that even possible? Someone's heart still lying around after two hundred years?"

"It was stolen and preserved by her family," Samantha said.

"Trish told me it was torn from her chest by locals and given to a priest."

"Legend," she replied.

"What *isn't* legend?" Stew asked.

"Helen Tarver's body *was* torn apart by locals. Apparently that part is true," Samantha said. "Her remains were to be cremated in a ceremonial fire not long after her death, but of course her heart was taken before the ceremonial fire took place."

"Was the Tarver family as nuts as she was?" Ryan asked. "Is that why they stole her heart? To carry on her work, so to speak?"

"On the contrary—the Tarver family changed their names to Moyer and left town soon after, wanting to abandon the bizarre religion, wanting to distance themselves from Helen's memory as much as possible. They felt Helen had taken their beliefs and practices too far. Before long, the heart's whereabouts—along with any surviving Tarvers, or Moyers, if you will—became a mystery."

"But Carol uncovered that mystery, didn't she," Stew said, more than asked.

Samantha nodded. "She found the heart in the hands of an elder Moyer. Took the heart by force and began to study."

"Did you ever *see* this heart?" Stew asked.

"No—she never let us see it."

"So it could all be BS."

"I suppose. But Mike and I never questioned it. After all, the things she was able to do for us, the power she wielded…we had no reason to doubt her."

"Wait, wait, wait," Ryan broke in. "Why didn't the elder Tarver, or Moyer, or whatever just destroy the heart? Why keep it?"

"Fear. Superstition. For centuries, many cultures have valued the human heart as a religious artifact for its connections to the soul. The Moyers were no different. Only they also believed that if the heart were to be destroyed, then the soul of Helen Tarver would be set free to inhabit another. They didn't want to take such a chance."

"But it's okay for us to destroy it and let her soul inhabit one of us?" Ryan said.

"That part's just superstition," Samantha said.

"Oh, *that* part is? Oh, okay."

"Ryan…" Stew said again.

"Would you stop trying to reel me in like my fucking mother, Stew?" Calmly, Samantha said: "If Carol believed there was the possibility that she could play host to Helen Tarver's soul, she would have found a way by now, and she would have done it happily. No—I believe Carol needs the heart to be whole. Locked away and safe from others."

"Is that why you keep yourself locked away here? Why you've refused to say a word to *anyone* about all of this?" Stew's tone was accusatory.

Samantha could only hang her head in shame. "A crazy hermit of a woman is of no threat to anyone. I trust it's why Carol has never come for me."

"Why did she marry?" Karl spoke up.

Samantha flinched and looked up as though she'd forgotten Karl was there. "She needed an ally. She needed accomplices. Her studies were laborious and time-consuming. So, she seduced my brother, gave him that first hit. My brother then came to me, and I got *my* first hit. You know the rest." She looked away, her eyes glazing over, her tone now soft and distant. "We had no idea we were being courted by hell itself."

Ryan rolled his eyes. Splayed a cynical hand. "Okay, fine—a two-hundred-year-old devil-woman's heart. Why not? How do we find it?"

"The boiler room," Stew said.

"It's not there," Ryan said.

"It must be."

"It's not there, Stew! I remember everything now, and it's *not there!*"

"Of course it isn't," Samantha said. "It's far too valuable to leave so far from home."

Ryan gaped at her. "Far from home? You saying it's at her *house*?"

"If I had to guess."

"But she has no problem keeping all of her other crazy crap at the school," Ryan said.

"Mere tools," Samantha said. "They enable her to carry out her rituals, but her strength—her *true* strength—stems from the heart. It is her conduit, her direct line to Helen Tarver's evil. Without it she has very little."

"So, it's in her house," Ryan said. "Christ, I was mere feet from it." He looked at Stew. "If we knew then what we know now, I could have just knocked her cold and destroyed the thing that night."

"Hindsight will only drive you crazy, Ryan," Stew said.

"Craz*ier*, you mean."

"My offer to kill the bitch is still on the table," Karl said.

62

Rebecca must have gone over her itinerary for the following day a dozen times, and it had nothing to do with preparation. Nothing was sticking. Every time she would start, the words would begin to blur, and she would start to think about Ryan.

She left her bedroom and noticed her mother's door was closed. Napping, maybe. Best to leave her be. Should she risk a cigarette? She had been jonesing for one ever since her odd conversation earlier with Ryan. *Was* her mother napping? Screw it, she would sneak one.

Rebecca grabbed the pack and lighter hidden in her dresser and tiptoed out onto the back deck. She got maybe two drags in when she saw her mother's bedroom door begin to open through the deck's sliding glass door. She quickly tossed the cigarette over the deck and ducked out of sight.

I'm screwed, she thought. No doubt her mother was currently wondering where she was. Her bedroom light was on, after all, and her school material for the next day was laid out on her bed. With no reply coming from her daughter anywhere in the house, Carol's next logical step would be to check the back deck.

She quickly stuffed the pack and the lighter into her back pocket with the plan to keep her mother in front of her when she inevitably did show, lest she spot the bulge in her daughter's back pocket. Now it was just a matter of hoping the deck didn't stink of smoke.

Or maybe go in and greet her first? She'd only had two puffs. The scent on her wouldn't be strong. Just don't get too close. Maybe say she had to use the toilet first? Hurry in and gargle and wash her hands—and pray she didn't spot the bulge in her back pocket—and hide the pack and lighter before coming back out? Ugh—such a song and dance for a stupid habit.

Rebecca peeked through the sliding glass door before making a move and …

…it appeared there would be no song and dance after all; her mother did not appear to be looking for her. In fact, Rebecca wasn't exactly sure *what* her mother was doing. What she did know was that her mother was carrying a shoebox and heading for the front door.

Where the hell is she going? And with a shoebox, no less?

Rebecca waited a solid minute after her mother had left before attempting re-entry. She put away her cigarettes and lighter and then paused. The shoebox. Her mother not saying goodbye before she left the house. All odd.

Or is it? The shoebox is probably filled with stuff for her classroom.

But not saying goodbye, or where she was going? And why take it to the school now? Surely it was something that could have waited until morning. She decided to snoop.

Inside her mother's room, a familiar smell hit her—faint but there. Wood chips? She'd had her share of hamsters as a child and knew the subtle smell of pine and cedar wood shavings well. Is that what was in the shoebox? A hamster or gerbil for someone? For her classroom maybe? A classroom mascot of sorts? That made sense, and yet it didn't. If the shoebox did contain such a thing, why not tell her about it? *Show* it to her before bringing it to school? She knew her daughter's affinity for hamsters.

She dismissed the thought entirely as her nose playing tricks on her, that no such hamster and its wood chip bedding existed—which of course brought less light to the contents of the shoebox, but oh well—and carried on snooping about her mother's room.

She spotted the great porcelain urn that stood alone on the top of her mother's mantel and quickly looked away. Her father's ashes. Rebecca could never bring herself to look at them for very long. The idea of his remains in such a way, so close, had yet to make her feel at ease, in spite of it being so common. Maybe one day.

But not today.

Rebecca suddenly felt uncomfortable, as though her father himself was judging her meddling behavior from the mantel. She went to leave, stopped, and turned back around. Something had caught her eye, only registering a second after.

The corner of a book was poking out from beneath her mother's bed. She went towards it. Pulled it out from beneath the bed. It was an old Highland Elementary yearbook. Had her mother been reading this? Rebecca casually flipped through the pages, the unsettling notion that some of the faces of students she was flipping past might long be

(*murdered*)

dead not escaping her. It was all getting too creepy. Her mother's odd behavior. The unnerving feeling that her father was somehow watching. The yearbook with potentially dead

(*murdered*)

faces smiling back at her. She went to close the book, but found that in her musing over all things unsettling, she had absently flipped towards the back of the yearbook. Towards one page in particular; that page displaying itself with little effort because it had clearly been tampered with. *Cut*, to be exact. It was the custodial staff page. Head custodian Karl Sandford's name, and name only, leading the row. All of the other subsequent names in that row had faces. Karl Sandford's did not. His face had been neatly excised.

63

"So, do we go back to the school?" Karl asked once they were all back in their car and heading west.

"I told you, I didn't see it in the school," Ryan said.

"Maybe you missed it, Ryan," Stew said.

"Yeah, son," Karl said, "you weren't exactly yourself at the time."

"Guys, I got a good look. I'll admit, I remembered zilch at first, but it's all coming back to me now. In fact, it *has* come back to me—all of it. I saw some pretty disturbing shit, but I didn't see anything that resembled a heart."

"At the risk of sounding cynical here, how on Earth would we even know what a two-hundred-year-old heart would look like?" Stew asked.

Ryan frowned. It was a good point. "Samantha said it was preserved," he said.

"Yeah, but preserved from two hundred years ago?" Stew said. "I would venture to say that preservation methods have become somewhat more advanced since then."

"Well, it has to be at least *partially* intact," Ryan said. "Carol's been getting some pretty fucking good mileage out of the thing."

Stew took his eyes off the road for a second and gave Ryan a disapproving glance.

Ryan knew what it meant. "Look, Stew, I'm worked up, and I'm scared shitless, all right? And when I'm worked up and scared shitless, I fucking curse. Deal with it, please."

Stew put both eyes back on the road and said nothing.

"So, does that mean we can definitely say that the heart is not in the boiler room?" Karl asked.

"All I can tell you is this: I saw every picture of every child murdered in that fucked-up 'altar' of hers. They lined the walls like celebrities in a teenager's room, for Christ's sake. I saw symbols and objects that I couldn't even begin to explain. I saw my name. I saw Trish's name. I saw John's picture. They're hazy sometimes, but I saw them. I saw crazy, crazy shit. Maybe I saw the heart, and maybe I didn't. But my gut tells me it isn't there. I think Samantha was probably right: The thing's too valuable to her not to keep it close. Maybe she carries it around with her somehow." Ryan gave an incredulous snort and chuckle. "I can't believe three grown men are having a rational discussion about the location of some two-hundred-year-old voodoo heart."

"Nevertheless…" Stew said.

"My guess is her home," Karl said.

"If it *is* in her home, how do we get it?" Stew asked. "I mean, do we break in and tie her up like criminals? Tear the place apart?"

"Screw it," Ryan said. "I'm calling Rebecca again."

"Why?" Stew asked.

"Maybe she'll *let* us in."

"And then what?"

"I don't know—" He gave the incredulous snort and chuckle again. "Start looking for a two-hundred-year-old fucking voodoo heart, I guess."

"And if Carol's there?" Stew asked.

"I'm good with the tying-her-up-like-criminals thing if you guys are."

Stew tightened his grip on the wheel and shocked both Ryan and Karl with: "Fuck it. Call Rebecca."

64

"Hello?"

"Rebecca, it's me again," Ryan said.

"I tried calling you back," she said. "You turned your phone off, didn't you?"

"Yeah."

"Why?"

"I was upset, I guess."

"I'm sorry. It just felt like the right thing to…I don't know. Did you understand where I was coming from?"

"I did. But I want you to listen to me for a minute, okay? I totally understand why you did what you did. If I was in your shoes, I probably would have done the same thing. Some pretty fucked-up things have been happening to me these past few weeks, and I've been trying to make sense of them all. Obviously it's been making me act like a whacko, no question, and I'm not even sure what to believe lately. But I *am* certain of two things. One is that I care for you very much. *Very* much. Of all the crazy shit that I've been experiencing these past few weeks, you are definitely not one of them. If anything, our time together has kept me sane."

"Ryan—"

"*Two*—and this is not me being a whacko here; please take my word on this, for whatever that means to you anymore—I have this incredibly strong belief that something very bad is going to happen soon."

"Bad?"

"At the school. Something very bad is going to happen again at the school."

"Like what? Another suicide?"

"Maybe. Maybe worse."

Ryan heard a deep sigh of frustration on her end.

"I know…there I go again, talking all crazy, but I need you to try to believe me on this. Please, Rebecca."

"Why were you asking me all those questions about my dad?"

How to play this?

"Curiosity, I guess. We never really talked about him much, and I noticed there weren't many pictures of him around the house. If we were heading towards something special, then I wanted to know everything about you."

Weak.

"But you only started asking all those questions *after* I told you I wanted to end it."

Shit.

"Maybe I thought there was still a chance for us."

"That's a lie. It was something else."

Shit, shit.

"Okay, fine—maybe I had other reasons." And then Ryan saw an opportunity. Quickly, he added: "Maybe we shouldn't discuss this with your mother in the house. I don't want her to hear our conversation. It might upset her." *And make the crazy bitch kill me sooner than later,* he added privately.

"She's not here."

Yes.

"Where is she?"

"I don't know."

"She didn't say?"

"No. In fact she was acting pretty weird before she left."

Ryan felt his pulse quicken, blood thumping in his ears. "Weird how? What do you mean?"

"I was out on the deck sneaking a smoke. She had been in her room with the door closed awhile, so I figured she was napping or talking to my dad or something and that it was safe…"

Talking to her dad?

"…but then her door opened, and I kinda ducked out of sight so she wouldn't see me, you know? She left the house without telling me where she was going. Left without even saying goodbye. She was carrying a shoebox. She had this…*look* on her face. She seemed very preoccupied with something."

"What was in the shoebox?"

"No idea. I went into her room after and found an old yearbook under her bed. It was kinda half-sticking out like she had just been reading it and tossed it under there after. At least that's what I thought."

"Yearbook?"

"Yeah. An old Highland yearbook. I was curious and started flipping through it. Your buddy Karl the janitor's picture had been cut out of it. I thought that was kind of odd."

Ryan's pulse quickened further still, thudding in his ears like tom-toms. "What did you mean when you said you thought your mom was talking to your dad? I don't get that."

Rebecca's voice grew softer. "You know my mom doesn't like to keep pictures of my dad in the house."

"Yeah?"

"But she does have his remains in a big urn on the mantel in her bedroom. She acts as though they aren't even there and hardly ever discusses them with me, but sometimes at night I can hear her whispering, and I just *know* she's talking to him. I guess it's her own little coping mechanism. Her secret. So, I show her that respect and leave it alone. I never mention it."

Jesus, it's in the urn. The fucking heart is in her dead father's urn.

"Rebecca, I need to see you."

"I don't think that's a good idea."

"I *need* to see you, Rebecca. Please. Can I come over?"

A pause.

"Rebecca?"

"I don't think that's a good idea."

"Rebecca, *please.*"

"I'm sorry." She hung up.

Ryan immediately called her back. Straight to voicemail. Now it was apparently she who'd turned off her phone.

"*Fuck!*" Ryan screamed.

"*What?*" Stew said.

Ryan ignored him. Tried calling back again. Straight to voicemail again. "God *dammit!*"

"*What?!*" Stew yelled.

Ryan sighed, dropping the phone into his lap. "It *is* at her house. She keeps it in a big urn that supposedly holds her dead husband's ashes."

"Rebecca told you that?"

"Of course not. But she did tell me that she hears her mother whispering to the damn thing in the middle of the night. Rebecca thinks her mother is whispering to her dead father, talking to him out of grief. But why the hell would she be whispering to the husband she killed?"

"Guilt?" Karl offered.

Ryan frowned back at him. "It's not *guilt*, Karl. It's not even the poor guy's ashes; I'd bet the house on it. She's whispering—chanting, praying, I don't fucking know—to Helen Tarver's heart."

"But to keep it in an urn that's supposed to hold her husband's ashes? Isn't that risky?"

"No. Much as it pains me to say, it's freaking brilliant. Who peeks in on the ashes of a loved one? The damn thing is literally hiding in plain sight."

"My God," Karl murmured in back.

"Then we go to her place right now and grab it," Stew said. "I heard you say the mother wasn't home, so we go *now*."

"Hang on a sec," Ryan said. "Rebecca said her mother left the house in a hurry, without saying goodbye. Apparently she was carrying a shoebox filled with God knows what. Guarantee you she's heading to the school, to her altar."

"Why?"

"Because along with God knows what in that shoebox, there is one thing I'm certain it contains. A photo of Karl."

"*Me?*"

Ryan told them about the yearbook Rebecca found. Karl moaned.

Ryan said: "We need to split up."

65

Carol Lawrence knelt before her altar, her incantations finished, the photo of Karl (drying blood of the rat smeared onto Karl's face in a precise pattern that would ensure he would suffer a brain aneurysm in the very near future) at her side.

Carol carefully lifted the photo by the edges and pinned it on the wall next to Barbara's. She turned to a small mirror on the opposite wall and caught a glimpse of her reflection. The flickering candlelight in the chamber cast shadows around the hollow contours of her cheekbones and eyes, making her face—she believed—resemble a skull. Death. The joy she felt was exquisite.

66

"*Me?*" Karl said again. "How the hell does she know about me?"

Stew was blunt. "Like you said, Karl; we put ourselves into her line of fire. It was only a matter of time before she found out."

"So, what do we do? What do we do?" Karl begged.

"Like I said, we split up," Ryan said. "We need to get to Rebecca's to grab the urn, and then get to that school to stop Carol from doing whatever the hell she's planning to do with Karl's picture."

"So who goes where?" Stew asked.

"Drop me off at the school," Ryan said. "You and Karl go to Rebecca's. Break the fucking door down if you have to."

"Why should you go to the school?" Stew asked. "If anyone's got a chance of having Rebecca let them in, it's you."

"I'm already screwed, guys," Ryan said. "And, Karl—there's a good chance you're about to be screwed too."

"First time I been screwed in thirty goddamn years and it's got to be like this."

Ryan went on. "I know where her altar is. I know where to find her. I've got to try something. Hell, I'll kick the shit out of her if I have to. And weird as this sounds, maybe there's something in the school that's willing to help me—something you guys won't be able to see, but *I* will."

Stew went to say something, but Ryan wouldn't let him.

"Stew, we can't risk me having another psychotic episode on the way to Rebecca's. Like I said, I'm already screwed. The heart is the most important thing right now. We need someone strong and reliable. That's you and Karl."

Stew silently digested Ryan's logic. Then: "Fine—where does Carol live?"

"I'll tell you when we get to the school. It's not far from there. After you drop me off, do whatever you can to get that urn from Rebecca."

"What if you're wrong about the urn?" Stew asked.

"I'm not."

Karl said: "Aww man... Am I gonna die?"

67

Carol was out of her altar and climbing the basement stairs when she heard the voices. People in the school. She froze midstep, listening intently. She recognized all three voices. Heard every word they were saying. Then the faint metallic sound of—coins? Keys?—hitting the tiled floor, followed by panicked shouts from both Stew and Ryan.

But not Karl.

Carol smiled.

———————◆———————

Stew pulled into the school lot. No protestors. No cars.

"I don't see her car," Stew said. "Maybe she's not here."

"She's here," Ryan said.

Stew took a deep breath and let it out slow. Glanced over at Ryan. "'Good luck' too cliché?"

"I'll take some luck. But you need to let me in first." He patted his empty pockets. "No keys."

His school key on the same ring that held his car key, Stew killed the engine and pulled them from the ignition. He then looked back at Karl. "Be right back."

"Like hell," Karl replied. "You two ain't leaving me here alone."

All three men hurried towards the front entrance. Once inside, Ryan gave Stew and Karl directions to where Carol and Rebecca lived.

"Go get the damn thing, guys," Ryan said. "Do whatever you have to."

"Do you even *have* a plan?" Stew asked.

Ryan looked around the dimly lit lobby. Dusk had arrived, and light was fading. To Stew, it seemed as though Ryan was gathering his nerve more than looking for anything in particular.

"The boiler room," Ryan finally said. "If she's anywhere, she's down there. At least I hope."

"The basement door to the boiler room will be locked," Karl said, rummaging through his pockets and producing a large ring of keys. He pinched one of the keys between his thumb and index finger, worked it off the ring, and handed it to Ryan.

"Thanks. Get to Rebecca's. Find that urn. Destroy that stupid heart."

Stew stepped forward and hugged Ryan hard.

"Jesus, man," Ryan said in his powerful embrace. "Why don't you hit the gym once in a while?"

Stew let go and tried acknowledging Ryan's levity with a smile. It felt all kinds of awkward on his face, the kind of reassuring smile you offered to someone on their deathbed.

Ryan turned to Karl, put a hand on his shoulder, and squeezed. Went to say something and stopped. Karl's eyes had rolled back into his head. The old man then dropped his big ring of keys and fell backwards, plank-like, onto the lobby floor, the back of his head ricocheting off the tile with a sickening crack.

Both Ryan and Stew screamed.

68

According to Carol, it couldn't have been scripted any better—Karl's aneurysm allowed her the precious time she needed to phone her daughter.

Carol crept back down into the boiler room, pulled her cell, and called Rebecca. It went straight to voicemail. She cursed lightly under her breath and dialed their landline. Rebecca answered on the third ring.

"Hello?"

"Becks? It's Mom."

"Mom? Why are you whispering? Everything okay?"

"No, sweetheart, it's not. I'm at the school. I came here to get some last-minute work done, and Ryan and two other men are here. They've gone crazy, Becks. I overheard them planning something really bad involving you and me."

"*What?* What are you talking about?"

"I don't have time to explain. I'm going to try to find a place to hide and call for help, but I had to warn you first. A man is on his way to our house, Becks—he's coming for your father's ashes."

"*Daddy's ashes?* Are you kidding me? What the *hell* is going on?"

"Becks, *please*—they think Daddy was *evil* or something, and they want to grab his ashes and get rid of them. That's why Ryan was asking you all those questions about your father and Aunt Samantha. I *told* you; Ryan lost his grip on reality. Didn't I tell you? Please don't let them take my husband's ashes, Becks." She feigned a crack in her voice, as though fighting back tears. "Take Daddy's urn and go. Go somewhere—*any-where*—and hide. Do it now, sweetheart. *Please.*"

"Okay, Mom, I'm going. I'm leaving right now. Do you want me to call the police?"

"No—just go, Becks. I'm calling them the second I hang up with you."

"Okay. Please be careful, Mom. I love you."

"I love you too, sweetheart."

Karl was breathing but comatose. Both Stew and Ryan had rushed to his side after his collapse, Stew attempting to lift him after checking his vital signs.

"You sure you should do that?" Ryan asked.

Both men were breathing heavily, adrenaline flooding their veins.

"Why?"

"Well, what if he's got neck trauma or something? Couldn't we make him worse?"

They both looked down at Karl. His eyes weren't open, but they weren't closed either; they were slits that only showed white. His mouth hung open. His fleshy skin was the color of salt.

"I'm not gonna leave him here on the lobby floor, Ryan. Did you hear his head hit?"

"Exactly. He might have damaged his neck. We could make it worse."

"I'm *not* leaving him out in the open like this." He pulled out his cell.

"What are you doing?"

Stew looked at Ryan as though it was obvious. "911. We need an ambulance."

"Hospital isn't going to help this, Stew. You *know* that."

"Well, then what the hell do we do?"

Ryan considered a moment. "Fine—we move him. Let's take him to the nurse's office. Lay him on one of the cots."

"Christ, Ryan, we've got to do something more than that."

"We *are* going to do something more than that. I'm going to find the psycho witch and knock her the fuck out, and you're going to go to Rebecca's and destroy that urn and whatever the hell's inside."

Stew motioned down at Karl. "You think that will undo what happened to him?"

"Banging his head? No idea. What made him fall and bang his head? We can only hope. Come on."

Both men gingerly lifted Karl and carried him to the nurse's office, placing him on a cot in one of two rooms therein. Stew lovingly rubbed Karl's bald head. "You're not going yet, brother. You're going to live to see it die. You *are.*"

Stew turned out the light and closed the door. Turned out the main lights in the nurse's office and closed that door behind them as well. Stew immediately started for the lobby. "Find the bitch," he said. "I'm gonna get that goddamn heart and feed her the fucking thing."

The hair on Ryan's arms stood. A pissed-off Stew was a frightening sight indeed.

69

The boiler room. Should he begin there as he had suggested to Stew and Karl? Common sense would say yes. Only if Carol had suspected he might be coming—a distinct possibility—she could be anywhere. If Ryan had learned one thing about Carol in the short time he'd known her, it was that she was crafty as they came. A world-class chess player always three moves ahead of her opponent. Just look at what she'd done to poor Karl. Checkmated the guy before he was even in the game.

Where then? While no high school, or even middle school, Pinewood was still a good-sized elementary school. So many places to hide.

If *she's hiding.*

(*Why wouldn't she?*)

Oh, she might be. But not for reasons of never being found.

(*Reasons for an ambush.*)

Boom.

The hair on Ryan's arms stood again.

I can handle a woman.

(*In a straight-up fight? Sure. But Carol isn't the type to play fair, is she? And let's not forget the whole black magic bullshit she has on you. For all you know, you could drop at any moment like Karl did.*)

The hairs on his arms weren't sitting anytime soon. He needed to hurry. Ryan started down the south wing towards the cafeteria.

———————◆———————

Much as it killed him, Stew did not speed to Rebecca's house. The last thing he wanted was to be pulled over and cause a delay. When he hit residential roads, where the speed limit was twenty-five miles an hour, his bladder taunted him for no good reason other than he was close and forced to go at a snail's pace.

"Here we go, baby," he soon said to himself, spotting the street sign Ryan had mentioned to him, turning onto the street and hitting his high beams without a care for any oncoming cars that might happen by. He cruised the street, repeating Ryan's directions aloud: "Pass four mail-boxes...fifth one is the one I want...number twenty-six...here we go..."

Number twenty-six was there. So was a white Honda Civic backing out of the driveway in one hell of a hurry.

———————◆———————

Rebecca hung up the phone and ran into her mother's room. Approached the mantel but did not touch the urn right away. It didn't feel right. Several times she reached for it only to pull her hands away. It was about to be the very first time she'd held the urn that contained her father's ashes. She felt the need to apologize.

"I'm sorry, Daddy." Rebecca took the urn from the mantel and held it tight to her chest, keeping it there a moment, embracing it. She felt tears coming. Again she said: "I'm sorry, Daddy."

She steadied her breathing, suppressed her emotions. Now was not the time. Rebecca hurried outside, placed the urn in the passenger seat first, made her way into the driver's seat, and started the engine.

Where to go? Her mother's panic had forced Rebecca to act without thought, but now she needed to formulate at least *some* course of action. Her mother had urged her to just take the urn and leave. Go anywhere. Just leave. Someone was coming for her. Someone her mother classified as crazy.

Crazy. Someone might be coming for her, but someone was already *with* her mother,

(*Ryan?*)

and they too were crazy. Rebecca suddenly knew one thing: she needed to help her mother. To protect her in any conceivable way she could.

She said she was calling the police. Do as she said; take the urn somewhere safe and hide.

And if the police didn't show in time? Or if perhaps she never even managed to call the police? What if the crazy people

(*Ryan??*)

got to her before she could make the call?

Rebecca put her car into reverse and gunned it out of the driveway. Her foot, heavy with panic on the accelerator, caused the car to swerve onto the lawn, and she found herself hopping the curb before screeching to a halt, instantly reaching for the urn with her right hand like a parent bracing their child before a potential accident.

And there *was*, Rebecca would suddenly discover with near paralyzing fear, a potential accident. A car was coming straight for her, high beams inexplicably on.

One of the crazy people. They were here.

70

Ryan stopped every few feet down that south wing towards the cafeteria to listen and look. The majority of the classroom doors were shut and dark inside, giving him nothing. Could she be hiding in one of them? Crouched and ready to pounce as he strolled by? No—that would mean a straight-up fight, giving him the advantage. Unless she had a weapon, of course.

A thought then hit Ryan. Should he turn around and head to his *own* classroom? If Carol, in her chesslike way of thinking, had predicted Ryan clever enough not to head immediately to the boiler room in his search, would she then assume he might head somewhere familiar in a place that was still largely unfamiliar to him?

What sense would that make? I'm here to find her, not to hole up somewhere safe and familiar.

(*Maybe you've only got it half right, then. Perhaps* she's *the one holing up somewhere safe, expecting your classroom to be the last place you would look for her. After all, we've already established that she doesn't need to lay any hands on you to do damage. Christ, for all you know, she's there now, clutching that canvas with animal blood and your own freaking cum spiraled all over your name, casting one of her stupid fucking spells.*)

Yes. Such a prospect held merit. His journey towards the cafeteria was, after all, somewhat random. Was in fact, in all honesty, an aimless start just to get his feet moving at a time when his feet felt leaden.

He would do it. He would head to his classroom. His gut told him something was there—*she* was there—waiting for him.

Ready or not, bitch; here I come.

71

Stew dove out of the way of the oncoming car, his huge body thudding onto the lawn, momentarily stealing his breath.

He had exited his car with the intentions of talking as rationally as possible given the bizarre circumstances, and he was halfway towards the car when he heard the engine roar and the tires screech, and he knew that the driver of the Honda meant to hit him if he didn't move.

The driver *had* to be Rebecca, and Carol had apparently gotten hold of her first—it was the only explanation that made sense. He would also bet his life that Rebecca had the urn with her in that car.

Stew rolled onto all fours and inhaled deep through his nose to regain his breath. The Honda was already turning out of the development, and Stew knew he was seconds from losing her. He found his feet and sprinted towards the driver's side door of his still-running car. In seconds he was speeding down the same road the Honda had turned onto, unsure of what his next move was.

––––––––––– ◊ –––––––––––

Rebecca sped down the road, steering with her left hand, her right still bracing the urn. Her mother had been right. A man had come for her, and the thought of ramming him with her car in order to escape did not even give her a moment's pause.

She needed to get to the school. She needed to make sure her mother was okay, help her in any way that she could. She entertained the idea of calling the police en route. She would say she was being followed. Was she, though? Had she lost him? She looked into her rearview mirror and saw darkness. No headlights. Should she call the police and tell them to go to the school? Her mother had told her that *she* was calling them. But what if, as Rebecca had feared earlier, her mother hadn't managed to? What if the crazy people had gotten to her first? And suppose Rebecca did call the police now? What would she say that didn't make her sound crazy herself?

You don't have to give them any backstory, girl. Just tell them to go to the school—its history is infamous to local police; ominous goings-on left and right—and that your mother is there and in danger.

But how long would *that* take? For the 911 operator to take down the report and for the police to show? And lest she forget, the school's history was infamous to police *and* locals. It was almost guaranteed that the police received more than their share of crank calls from those outraged locals after Pinewood had been erected, many understandably unstable from grief and loss, claiming who knows what? It would all be so time consuming. Her mother needed help *now*.

"*Shit!*" Rebecca cried out in frustration. She stomped the accelerator. She was nearly there.

Stew had grown up in the area surrounding Pinewood. Lived there all his life. This helped immensely as he followed Rebecca's car with his head-lights off.

He did not attempt to pass her. The girl had tried to run him over, for crying out loud. If he sped up alongside of her, urging her to pull over, the girl might damn well try to run him off the road. To Stew, the best course of action was a stealth approach, hoping to follow her unobserved.

So far he had kept up well, but she was moving fast on roads not designed for such high speeds. A few sudden turns on those compact roads—she of course was *not* using turn signals—made his tires screech, and he feared such a sound might give him away. But after a few more of those sudden turns, it became glaringly obvious to Stew as to where the Honda was heading. He breathed easier as he knew he would not have to follow so close. Stew could make it to Pinewood with his eyes closed.

72

Ryan doubled back towards the lobby and then headed west down the familiar fifth-grade wing. His footsteps were quicker now and not nearly as cautious. He passed Trish's room and did not feel sorrow. He felt a righteous fury. He would make this woman suffer for what she had done to his friend. Ryan had never hit a woman before in his life, but right now he wanted nothing more than to do it. Not just hit her, but beat the everloving crap out of her. Take his time about it, too.

And if she has a weapon?

(*What had Stew said about the heart? Feeding her the fucking thing? I'll feed her that fucking weapon first.*)

And the other thing? Her being able to hurt you without laying hands on you?

Ryan's classroom door was closed, the interior dark. He gripped the doorknob and hesitated. Was she really in there, waiting for him?

You know she is. So don't go trying to be sneaky and creep on in, giving her a chance to steel herself for the attack. Rip that damn door open, hit the lights, and storm your ass inside, give her one hell of a surprise.

Ryan did just that. He did not see Carol Lawrence anywhere in his classroom. What he *did* see froze him. Something that simply made no sense.

His classroom was a burnt and barren hole. There were no desks, no chairs. The walls were charred black and gray. Ash and rubble littered the filthy tiled floor. The faint smell of sulphur hung in the air. Ryan stood in a room that appeared to have been the victim of a terrible fire long ago.

"Do you finally see it now?" a voice behind him asked.

Ryan spun and found himself looking at Carol Lawrence. She stood in the doorway, her face both sympathetic and grave. Ryan did not lunge for her. He was too dumbfounded to even breathe.

"Do you finally see the *truth*?"

73

"Truth?" Ryan said. His righteous anger was paused, his current surroundings cancelling out all previous intentions, demanding explanation.

"Yes, Ryan, the truth." Carol stepped into the ruins of his classroom. "The truth about what we've been working on all this time. About what I've been getting you to accept, to come to terms with."

Ryan's eyes were wide and unblinking, his mouth hanging open slightly. His head throbbed, the familiar sickness stirred. He fought hard to regain his initiative.

"You're a sick woman," he said. "I know all about you."

"You know what you *want* to know about me. You have resentment towards me because I've been helping you bring something to the surface that you've been trying to keep suppressed for a very long time. It's why you've recently labeled me as your antagonist."

"What the hell are you talking about?"

"Look around you, Ryan. You're standing in a school that was burnt to the ground five years ago. You were *convinced* that a new school stood in its place. You were *convinced* that you worked there. How long have you been coming here? How many times have you stood in this classroom—your *daughter's* classroom—seeing something else entirely?"

74

Ryan's face twitched. "Daughter? I don't *have* a daughter."

"You *did* have a daughter. You lost her here. She was taken from you in this very classroom by another student."

He barked out a laugh. "*What?*"

"People often repress painful memories they can't cope with on their own, Ryan. They often fabricate alternate explanations to help them cope. You couldn't handle your daughter's death. You were a young, single father forced into counseling with me to help you manage your crippling grief. Before long, your grief was so strong that you refused to accept the truth. Your mind concocted an elaborate story as a defense mechanism to protect you from that truth. Before long, you had forgotten about your own daughter's very existence."

Ryan closed his eyes and shook his head. His head throbbed; his nausea surged, flu-like. "No—no, you're fucking with me. You're inside my head, and you're fucking with me. I never had a daughter." He opened his eyes. "You're related to Helen Tarver. *You're* responsible for what happened here. Stew is real. Karl is real. Trish was real. It's *all* real. I'm…I'm dating your fucking daughter!"

"Listen to what you're saying, Ryan. Yes, those people you mentioned *are* real; they were all employed by Highland. You knew them well and were quite fond of them. Especially my 'daughter.' Rebecca Lawrence was *your* daughter's teacher. You were especially fond of her, and she you."

"Bullshit, bullshit, bullshit."

"Look around you, Ryan—" She waved a hand over the classroom, the devastation therein. "My goodness, it's all the proof you need—you're *standing* in it."

Ryan looked in all directions and then closed his eyes again. "It wasn't like this before…"

"You didn't allow yourself to *see* it like this before."

He opened his eyes again. "I saw things in this school. This is Pinewood Elementary. It used to be Highland Elementary. I *saw* things here. I know what's going on." His voice was growing desperate.

"There *was* a Highland Elementary, Ryan, but there is no Pinewood. Listen to me, please. Your daughter was murdered."

"No."

"Think about it, Ryan: even your *age* makes sense. You're not some twenty-two-year-old boy, fresh out of college and looking for a job. You're a thirty-year-old man. You were a young father with a daughter starting first grade…."

"*No.*"

"First grade—the same grade that Rebecca Lawrence taught."

"You're Carol Lawrence. Rebecca is your daughter."

"Your daughter was murdered by another student. You could not cope with the truth—"

"No."

"—and you created an alternate reality for yourself. You even believed that you yourself were a schoolteacher."

"I *am.*"

"You created an alternate reality, Ryan," she said again. "I've been trying to get you to realize what *really* happened for some time now. The more I did, the more you resisted. Eventually, you began to see me as your enemy."

"Please stop."

"You are standing in the remains of Highland Elementary. Your daughter was murdered. You have been in therapy for the past five years trying to deal with that loss. All that you knew is not the truth, Ryan." She waved her hand across the interior of the room again. "*This* is the truth."

The pounding in Ryan's head felt as though his skull might crack at any moment. He tasted bile in his throat, demanding release.

"No," he wept. "I know what's going on. I know who I am. I know what's real."

She strolled towards the chalkboard. "*This* is real—" She rapped her knuckles on the board five times—one; one, two, three; one.

Ryan dropped to his knees and pitched forward, his forehead pressed into the dirty floor. His head swam; unconsciousness felt one or two heartbeats away.

"I know what's real," he wept one last time before rolling onto his back and passing out.

Carol Lawrence smiled, turned, and exited Ryan's classroom.

75

Ryan dreamt of a little girl.

He kneels before her, and she rushes into his arms, nearly knocking him over. He teeters backwards, catching himself, laughing. The little girl then kisses him on the cheek and wraps her tiny arms around his neck, squeezing in a loving embrace.

Now Ryan watches the little girl sleep in her bed, her eyelids fluttering from a dream, her mouth slightly open, emitting shallow, tiny breaths that make the belly of her pink pajamas rise and fall. He watches her sleep for what seems like hours, treasuring the moment with impossible love.

Now Ryan walks the little girl to her first day of school. Her small, delicate hand grips his own, her palms sweaty with anxiety as Ryan walks her to her classroom, passing children equally stuck to their parents, equally anxious for their first day.

Ryan and the little girl enter the classroom and meet the teacher—a young, pretty woman with strawberry blonde hair. She introduces herself as Miss Lawrence. Her beauty is such that Ryan takes note that it is *Miss* and not *Mrs.* Lawrence.

Ryan gets down on his knees to kiss the little girl goodbye. He sees terror in her eyes, her fear palpable. Ryan leans in to hug and kiss her again, to tell her it will all be all right, and the little girl clutches onto him as though the two were teetering on the edge of a cliff.

Ryan pries her off and assures her all will be well again. She is crying now, scared beyond reason. She tells him this. Tells him that something bad is going to happen. He assures her yet again that all is well; he will be back to get her soon.

Ryan leaves, is halfway down the hall when he hears a blood-curdling scream. He spins and runs back to the classroom. The little girl is lying on her back, eyes closed, a knife sticking out of her chest.

Ryan rushes to her side and cries out. He looks up for help, and Miss Lawrence looks down at him with disgust. "Why did you leave her if you knew this would happen?" she says.

Ryan stammers, searching for words. He then feels the little girl twitch in his arms. He looks down and sees that the girl's eyes have opened. She looks up at Ryan with the same look of fear and terror from just moments ago, only now, unable to speak, the knife taking her breath, her eyes convey something else, not unlike the same question Miss Lawrence had posed; of this Ryan was sure: *why did you leave me?*

Ryan cries out again and pulls the little girl into him. Her body goes limp, her eyes rolling back into her head. Ryan cries out again, apologizes profusely, begs for her to come back.

And she does come back. It all comes back. The scene begins anew: Ryan hugging and kissing the little girl goodbye in the classroom once again. Her look of terror is like before. Her words that she is afraid and that something bad is going to happen are as before. And Ryan assures her all will be well and leaves as before. And then the blood-curdling scream, spinning him on the spot, Ryan rushing into the classroom and seeing the little girl lying on the floor with a knife in her chest, taking her into his arms and crying out, looking up for help, Miss Lawrence looking down on him with disgust and asking, "Why did you leave her if you knew this would happen?", the little girl looking up at him, unable to talk, her eyes asking *why did you leave me?* before she dies in his arms as before.

And then it starts over again, and again after that, each time eroding the layers of Ryan's sanity.

One floor below, back at her altar, the director was directing again, kneeling and sitting back on her heels, her eyes rolled back white, seemingly unable to see, but seeing all too well—seeing the dream she was directing with exquisite glee.

Behind her, Ryan's canvas hung on the wall. On that canvas was something new. Underneath the spirals of dried chicken's blood and semen across his name was a crude line drawing: a little girl with a red dot in the center of her chest.

Carol Lawrence was now quite sure that if Ryan woke up, and she highly doubted that he would, his mind would be far, far gone.

76

Carol Lawrence left her altar and now walked through the deserted hall-ways of Pinewood Elementary. She poked her head into Ryan's classroom to ensure he was where she had left him—and he was. She smiled as she watched him twitch and whimper in what was now a fetal ball on the tile floor. She blew him a kiss, left his classroom, and then dialed her daughter's cell phone number as she walked towards the lobby.

"*Mom?*" Rebecca answered with what was practically a yell.

"I'm here, sweetheart. I'm here."

"Are you okay?"

"I'm okay. Where are you?"

"I'm thirty seconds from the school. I'll be right there."

Carol frowned. She had explicitly told her to go someplace safe. Would Stew be following her?

"Sweetheart, I told you to go somewhere and *hide*."

"I know, I just—"

"It's okay—I understand. Do you have your father's ashes with you?"

"Yeah, I've got them. But you were right—someone *did* come look-ing for them. I got away, though."

Carol closed her eyes and smiled, exhaling slowly.

"He might be following me though, Mom. We should call the police."

"I already did, sweetheart," Carol lied. "Come here now—it's safe. Bring the urn with you and be very careful with it, please."

"What about Ryan and his friends?"

"They're gone. They left in a hurry for some reason. Everything's okay, I promise. Just come to the main entrance. I'll be waiting for you."

———— ◆ ————

The first thing Carol did when Rebecca met her at the main entrance was take the urn from her. Once the urn was secured to her chest with her left arm, she reached forward with her right and hugged her daughter.

"I'm so glad you're safe, honey. Are you okay?"

Rebecca nodded and then looked warily around the dark lobby. "You're sure they're gone?"

"Yes, honey, I'm sure. But there's always a chance they could come back. So I want you to—"

"You called the police, right?"

"Yes, I did. But listen to me: I can't guarantee the police will get here soon, and Ryan and his friends may come back. I want you to hide until the police arrive."

"I'm not leaving you."

"Rebecca, please!"

Rebecca recoiled, her mother's sudden fury uncharacteristic.

"I want you to *hide*, do you understand me? I am going to go put your father's ashes somewhere safe. I do *not* want you to move from wherever you are hiding until the police get here. Do you understand?"

Rebecca's head bobbed, her face innocent like a child's.

"Good. I'm sorry I yelled, sweetheart. It's just…I'm afraid. I'm worried about your father's remains."

Rebecca nodded again, still mute like the scolded child.

"That's my good girl," Carol said. "Find someplace safe and stay out of sight. I'll call you when the police arrive."

Rebecca finally spoke, her voice soft and tentative. "Where will *you* be?"

"I'll be okay, honey; I promise."

Carol turned and left with the urn. Before long, she was gone.

Rebecca spun slowly in the lobby, eyes going all over. Where to hide? Her eyes settled on the nurse's office. She hurried towards it and entered. Before her was the main desk, beyond that, the nurse's station. To her right and left were doors, each leading to a room with a cot; she remembered this much from the tour that had come with orientation. She would be safer in one of the cot rooms; out here she was in plain sight. Speaking of plain sight, she thought it wise to hit the lights. Even with the door shut, someone in the darkened lobby might notice the light on under the door. And wasn't it possible that that someone

(*Ryan???*)

might be here now, looking for her? That they'd arrived a second after she'd closed the nurse's office door behind her?

Rebecca hurried towards the wall and turned off the light. Total blackness in the nurse's office now. She closed her eyes and tried to envision the precise outlay of the office she'd just gleaned seconds before. Took short cautious steps forward, hands outstretched and aimed slightly downwards, probing, looking for the main desk.

Her toes found it before her hands did, the big toe of her right foot banging the leg of the desk hard enough to shift it—she could hear the subtle squeal of metal on tile—and hard enough to hurt. She cursed lightly.

Rebecca then bent forward at the waist and placed both hands on the desk. It felt good, gave her a sense of security.

Okay, first leg of the journey is done, she thought. *Now—left room or right?* And then a second thought: *Does it really matter? Pick one, and quickly.*

She went left, again groping blindly, hands outstretched.

No toe casualty this time; her hands found the door first. She opened the door and then closed it behind her. Got down on all fours—and this too gave her a better sense of security, being so low to the ground, the stability of moving on four wheels instead of two—and crawled slowly forward, one hand out in front, oscillating back and forth, searching for the cot.

She soon found one of the cot's legs and the ample space beyond, underneath the cot. Flat to her belly now as she wormed her way beneath the cot, and soon, this too gave her a better sense of security. And why not? It was almost cliché—hiding from the boogeyman under the bed.

She lay there, flat on her stomach, chin propped beneath both hands. She slowed her breathing to minute breaths from her nose, keen to block out any noise that may prevent her from hearing any goings-on in the lobby. Hoping such goings-on would be the sounds of men and women entering the building, claiming to be police. Hoping it might then be her mother's voice calling for her, telling her everything was okay, that it was safe to come out of hiding.

The absolute last thing Rebecca had hoped to hear was a broken snore coming from the cot above her.

77

Rebecca screamed.

She banged her head on the metal frame of the cot while scurrying out from beneath it and didn't feel a thing, fear anesthetizing her.

On her feet now, she lunged blindly for the door, colliding with it, groping for the handle, finding it, cranking it, ripping the door open and darting out into blackness, making a hard right towards the main door of the nurse's office that led out to the lobby, colliding too with that door, banging her shoulder hard, again not feeling anything, groping frantically for a handle again, finding it again, ripping the door open again and rushing out into the lobby and into the immediate arms of a powerful man.

———— ♦ ————

Stew took hold of Rebecca around the waist with his left arm and clasped a firm hand over her mouth with his right. She screamed all the same, fought and struggled, and Stew clamped down harder, squeezed her waist tighter, spoke quickly and urgently in what was a loud whisper into her ear.

"Listen to me very carefully, Rebecca. My name is Stew Taylor. I am the gym teacher here at Pinewood. I taught at Highland for several years before that. We have actually met before, but only briefly. Do you remember?"

Rebecca stopped struggling, stopped screaming, clearly realizing the futility of trying to escape Stew's hold on her. She eventually nodded, Stew's hand still covering her mouth.

"Good. I don't have time for small talk, so I'm afraid I'll have to be very curt with you. I ask for your forgiveness in advance. Ryan is hurt. He's unconscious in his classroom. The man lying on the cot in the nurse's office is Karl Sandford, the janitor at Pinewood. I believe you know him too. He is also hurt and unconscious. Your mother is responsible for this. She is not who she appears to be. We are not here to hurt you *or* her; we're only here to stop her and save future lives."

Rebecca remained quiet and still. This concerned Stew, made him feel as though she may be playing possum, lulling him into a false sense of security so that he might let go of her so she could make her escape.

"I don't expect you to buy this right away, Rebecca, but I *will* ask you to use common sense. Why do you think your mother wanted that urn so badly?"

Rebecca finally spoke, mumbling into Stew's palm. He immediately pulled his hand away but kept a firm grip around her waist.

"Those are my father's ashes," she said. "My mother said you and Ryan wanted to destroy them."

"We did not want to destroy your father's ashes," Stew said. "In fact, we *couldn't* destroy his ashes, and do you know why?"

Rebecca shook her head.

"Because your father's ashes aren't *inside* that urn."

Rebecca tried looking over her shoulder at Stew. "What the hell are you talking about?"

"Bear with me here, all right? There's something else inside that urn—something that means a *heck* of a lot more to your mother than your father's remains."

"What?"

"A heart."

"A *heart*?"

"Yes."

"Like a *real* heart? A *person's* heart?"

"Yes."

"You're crazy."

"Have you ever looked inside the urn?"

"Of course not. Who looks at the ashes of a loved one?"

Stew instantly flashed on Ryan's similar sentiment: *Much as it pains me to say, it's freaking brilliant. Who peeks in on the ashes of a loved one? The damn thing is literally hiding in plain sight.* And it was a damned good point. Stew made up a quick lie on the spot.

"Lots of people. Many request that their ashes be sprinkled somewhere important to them after they've passed on." And this was also a damned good point, one he hadn't thought of when Ryan had expressed his. Stew was proud of the lie, in spite of the situation's gravity.

"Well, my father didn't want his ashes sprinkled anywhere, at least as far as I know."

"Nevertheless…"

"So what are you saying? Are you saying my mother has a *human heart* in my father's urn?" She snorted. "Why the hell—"

"It's the preserved heart of a very bad person from hundreds of years ago. It's a source of strength for your mother. She uses it to…" *To what? How to say it?* "…to get people to do things…to commit suicide…to make children murder children."

"This is ludicrous. You're trying to tell me my mother is some kind of witch?"

"I don't know what to call her. But she *is* responsible for multiple murders…including your father's."

Rebecca started struggling again. "*Let me go! You're fucking crazy!*"

Stew placed a hand over her mouth and tightened his hold on her waist again. He put his lips to her ear and in that loud whisper again: "*Stop it and use your head, child!*" He then dragged her into the nurse's office and hit the lights. Walked into the cot room on the left and hit those lights. Pointed down at a still very unconscious and chalk-white Karl. "Who did that to Karl?" Rebecca gaped down at Karl. Stew then released his hold on her waist and took her by the wrist, dragging her back out into the lobby. He pulled her close so she could see the severity in his eyes, pointed towards the fifth-grade wing. "Go on down and check out your boyfriend in his classroom—it looks like he's being cooked from the inside out. I tried *everything* to wake him. Who did that to him, you think?"

Rebecca started to say something, but Stew went on.

"Your mother knows why we're here, and she's trying to stop us. She stops *anyone* who is a threat to her. Is it a coincidence that your father died when he became born again? He was a threat to her, Rebecca. He *knew* what she was into, and he wanted her to *stop*."

Rebecca had closed her eyes, was shaking her head with every word Stew spoke. Stew's frustration grew. He tightened his hold on her wrist enough to cause her to wince from the pressure and open her eyes.

"Figure it out for yourself then, goddammit! Go find your mother! Ask her where the urn is. Ask her why it was so important for you to bring it here."

"It's her husband's remains," Rebecca protested. "She didn't want them to be destroyed."

"*Then bluff her!*" Stew yelled. He immediately caught himself and went back to a loud whisper. "Tell her you already *looked* inside the damn urn. Ask her why there was a fucking heart in there instead of your father's remains."

"I'm not going to lie to my mother."

Stew gritted his teeth. *She's in the boiler room. In her altar. She has to be. It would be the only place she felt safe to take the heart. Drag her daughter down there and* demand *she show herself. End this shit* now.

Stew started to drag Rebecca down the hall, towards the boiler room. "You and I are going for a little walk, child. You need to see for yourself."

78

Carol Lawrence was on all fours, crawling out of the small square entrance behind the great boiler that led to her altar, when she suddenly froze halfway. The basement lights had come on; someone was coming down the stairs. Before Carol could get to her feet, she spotted Stew Taylor and her daughter roughly ten feet away, watching her. Stew gripped Rebecca's arm, but she was not struggling. She was transfixed by her mother, by the mysterious hole in the wall she was crawling out of.

"Mom?" Rebecca said, eyes going from her mother to the square hole in the wall, then back to her mother again. Carol did not appear to have the urn with her.

My God, Stew thought. *That's it. That's the entrance to her chamber, her altar. The whole damn time, that seemingly innocuous steel panel in the wall was the entrance to her altar* the whole damn time.

Stew knew in his bones that she had just placed the urn safely inside and was now exiting, hopefully unobserved. *Well, tough shit, lady. You've been observed. You've been* observed. *Try talking your way out of this one.* He contemplated rushing forward, subduing Carol, and then crawling inside that chamber to grab the urn himself. Only he stopped when he noticed the bewildered look on Rebecca's face, the myriad of questions it held. This needed playing out first.

Carol got to her feet. "My God, sweetheart, are you all right?"

Rebecca nodded, but could not take her eyes off the square opening, its passage, at the base of the wall her mother had just emerged from.

"Take your hands off my daughter, Stew—the police will be here any minute," Carol said.

"You didn't call the police," Stew said. "Not yet anyway. I'm sure you would have called them after you were finished with us—but not now. Not when there are so many loose ends to tie up first."

"Mom?" Rebecca said again. It seemed all she was capable of for the moment.

"It's okay, Becks. Let my daughter go, Stew. Becks, come over here."

"I'll let her go, Carol. But I've got one little condition first. Let her look inside her father's urn. Better yet—let her take a good long look inside that little cubbyhole you've got there. I'm sure she'll find it all very enlightening."

Carol's face darkened. "There's nothing in there. I'm trying to hide my husband's remains, which you sick bastards are trying to take from me."

Stew actually smiled. "Okay then, you've got my word—I won't touch those remains. Just show your daughter. Let her see those remains for herself."

Carol's nostrils flared, her eyes like daggers on Stew. "My daughter doesn't *want* to look at her father's ashes. And I'm certainly not going to force her to look now because a crazy man like you is making her—"

"I already looked," Rebecca said.

Carol's eyes snapped onto her daughter, wide and intense. "You looked?"

Hot damn, she's taking my advice. She's bluffing her mother.

"Yes."

Carol started inching towards them. "*When* did you look?"

"On the drive over here."

"And yet you never mentioned it earlier."

"No."

"You looked inside on the way over here, and yet you never mentioned it. I see."

"I was…I was scared…confused."

"And why was that?"

"Because I didn't see Daddy's ashes…"

"No? What *did* you see?"

Rebecca hesitated.

Say it, child.

"What did you *see*, Rebecca?" Carol said again.

"A heart."

Fucking hallelujah.

Carol was eerily composed. Stew didn't like it.

"A *heart*?"

"Yes. An old one. It was preserved."

"Are you sure that's what you saw, Rebecca?"

"I—yes."

"I see. Well, perhaps you better look again."

Stew frowned. It was the very last thing he had expected Carol to say.

"Come over here, Rebecca—it's time we put this nonsense to rest once and for all. Oh, and might I add," she said to Stew, "that when this is all over, I suggest you and your friends find a very good lawyer."

"My friends are likely dead," Stew said. "As I'm sure you know."

Carol ignored his comment, kept her gaze on Rebecca.

"Come over here, Rebecca," she said again. "You want to see for yourself, don't you? Come on over here; I'll show you what's inside the urn myself. I'll show you that what you *think* you saw was nothing more than your mind playing tricks on you, fueled by the nonsense this crazy man and your boyfriend have been poisoning it with."

"It's a trick," Stew said to Rebecca. "She has the ability to alter perception. She'll make you see the goddam Easter bunny inside that urn if she wants to. Don't do it."

Rebecca ignored him. "Where is it?" she asked her mother.

Carol pointed to the square opening at the base of the wall, the narrow passage beyond. "In there. A safe place I happened to discover years ago at Highland. It survived the fire. The urn is in there. Your father's *remains* are in there."

Rebecca looked at Stew. Stew shook his head at her.

This is playing out all sorts of wrong.

"Come on, sweetheart," Carol beckoned. "Let's get this over with." She pointed at Stew. "*You* stay put. If you have any decency in your body, you'll *stay put*. This is strictly a family matter."

Let her go and see for herself. The crazy bitch may be able to alter perception of what's inside that urn, but the entire contents of her lair that Ryan spoke of?

(*Why not? There's no guidebook for how this insanity works.*)

Okay, fine then—let her go. Let the girl see Disneyland inside that lair if that's what Carol is capable of managing. You know the truth, and if she alters Rebecca's perception of that truth, it doesn't change a damn thing. In fact, better Rebecca not be here when you rush the bitch.

Stew released his hold on Rebecca's arm. She slid slowly out of his grasp and started towards her mother. Carol smiled and gestured towards the square entrance at the base of the wall. "Go on, sweetheart," she said lovingly. "It's all right; you'll see."

Rebecca got down on all fours and poked her head inside the opening, pausing there. "It's dark," she said. "I can't see anything."

"Go on, Becks—it's a straight shot all the way through. The passage opens up after ten feet or so. You'll be in a room. In that room there will be a flashlight to your immediate left along the wall."

Rebecca looked up at her mother. Her face was a frightened child's.

"It'll be okay, sweetheart," Carol said.

Without further delay, Rebecca began to crawl into darkness.

"I heard what you said upstairs in the lobby earlier," Carol said to Stew. "About feeding me a heart?"

"That's right. I hope you're hungry."

"I'm afraid I'm not." Calmly, Carol bent, retrieved the steel panel, and then clicked it into place, sealing her daughter inside the chamber. If she had made any sudden movements, Stew would have pounced. But she hadn't; she'd simply bent and secured the panel back in place as casually as you please.

Rebecca's scream from within was instantaneous. Her only source of light on her journey deeper into the wall had been the square of light behind her from the boiler room. Now it had been sealed off.

Stew rushed towards Carol—and then stopped on a dime. The boiler room was suddenly black, all source of light gone. The faint laughter of Carol nearby.

All two hundred and sixty pounds of Stew Taylor was terrified.

79

Stew crept forward, arms outstretched and waving in all directions so as not to collide with anything in the blackness of the boiler room, chief of them Carol. Or maybe it would be good to collide with her. He was confident that if he could get his hands on her, he could choke her right out, even in the dark…assuming she didn't have a weapon.

And you know she does.

Stew's terror climbed a notch. He continued to carefully shuffle forward, Rebecca's muffled screams from within Carol's chamber his guide to the precise spot behind the boiler. He soon found the boiler and then, beyond that, the wall. He ran both hands down the wall until they settled on the steel panel, his fingers locating the edges, working furiously on those edges in a bid to rip the panel free. Rebecca's screams grew louder, and Stew worked faster. Even with his considerable strength, it was a futile task. He would need a crowbar or something similar to pry the damn thing off.

Look for one?

(*In the dark?*)

All of Stew's attention was momentarily focused on freeing Rebecca. None of it was on Carol. This revelation came a second too late. Stew felt her presence behind him, an icy feeling of dread that tickled his very soul. He leapt to his feet and spun. His eyes, growing somewhat accustomed to the dark, spotted Carol's silhouette before him, but he did not react. Could not react. The red eyes

(*they're red. RED!*)

that burned like embers held him whole, paralyzing him with terror he did not think capable of being surpassed until now.

An angry hiss, not unlike a cat's, and the red eyes jumped with movement, a searing pain following as something sliced into Stew's abdomen. He cried out and clutched his stomach with both hands, felt the immediate dampening of his shirt from his own blood. He looked down at his stomach but of course could see nothing. He looked up again, and the red eyes—the only absolute in the cruel darkness—were gone.

A second angry hiss from behind him now. Waist level. He spun towards it. The red eyes were there. He went for them and got nothing. Felt the blade slice into his hamstring a second after, bringing him down to one knee. He cried out again.

Laughter echoing all around him now, as though coming from multiple spots at once. He looked up, desperate to spot the red eyes. They were gone again. But the laughter was still there. She was still there.

⚬ ◆ ⚬

Rebecca—who until now had been curled into a tight ball while she cried for help—slowly uncoiled herself within the walls of the chamber. She could hear Stew's cry of pain. And then a second cry, this one more intense. Something was happening to him. Someone was *hurting* him. A reluctant logic: who else could it be besides her mother? *She* had been the one to wall her in. Was it to protect her from Stew? He had been no immediate threat. Did, in fact, seem keen on having Rebecca venture into the wall to retrieve the urn—it had all been his idea from the start. So why had her mother walled her in? Why was she now attacking Stew? And how *could* she attack Stew with any measure of success? She stood no chance against such a man. None of it made sense.

Rebecca crawled throughout the cramped confines of the chamber, went to the wall where her mother had assured her a flashlight would be. It was not there. She continued to search blindly on her hands and knees, searching for something, *anything* that might be a source of light.

She felt many things, all of them unfamiliar, and released them immediately to continue her search. Her hands soon stumbled upon something that was familiar, and as she snatched what felt like a very small cardboard box and felt the rough strip on one side, shook the contents and heard the rattle of wooden matches therein, she knew she had found her source of light.

Rebecca immediately slid open the box and removed a match, blindly fingering the side of the box with the rough strip with one hand to guide her other in lighting the match.

There were plenty of things within those walls that Rebecca could have illuminated with that first match. She happened to illuminate her father's picture. Her father's picture with a necklace of small needles encircling his throat. The word "stroke" written on his torso in something red. Rebecca could only stare at the picture in disbelief, the flickering light from the match adding ominous impact to a moment that needed none.

The match died, and she lit another, and her father was there again in that wavering light of the match. The needles. The word "stroke" written on his torso in something

(*blood*)

red. Rebecca started to cry. She caressed the parts of the photo that were not desecrated. The match went out, and she lit another, forcing herself to look away from her father's picture and take inventory of the room's remaining contents. And she only cried harder when she did. The things she saw—the *horrors* she saw.

The match died, and she lit another. As though scripted, the last item she spotted in the far corner of the room was the very reason for her trek. It was the urn.

80

Rebecca's fourth match had maybe twenty seconds left, but that was enough time for her to locate the small entrance at the base of the chamber wall from which she'd emerged. She placed the urn inside, blew out the match, stuffed the box of matches into her waistband, and crawled on in. Once inside the narrow passage, she managed to turn herself around so that her feet were leading the way, the urn now carefully balanced on her lap. From there, she scooted forward on her butt, one hand holding the urn tight to her lap, reached the end of the passage where the panel was still blocking her exit, brought her knees up, and then thrust her legs forward, soles of her shoes banging the panel. The panel did not give out entirely on the first blow, but it did give. Two more powerful thrusts and the panel came free.

Rebecca crawled out into total darkness and stood, urn gripped tight in both hands. "Stew?" she called.

Nothing for a moment—and then her mother's voice: "Rebecca?"

Rebecca readied a second bluff. "Mom? Is that you?"

The voice grew closer, maybe twenty feet away. "Yes, it's me. Are you all right?"

"I can't see, Mom. I need to show you something. I need to show you something really important, but I can't see."

An excruciating pause. Rebecca could almost hear her mother thinking, considering, judging.

The boiler room came to life with light. Rebecca squinted as her eyes tried to acclimate. She did not see her mother in her immediate field of vision.

"Mom?"

Carol rounded the corner, her footsteps slow, casual, confident.

"You wanted to show me something, Rebecca?" No "sweetheart," no "honey," no "Becks." *Rebecca.* Her full name was always reserved for times of seriousness or scolding. Now it seemed to carry a different connotation, as though her mother was politely addressing a stranger she'd just met. It frightened Rebecca that much more.

Rebecca brandished the urn. "I know what this is…I know what you've been doing…" She bit down on her inner cheek to keep from crying. "…I know you killed Daddy."

Carol's expression was ice. "Rebecca, you have an opportunity in front of you now that no other person in this world has. You have the opportunity to gain infinite power." She pointed a finger at her daughter. "It's in your blood." She brought the finger to her own chest. "It's in *our* blood."

Rebecca kept quiet.

"You have the opportunity to attain any and all you desire, Rebecca. The opportunity to feel the unparalleled rapture you can only feel when you consume the essence of something so pure and unspoiled…and I can give it to you. I can *teach* you."

"You kill children."

"I've never killed a child in my life."

"You *made* them kill each other."

Carol shrugged. "Semantics."

"That's sick."

Carol shrugged again. "Am I any different than the puppet master people call God? God kills all the time, and he is indiscriminate in his choosing. Young, old, *devout.* And it is the devout fools that perhaps he takes the greatest pleasure in killing, for they continue to worship him after, convincing themselves that his choosing to take their loved ones was all part of some grander plan." She laughed. "It really is all so amusing."

"You're not God."

"No—nor do I want to be. But I have embraced his way. I too can kill indiscriminately to feel his exquisite sense of power. And my rewards are far greater than any sense of power. It *is* power. A power that grants me…" She closed her eyes and exhaled with perverse delight; a woman on the cusp of an orgasm. "…oh, Rebecca, the ecstasy that power grants me…"

"Why did you kill my father?"

Carol opened her eyes. "Again, I should remind you that I've never technically killed anyone—except maybe poor Stew just now." She giggled.

"Stop it, Mom."

Carol cocked her head. "All right then. Your father was a traitor, Rebecca. A hypocritical traitor. He delighted in wickedness and then ultimately asked forgiveness from God for that delight. He asked forgiveness when everything else in his life was in chaos, and isn't chaos the true nature of man? It certainly isn't order. Your father never went to God out of true faith. He went out of fear—no different than an atheist asking, *begging*, for salvation on his deathbed. What God would embrace such hypocrisy? I do believe God would actually *thank* me for taking him as easily as I did." She laughed.

"I can't believe this. I can't believe *you*."

"I know it's painful for you now, Rebecca. But if you let me show you…if you allow me to let you *taste* what's possible…"

"What did you do to Ryan?"

"Oh, please don't tell me you're shedding any tears for a boy you've only known a few weeks, Rebecca."

Rebecca said nothing.

"He was a threat, Rebecca. He had that damned ability to *see*, just like the others. Though I must admit, he was a hell of a lot tougher than the others. I thought he was mine as soon as I obtained his semen after you two snuck out onto the deck for a cigarette the other night. Thank God"—she chuckled softly at her own hypocrisy—"for the boy's drunken carelessness of leaving a used condom on the floor. Pretty classy fella, Rebecca, I must say." Her face then darkened. "Oh, and I must also say, I'm very disappointed you started smoking again. It's *weak*, Rebecca. It shows weakness. But we'll make you strong again."

Rebecca hung her head and bit down on her cheek again to keep from crying. It was futile. Tears rolled down her cheeks against her will.

"Well, then I'm sure you're going to love this." Rebecca set the urn on the floor and dug into her back pocket, where her crumpled back of Marlboro Lights still hid. She plucked one from the pack and placed it between her lips, pulled the box of matches from her waistband, lit one, lit her cigarette, and inhaled deeply.

Carol looked on without expression, seemingly refusing to give her daughter the satisfaction of visible disappointment.

Rebecca took a final drag, long and slow, and then flicked the cigarette at her mother. Carol flinched and turned away. Rebecca quickly plucked another match from the box, lit it, tipped the porcelain urn over onto its side with the toe of her shoe, and then brought her heel up and then down onto the side of the urn with a mighty stomp, shattering it, keen on setting its horrific contents ablaze, for it had to have been—*had to have been*—preserved in something flammable all these years.

Only Rebecca set nothing ablaze. The match burning idly between her thumb and index finger, Rebecca set nothing ablaze because there was nothing *to* set ablaze. The urn was empty. She could only gape down at the nothing within the shattered remains of the urn before eventually lifting her head and locking eyes with her mother.

Her mother raised both eyebrows, splayed a hand—and was there not the tiniest bit of smugness in that gesture? Mockery, even?

Rebecca dropped the match to the floor, where it burned and soon died, sulphury smoke rising right after.

"It's empty," Rebecca said, dropping her gaze to the shattered remains once again. She spoke these words, not to her mother, but to herself, as though she had betrayed her own virtue.

"Empty," Carol said.

Rebecca raised her head and looked at her mother once again.

"Earlier, I overheard your partner in crime, Stew, telling Ryan he was going to feed me Helen's heart," Carol said. "I found it deliciously—pun most certainly intended—amusing. He reiterated this threat only moments ago. I told him I wasn't hungry." She licked her lips and patted her belly.

"*Oh my God...*" Rebecca slapped a hand over her mouth, sure she was going to vomit.

"From the day I started, it had always been the endgame for me, Rebecca." She explained it all so casually, as though discussing her aspirations within a sane vocation. "Believe me, it would have been far easier to do it sooner than later, only I wasn't ready. I hadn't *earned* it. I took a chance tonight." She smiled. Her eyes were red. And then they weren't. Rebecca blinked hard, certain she'd seen wrong. "I'm glad I took that chance. Helen's soul resides in me now, sweetheart…"—again, these words, so casual, as though such a perverse undertaking was an everyday thing—"and I look forward to the infinite rewards it will offer. Please, please allow me to share it with you. *Please*."

"No."

"I can undo what I did to Ryan," she said. "I can make him love you unconditionally. All memories of what has transpired over the course of these past few weeks can be erased. He will be yours and yours alone until you deem otherwise."

"What about *my* memory?"

Carol tilted her head, screwing her gaze into her daughter's, a probing, testing gaze for what she was about to say. "I can change that too."

Rebecca started to cry again. "You're crazy…"

Carol sighed and pulled her knife. "I want you to know, sweetheart, that despite what you might think of me, I take no delight in this whatsoever—" She wiped the blade free of Stew's blood onto her shirt, as though killing her daughter with a blade soiled in another's blood was disrespectful. "I love you."

Carol lunged.

Rebecca screamed.

Stew rounded the corner from where Carol had left him to die, shoved Rebecca out of the way, and met Carol's charge with a sledgehammer right cross on the point of her chin, dropping her like dead meat.

Panting, doubled over in pain, Stew spat blood on Carol's unconscious body. "That's for my boy John, you crazy bitch."

81

Rebecca and Stew did not speak at first. Both just stared down at the un-conscious Carol Lawrence, Rebecca weeping, Stew still panting, doubled over again, clutching his stomach with one hand, his hamstring with the other.

"I'm sorry I hit your mom," he said.

Rebecca turned to Stew. Took in his wounds. "Did she do that to you?"

Stew reached down and grabbed the discarded knife by Carol's side and showed it to Rebecca. She acknowledged it with a dejected nod.

Stew slid the knife into his back pocket and then turned his attention onto the shattered remains of the urn and, more importantly, the nothing therein. "Did I hear right?" he said. "Did I hear she actually *ate* the heart?"

"Yeah. My guess is that she did it while you and I were upstairs by the nurse's office. When we came down here and caught her crawling out of her…" Rebecca swallowed hard, glanced over at the boiler and the en-trance to her mother's chamber beyond. "…*whatever* the hell you call it, she must have just finished."

"My God…how does one eat a two-hundred-year-old preserved heart without getting sick?"

"She said it was always her intention—even from the very start. My guess was that she—I don't know—knew a way with all her mumbo-jumbo stuff." Rebecca snorted incredulously. "And I brought it to her…served it right up like some delivery boy."

"You had no way of knowing," Stew said.

Rebecca looked at Stew, his wounded state. "We need to get you to a hospital."

"That would be nice."

"What do we do with my mother?"

"Let's get her upstairs. Call the police for real this time."

"You sure you can lift her?" she asked, gesturing to his injuries.

"I think the two of us should be able."

Rebecca and Stew carried Carol Lawrence's unconscious body into the lobby and placed it on one of the sofas.

"She never *did* call the police, did she?" Rebecca asked.

Stew, who had quickly ducked into the nurse's office soon after laying Carol on the sofa and was now dressing his wounds with supplies he'd found there, replied: "No—I highly doubt it."

Rebecca watched Stew attend to himself. "We really need to get you to a hospital. You were unconscious for a spell, weren't you?"

Stew nodded. "Not from these, though," he said, waving a hand over his stomach and leg. "She whacked me good on my noggin with something soon after she sliced my hamstring."

"Then you could have a concussion to boot."

"Wouldn't be surprised."

Rebecca looked down at her mother. "What do you think will happen to my mom?"

Stew sighed. "I honestly don't know."

Rebecca looked away, tears welling up and then breaking free, rolling down both cheeks.

"What's going on?"

Both Stew and Rebecca spun.

It was Ryan, stumbling out of the fifth-grade wing and looking as though he'd been on one hell of a bender. He spotted Carol on the sofa. "Is that…?"

Stew nodded.

Ryan looked at Rebecca. "What are you…what is…*what the hell happened?*"

Rebecca said nothing. She didn't have to; her face said it all.

"Oh, Rebecca, I'm so…" He stopped. Looked at Carol again. "Is she…?"

"She's alive," Stew said.

"And the heart?" Ryan said. "You found the heart? You destroyed it?"

"Didn't have to," Stew said. "She ate the damn thing."

"She *what*?"

Stew didn't repeat himself, just looked at Ryan with raised eyebrows and a face that said: *Yup—crazy, huh?*

Of all the things Ryan might have said next, neither Stew nor Rebecca could have predicted what he did utter: "We have to kill her."

Simultaneously, Rebecca and Stew said: "*What?*"

"Jesus, Stew—*Samantha*," Ryan blurted. "Don't you remember what she said? The Moyers never destroyed the heart because they feared Helen Tarver's soul would be set free to inhabit another. You're telling me Carol actually *ate* the fucking thing? Do the math!"

Rebecca looked at Stew, afraid. Stew returned an uneasy glance, then turned back to Ryan, showed him his palms, and patted the air. "Whoa, whoa—slow down there, Ryan. Samantha also said the Moyers' beliefs about that were superstition."

"Then why would she eat it? Can you think of a more intimate way for her to embody Helen Tarver's soul?"

Palms still up and patting the air, Stew said: "Ryan, you're not yourself. You just had one hell of an ordeal in your classroom. I'm not really sure what happened to you in there, but you were unconscious for a while and in obvious pain." Stew paused a moment. "Do *you* remember what happened?"

"I…no. No, I don't remember. But please stop and think about—"

"No, *you* stop and think for a minute, Ryan. If Carol was still capable of wielding the heart's power, why are you awake and out here with us? Wouldn't you still be unconscious in your classroom?"

Ryan pointed at Carol. "Maybe it's because *she's* unconscious." Ryan's eyes, nervous, frantic, skittered all over the lobby, settling on the nurse's office in the distance. "What about Karl? Have you checked on Karl? Is *he* awake?"

"I haven't checked on him yet. But he banged his head on the floor pretty good when he fell, Ryan. You were there. If he's still unconscious, it's likely because of that, not because Carol is making it so."

Only Stew wasn't necessarily sure of his own convictions. Dazed as he was, Ryan's points were valid. Valid because Stew was coming to when he caught Carol's words to Rebecca before she'd attacked her: *From the day I started, it had always been the endgame for me, Rebecca. Believe me, it would have been far easier to do it sooner than later, only I wasn't ready. I hadn't earned it. I took a chance tonight. I'm glad I took that chance. Helen's soul resides in me now...and I look forward to the infinite rewards it will offer.*

"Ryan..." Stew started, but the uncertainty in his voice, in his eyes, betrayed him; Ryan's point grew more and more valid by the second. Carol had clicked off the lights in the boiler room without being anywhere *near* the damn switch. And those eyes...those *eyes*...he hadn't imagined that. Knew in the deepest recesses of his own soul that he had not, had *not* imagined that.

He flashed on Samantha's words when Ryan had asked why it was so important to keep the heart close when she kept all of her "crazy crap" that she used to carry out her rituals in the school: *Mere tools,* Samantha had said. *They enable her to carry out her rituals, but her strength—her true strength—stems from the heart. It is her conduit, her direct line to Helen Tarver's evil. Without it she has very little.*

And now she had ingested that evil. It was inside her. Believe what you will—and at this point, it was safe to say no one knew *what* to believe anymore—but was it not possible that Helen Tarver's soul was inside Carol now? Granting her infinite power far beyond what she was previously capable of?

"You know I'm right, Stew," Ryan said.

"You're not killing my mother!" Rebecca yelled.

"She's not the woman you thought she was, Rebecca," Ryan said.

"You're not killing her!" Rebecca pulled her phone. "I'm calling the police." She flipped open her phone. Frowned. Hit the power button several times and frowned some more.

"What's wrong?" Stew asked.

"It's dead," she said, still fiddling with the phone, removing the battery, snapping it back in, and then trying it again to no avail. "What the hell…"

Stew pulled his phone. It too was dead. He told them so.

"*Coincidence?!*" Ryan yelled.

Rebecca spun on him. "*Yes!*" She started towards the main office. "I'll use the school line," she said over her shoulder.

Ryan and Stew tracked her march.

"Why bother?!" Ryan called after her. "*Rebecca!*"

"*HELP ME! SOMEONE, PLEASE HELP!*" Karl's voice in the distance, crying out from within the nurse's office.

"*Karl,*" Stew said. He hurried towards the nurse's office. Opened the main door, hit the lights, and then opened the door to his left that held Karl, hit those lights. What he saw paused him like a button. Karl was still very unconscious.

82

"*HELP ME! SOMEONE, PLEASE HELP!*" Rebecca and Ryan heard Karl cry once again, their eyes fixed down the hall, towards the nurse's office. Had they looked behind them, they would have seen Carol, awake now, silently mouthing and thus projecting Karl's cries in the distance with a delighted little smile.

And then Rebecca did glance back at her mother. Carol's eyes were open. She grinned up at her daughter. Silently mouthed "*HELP ME!*" again, and Karl could be heard crying out those very same words again in the distance.

Rebecca screamed.

Ryan spun.

Carol leapt from the sofa, dove into Ryan's waist and knocked him to the floor, she on top. She screeched, animal-like, and clawed at Ryan's eyes; she bit into his neck; she grabbed his hair and repeatedly banged the back of his head against the tiled floor; her wild grin—big, impossibly big—constant throughout.

"*Mom, stop it!!!*" Rebecca screamed.

Carol did anything but. Ryan fought futilely beneath her, Carol's savage fury overwhelming him. She gripped his hair again, banged it on the tiled floor again. "*DIE!*" she screamed, and banged his head again. "*DIE!*" Bang. "*DIE!*" Bang.

Rebecca grabbed hold of her mother's hair with both hands, jerked with all her might—and ended up tumbling backwards onto the seat of her pants with two fistfuls of her mother's hair and scalp, Carol never flinching once; her daughter might as well have plucked a wig from her head.

"*DIE!*" Bang. "*DIE!*" Bang. Ryan was unconscious, and Carol's impossibly wide grin stretched that much wider, tendrils of saliva dangling from both corners of her mouth now, spit spraying with each "*DIE!*" she gleefully screeched.

Stew on the scene now, rushing forward, the knife Carol had used on him tight in his meaty fist. He plunged it deep into the center of her back, and unlike Rebecca's partial scalping job, this attack produced a significant effect.

Carol cried out, sat upright atop Ryan's chest, back arched, stomach protruding, and feebly tried to bring both hands behind her back to clutch the wound.

Stew plunged the knife again, this time into her chest, and Carol cried out again, finally rolling off of Ryan and onto her back, her grin gone, in its stead an agonized grimace.

Ryan started coming to. He staggered to his feet, swaying, dazed, eventually stumbling back against the wall, which he slid down onto his butt.

Carol slowly rose to *her* feet, her shirt soaked red in front and in back. She stood, hunched over, wheezing, one hand on her bloodied chest, her gaze fixed on Stew.

Stew held the knife out in front, both in threat and in preparation to follow through with that threat.

Carol spat blood. "Oh, Stew…" she wheezed, the tendrils of saliva that hung from her chin now pink as they mixed with her own blood. "…the things I'm going to do to you…"

"*Mom, please!*" Rebecca cried.

Carol looked over at her daughter. "Oh, go fuck yourself, Rebecca. You're a bigger disappointment to me than your father ever was."

Rebecca suddenly looked as though *she* had been stabbed. Her chest sank, her shoulders sank, her face sank.

"Well, what are you waiting for, Stew?" Carol said, fixing her gaze back on him. She waved him on, her bravado contradicting her weakened state. "The sooner you come and take your medicine, the sooner your balls will be frying in hell along with your little buddy John."

Stew readied the knife.

"*Wait!*" Ryan called from his seat against the wall. Ryan struggled to his feet, his gaze not on Stew and Carol and Rebecca, but on something *behind* them.

83

Stew looked behind him. Rebecca looked behind Stew. Even Carol looked.

Stew saw nothing, as evidenced by the splay of his knife hand and then a quick look in Ryan's direction.

Rebecca saw nothing, as evidenced by her gaze ping-ponging between Ryan and the distance behind Stew, and then back on Ryan again, her previously deflated face now scrunched with mystery.

But Ryan saw it, and judging by the horrified look on Carol's face—to Ryan's great delight—she saw it too.

It started from the south wing—a slow and steady march of children towards the lobby, John Gray leading the march.

From the east wing another slow and steady march of children emerged, Jane Ballentine, the art teacher, leading the way.

The north wing, more children, Mike Johnson, the science teacher, leading.

And then finally the west wing, Trish Cooke leading.

Stew turned to Ryan. "*What?*"

Ryan only smiled back at Stew.

Revelation clicked on Stew's face. "*What do you see, Ryan?*"

Stew's words were like a starter's pistol. The children's march became a full-on sprint towards Carol, the four teachers strolling casually behind as the children rushed past them, content to amble and watch that which was about to unfold.

Carol screamed as the children pounced. They tore off her arms. They tore off her legs. They tore off her head. They took turns jumping on her headless, limbless torso as though it were a trampoline, a fitting analogy as any, Ryan mused—the children were clearly enjoying themselves.

⸻ ◆ ⸻

Stew watched Carol, now flat on her back, as she screeched and thrashed and fought something he could not see.

He spun towards Ryan again. *"Ryan! Ryan, what's happening?! What do you see?! WHAT DO YOU SEE?!"*

When Carol stopped screaming, when her arms dropped limply to her sides, when her legs stopped thrashing, and when her eyes, still open, went several beats without a blink, Ryan looked at Stew, smiled again, and said: "Vengeance, my friend. Long, long overdue vengeance."

⸻ ◆ ⸻

When it was finished, Ryan watched the children file their way back down the halls from which they'd emerged, the teachers once again leading the way. It was all so orderly and cavalier in its construct that it might have been a teacher guiding his or her students from lunch back to the classroom—had those students and teachers not begun to dissipate on that march before slowly fading away entirely.

The last to dissolve was Trish. She had let her students file on ahead before her. When they were gone, she locked eyes with Ryan, smiled her loving, cherubic smile, and blew him a kiss.

84

Pinewood Elementary started two weeks late. Though it was quite an undertaking—administration having to contact the family of each and every student due to attend the following day—a BS excuse about asbestos issues was used as the official reason.

Everything that had occurred in the weeks prior, and especially on the infamous night of, was kept as hush-hush as humanly possible. Even the police were willing to remain tight-lipped to the press for the better of the community. Leaks occurred, of course, but nothing could be substantiated, and each leak varied greatly, causing them all to ultimately lose credibility in the coming days.

Carol Lawrence's chamber, and the altar therein, was destroyed and sealed in forever. Despite Carol's knife wounds—all legally justified in the eyes of the law once all stories were told and corroborated—an autopsy ruled that a heart attack was the culprit in taking her life.

Ryan didn't think any sweeter irony was possible.

Karl never did recover from his fall. Unfortunately, it wasn't Carol's work that did him in, but significant bleeding in Karl's brain as a result of his head bouncing off the tiled floor when he'd fallen (though Ryan and Stew would agree later, with both great sorrow and anger, that technically it *was* Carol's work that did Karl in; after all, it was her damned spell that had caused him to fall).

Although Karl had not been conscious at the time of Carol's demise, Stew had leaned into the open casket during the janitor's funeral and whispered: "You were there when she died, brother. You were *there*."

Barbara Forsythe's body was eventually found, and her cause of death, like Carol's, was also ruled a heart attack. Fortunately (though again Ryan and Stew would discuss, *not so* fortunate for poor Barbara; they knew the truth), Barbara's advanced age meant not many eyebrows were raised over potential foul play.

Rebecca and Ryan resumed dating, but not right away. There were too many open wounds at first. They took their time and eased into things, letting it occur gradually. Once things did eventually get up and running, there weren't many times the two were apart. And of course Ryan now always, *always* made sure to flush a used condom immediately after they finished having sex. Call it superstition, but he simply couldn't fall asleep afterwards unless the ritual was done.

Stew and Ryan became quite good friends after their shared tragedies and made it a habit to hang out at least once a week for a few laughs as long as Ryan promised not to curse so much around Stew. Ryan agreed, but only if Stew would break down and have one measly beer with him from time to time.

85

The year was halfway done and without incident. Even the locals were beginning to mellow. The one significant problem—if it could be called that—was Barbara's absence. She had been such an adept secretary that each replacement they attempted in the five months since school started had failed so miserably they were asked to leave. Some even chose to quit.

Miss Gates, the new principal of Pinewood, was becoming desperate for a head secretary who could come even remotely close to filling Barbara's shoes, and the knock on her office door now would, she hoped, be the answer to her prayers.

"Come in," the principal said.

A pretty woman, late forties, light brown hair, and dark blue eyes, walked into the office and took a seat. In her left hand was a résumé. Tucked under that same left arm was a small wooden box. The woman, meticulously dressed in a beige business suit, stood upright and to attention as though she was military.

As the two shook hands, Miss Gates found herself silently marveling at the strength the woman carried in her manner. Genuine confidence and assuredness that other hopefuls had tried to project, but that Miss Gates regretfully saw through.

"Deborah Gates," Miss Gates said as they shook hands.

The woman smiled. "Susan Rose."

Miss Gates took her seat behind her desk, then gestured for the woman to take hers in front. "Please."

The woman smiled, thanked her, and sat. She handed Miss Gates her résumé. Miss Gates glanced at the résumé and frowned slightly. "It says *Moyer* here," she said.

"Moyer is my maiden name," the woman said. "I recently married." She then waved a playful finger at Miss Gates. "Don't let anyone tell you it can't happen after forty."

Miss Gates laughed. "Well, I suppose congratulations are in order. Good man?"

"Oh yes. Very obedient."

Miss Gates laughed again. Her gaze then fell on the small wooden box, now in the woman's lap.

The woman noticed, looked down at the box herself, and smiled. "A good-luck charm," she said. "Something very near and dear to my heart."

Miss Gates smiled. "Hey, whatever works, right?"

Susan Rose smiled back. Pleasantly recalled how she had seduced the lonely man at the morgue, now her husband, and thus obtained Carol Lawrence's heart after her autopsy. She then stroked the contours of the wooden box that held Carol Lawrence's heart, gave it a tap on the lid, and said: "Whatever works."

ABOUT THE AUTHOR

A native of the Philadelphia area, Jeff Mena-pace has published multiple works in both fiction and non-fiction. In 2011 he was the recipient of the Red Adept Reviews Indie Award for Horror.

Jeff's terrifying debut novel *Bad Games* became a #1 Kindle bestseller that spawned four acclaimed sequels, and now the series has been optioned for feature film and translated for foreign audiences.

His other novels, along with his award-winning short works, have also received international acclaim and are eagerly waiting to give you plenty of sleepless nights.

Free time for Jeff is spent watching horror movies, The Three Stooges, and mixed martial arts. He loves steak and more steak, thinks the original 1974 *Texas Chainsaw Massacre* is the greatest movie ever, wants to pet a lion someday, and hates spiders.

He currently lives in Pennsylvania with his wife Kelly and their cats Sammy and Bear.

Jeff loves to hear from his readers. Please feel free to contact him to discuss anything and everything, and be sure to visit his website to sign up for his FREE newsletter (no spam, not ever) where you will receive updates and sneak peeks on all future works along with the occasional free goodie!

CONNECT WITH JEFF ON SOCIAL MEDIA:

http://www.facebook.com/JeffMenapace.writer

http://twitter.com/JeffMenapace

https://www.linkedin.com/in/JeffMenapace

https://www.goodreads.com/JeffMenapace

https://www.instagram.com/JeffMenapace

FOLLOW JEFF ON BOOKBUB AND AMAZON TO GET THE LATEST ALERTS ON NEW RELEASES!

https://www.bookbub.com/authors/jeff-menapace

https://www.amazon.com/-/e/B004R09M0S

OTHER WORKS BY
JEFF MENAPACE

Please visit Jeff's Amazon Author Page or his website for a complete list
of all available works!

http://author.to/Jeffsauthorpage

www.jeffmenapace.com

AUTHOR'S NOTE

Thank you so much for reading *Dark Halls*, my friends. Perhaps you'll never look at an elementary school the same way again, yes?

Please know that every single reader is important to me. Whenever I'm asked what my writing goals are, my number one answer, without pause, is to entertain. I want you to have fun reading what I write. I want to make your heart race. I want you to get paper cuts (or Kindle thumb?) from turning the pages so fast. Again—I want to entertain you.

If I succeeded in doing that, I would be very grateful if you took a few minutes to write a review on Amazon for *Dark Halls*. Good reviews can be very helpful, and I absolutely love to read the various insights from satisfied readers.

Thank you so very much, my friends.

Until next time…

Jeff

Made in the USA
Middletown, DE
26 January 2020

83777222R00175